WE BEND NO KNEE

THE STEEL CLAN SAGA, BOOK THREE

T. THORN COYLE

Published by PF Publishing,
An imprint of Triple Flame Inc
3439 SE Hawthorne #203
Portland, OR 97214

Printed and bound by IngramSpark.
Australia: Ingram Content Group AU Pty Ltd, Melbourne, Victoria.
US: Lightning Source LLC, La Vergne, Tennessee / Allentown, Pennsylvania / Jackson, Tennessee, United States. UK: Lightning Source UK Ltd, Milton Keynes, United Kingdom. Europe: Lightning Source UK Ltd, with facilities in Germany, France, and Spain. The authorized representative in the European Economic Area is Lightning Source France, 1 Av. Johannes Gutenberg, 78310 Maurepas, France. compliance@lightningsource.fr

THE STEEL CLAN CREED

We seek no kings, no presidents, no rulers.

We seek no authority but the spark that dwells within.

We seek no bonds but friendship.

We seek no sovereigns but earth, water, and sky.

None shall rule over another.

We shall share what we have,

And ask for what we need.

We shall lead with open hearts and minds.

But shall you cross us?

Or attempt to enslave others?

With steel to hand we ride.

With steel to hand we strike.

No rulers. No masters.

The Knights of Anarchy will cut you down.

We seek no kings, no presidents, no rulers.

We seek no authority but the spark that dwells within.

We seek no bonds but friendship.

We seek no sovereigns but earth, water, and sky.

CHAPTER 1

TEGAN

Tegan rode, thighs resting easily on the rumbling machine, sumac-dyed-leather-covered knees scant inches from the warm tank that sent a fried potato smell wafting into the clean forest air. Tegan's stomach grumbled in harmony with the growl of per hog, and the sound of the big bikes flanking per own.

A snatch of song, bellowed by the big Sikh Haryath, was caught by the wind and whirled past Tegan's head. It was a new song about the dragons who set fire to New Salem and burned the city to the ground.

Which was not strictly true, but a person couldn't trust bards, now, could they? Bards embellished every fracked-earth thing. The battle of New Salem had been terrifying. Tegan's heart still thumped at the memory of strange magic, the gates cracking open, the roar of dragons, and the rolling of the earth beneath per boots.

The aftermath would be felt for a long time.

But meanwhile, the bards who had not even been present for the cataclysmic event warbled on about it in the big public house as elves, trolls, and humans banged their tankards on the wooden tables. A new song was better entertainment than an axe-throwing competition or the ridiculous knife juggling some of the younger knights had recently decided was great fun.

It was all fun until some fool lost a finger.

Tegan grinned, hearing the echo of per mother Inaya's voice inside per head. Tegan missed per moms, and even missed per father, Angel, Go No More's horse whisperer.

He would be busy, Tegan was sure, helping settle Jimena, Cualli, and his other relatives who had made the journey north with horses, people, and a strange, uncanny priestess who made Tegan glad the woman was on their side.

Seriously shivery, that one. Attractively shivery. Not that anything would get Tegan into her bed. Nope.

Tegan would stick to casual rolling about in the blankets with more ordinary humans and the occasional troll. Besides, Tegan hadn't felt much like rolling around at all lately. Per was in a slump and trying hard to chalk it up to being busy fighting off Queen Silverhair's minions and keeping the township safe.

Per squinted into the wind, enjoying the moist air and willing per thoughts away. Tegan had never been one for much rumination, but lately, couldn't seem to stop.

Huh. Perhaps a good fuck was not only long over-due, but necessary.

As if he'd heard per thoughts, Case roared past, flipping per off. Tegan returned the gesture, smiling beneath per kerchief. Yeah. If Tegan was going to bed anyone, it would be Case.

But that felt too messy, didn't it? Less than casual.

And the urgent longing for less-than-casual was newer than that fracked-earth dragon song. It gnawed at Tegan's belly in the night, until per was sweating in per bedroll, and willing per usually clever fingers to scratch an itch that Tegan just couldn't quite reach.

Tegan's motorcycle coughed, calling per attention back to the moment. Per adjusted the throttle, increasing speed on the cracking PR highway. The black ribbon snaked through the forest, with spruce, Douglas fir, and and coastal hemlock towering on each side. Year by year, the forest encroached on the old, Pre-Reckoning spaces, dragging what was left of the old human civilizations back into the wild.

Tegan roared ahead of Case, flipping him off as per bike sped by. The bike seemed to be doing better at increased speed. Might as well keep it that way for a while. Get home quicker.

Due south, a herd of elk thundered on the flat expanses of wildflowers and grasses, racing past the strange, green humps that used to be human dwellings and gathering places. The occasional sign made of brit-tle, PR material poked up, advertising things that had not existed in many decades.

Generations after the Reckoning, and the old cities and strange, sprawling settlements had slowly been torn apart by forest and all the creatures that called such places home.

Gone to green, Tegan's mothers called it. Gone to green was a good thing. More habitat for elk, buffalo, and beaver, not to mention nagini, dryads, dragons, and the other magical spirits that appeared when the great conflagration tore the human realms asunder, ushering in a new age between the realms. Some called the spaces the nine worlds, but others? They knew that the multiverse was more complex than could ever be described.

Gone to green meant cleaner water and softer air than was talked about in the books in Tegan's mother's schoolroom. But if the main arteries linking small cities and other enclaves were to remain open, Go No More township was going to have to get some people out here to cut things back again. Tegan's own hands itched to grip per machete and get on with it. If the dragoons weren't heading home now, Tegan might have called a stop for an impromptu work party.

As it was, per circled one arm and pointed forward, signaling to increase speed and get the heck back to their loved ones, the bathhouse, a smoke, and some beer. And the proper meal Tegan's stomach was clearly looking forward to.

Besides, Tegan's hog needed work. The coughing had started up earlier in the day, a couple dozen klicks back. And a worrying rattle jarred somewhere around per knees.

Tegan rode in convoy with half a dozen knights roaring behind, trailed by two provisions bikes that mostly carried biofuel and extra tools. Per sumac-red leathers, helmet, and boots were part of the clan's adopted uniform, though each knight had their own particular style. Tegan adjusted the scarf tied over per face and squinted into the wind. Per goggles had cracked a few days into the trip and Tegan missed them.

The dragoons patrolled, assessing new damage to the roads and not so coincidentally keeping an eye out for bandits, sickness, or would-be warlords and horse thieves. Mostly, the Knights of the Steel Clan were returning from a meeting with the Sovereign and Confederated Tribes. They needed a more solid plan to deal with the New Salem refugees that Go No More had taken in after the battle against Wulf and his minions. The bards got one thing right: New Salem itself was a wreck, between the magic Tegan's comrade Bocan had used to shake its foundations on a crash of rolling earth and the fire from the dragons.

Scout Litha rode ahead, along with Wasco apprentice Jessie Thomason, who had been a great help in talking with the confederated tribes. Tegan's best comrades Jenny and Bocan had stayed in Go No More. The township needed as many bodies as possible on the ground to help train the refugees in the basic combat all townspeople learned. And extra muscles were useful with the new building and infrastructure projects. The engineers and carpenters had their work cut out for them, as did Tegan's mother Winney, who was in charge of the township's school. Luckily, the New Salem refugees included many skilled people who'd been chafing beneath the so-called warlord's rule.

But others seemed to resent the egalitarian spokescouncil system the township ran on. Minor skirmishes for power had already erupted here and there. If that kept up, some people were going to be escorted elsewhere. The founders of Go No More were clear: none would rule over any other. Anyone who didn't like that? Could leave.

Tegan's mouth set in a thin line when per thought about it. The founders had worked hard to leave a legacy of communal effort for the common good and to see people who should be grateful to be out from under a pig fucker's iron hand challenge that? Well, it stuck in per craw.

Tegan's bike evened out on a long stretch of road just as a flicker—one of the medium-sized woodpeckers with bright orange tipped wings—sped in front of Tegan's hog. Tegan's eyes darted to the left, following the bird's flight.

And there, off the side of this ancient road, was something that most certainly should not have been there. A shimmering, bright seam of silver glowed from the depths of the forest.

This time, Tegan held up per right hand, fist closed to signal *stop*, and pulled over, waiting for per comrades to catch up. Per killed the big machine and grabbed the waterskin slung on the seat, squirting a long swallow of clear creek water down per grateful throat. Tegan gave a silent thanks to the spirits of the creek, and was glad to have left a small carving with the naiad who had allowed the convoy to drink their fill that morning.

Case rumbled up beside her and planted his heavy boots on the old tarmac, pulling down his own face scarf.

"What's happening?" he asked, dark brown eyes flashing beneath his goggles.

"I think I saw a gate back there."

The sound of two hogs approaching from up the road signaled the return of Litha and Jessie. Litha pulled her bike up, nose toward Tegan's. The scout pulled her goggles onto her helmet and pulled down her scarf. The creamy skin that matched her blond hair was red where it had been exposed to the wind, making her almost as ruddy as Case.

The scouts must have seen Tegan's signal in their rear mirrors.

"Did we miss something?" Litha asked with a frown. It was a good question for a scout, but Tegan could not expect anyone to have caught that shimmering seam. If it weren't for that flicker, Tegan wouldn't have seen it either.

Per jerked per head. "A gate. Quarter klick back."

"No shit," Jessie whistled, fiddling with the end of her long, dark braid. The Wasco apprentice was young still, but a terrific tracker and good with both axe and bow. "We gonna check it out?"

Tegan arched per scarred right brow.

"Right. Foolish question," Jessie said.

"Lead on," Litha said, snapping down her goggles and pulling up her scarf.

Tegan kicked per bike to life with a throaty rumble, and peeled out, heading back toward that shimmering slice of magic.

Wondering what in the nine worlds was going on.

CHAPTER 2
CASE

Case gave his bike a pat and paused to drink some water from the skin Tegan handed him. His comrade had a wary look in per dark eyes and had shucked the helmet that usually covered the grid pattern of elaborate knots that made up per hairstyle. It was some traditional style from a massive continent too far away to even think of. Sometimes his adventuring heart wished to see lands other than this verdant place he and his son called home.

But such things were distant dreams, and besides, there was plenty of excitement to be had dealing with the random pig fuckers who wanted to lord it over others instead of simply enjoying the peace and abundance of the rivers, mountains, and fertile land.

And there was still Underhill to contend with, too, though the battle of New Salem had dealt the gilded-arsed queen a mighty blow.

Case looked around at his comrades, all waiting to hear exactly what had them stopped in what had once been a smaller roadway that cut off the main highway and now was a choked-off artery to nowhere.

Despite Tegan freeing per shapely head, he kept his own helmet on. No telling how long they'd be here, and besides, it was good protection in case some bandits were about. Or even an angry squirrel.

Case had been pelted with nuts often enough to be wary of the little fuckers.

The cooling bike engines ticked, cooling in the moist, gray air.

He checked in with the Steel Clan amulet that rode beneath his leathers and loose hemp shirt. The elaborate metal knot was a small, comforting bump against his collarbone. It didn't buzz of magic, though.

Case's magical senses weren't the strongest, but he had enough to get by. His regular six senses were usually enough. Especially his sense of smell and hearing, along with the parent's intuition that had expanded his other intuitive abilities along the way. Having a child really made a person pay attention.

Litha and Jessie were already down the small deer path snaking between the tall trees. The scent of decaying leaves and moist earth was strong. Was there something else? He slowed his breathing down and deliberately softened his edges, opening his senses to the forest. He heard some animals scratching. Likely skunk or opossum. The *tok tok* of a pileated woodpecker, and the long, steady call of a flicker.

Farther away was the rumble of a herd of large beasts. The hoof cadence sounded like bison, rather than the elk they'd seen a while back.

He followed Tegan down the path, checking out per tight ass in sumac leather trousers that were starting to bag a bit from wear. If Tegan wore a shapeless sack, Case would still find his comrade intriguing. They'd danced around being lovers for a few years now, but neither of them had bothered to step across the line.

Case's last fling was with Jerrod, who took up his flank, along with the Sikhs, Haryath and Amarpal. Jerrod—tall, and handsome as a summer's day was long with his close-cut tight curled hair and broad nose—was bisexual, but gravitated more toward women, whereas Case was, and always had been, as omnisexual as the Gods made possible.

His boots crunched through the layers of leaves, fir needles, and other detritus. His ears were still open, and he sniffed the air occasionally, not catching much more than damp earth, woody fir, and the balsam and citrus combination of western hemlock.

And rose. That was strange. What were roses doing growing in the middle of this forest? The soil composition would be all wrong and there shouldn't be enough sunlight for a plant like that. The perks of dating someone from the Green Clan is that you picked up useful information like that. Case had cross-trained with Hakim L'Ouverture and the rest of the Green Clan for a year or two, expanding his knowledge.

That scent of rose and what it portended was further proof that the founders had been correct in insisting that cross-training was vital to the health of the township in more ways than one.

"Halt!" he called out to his comrades up ahead, planting his boots on the path. Jerrod swore softly, metal clanking as the tall, dark knight pulled up short.

"Give a man some warning next time, won't you? I almost plowed you down."

Case looked over his shoulder at his friend and grinned. "I thought halt *was* the warning."

"Pig fucker," Jerrod muttered, though without any heat behind the words.

Tegan had turned, arms crossed over per narrow chest, waiting for Case to explain, as Litha and Jessie ghosted back down the trail. Damn, those two were good. Silent as the coastal mist when they needed to be.

"I smelled roses," Case said.

"Roses?" Jerrod groused. "What, you stopped us to enjoy life in the moment? Come on, man."

Jessie cleared her throat. "He means that roses shouldn't be growing here."

"So, what does it mean?" asked Amarpal, speaking around a mouthful of fruit jerky.

"It means Underhill, that's what it means." Tegan's lips were screwed up as if per tasted something rotten. "It means I was right about seeing a gate."

Jerrod groaned. Case didn't blame him. All any of the Steel Clan wanted was to get back to Go No More, wash off the dirt of the road, eat something, kiss whomever they needed to, and get some decent sleep. No matter how much Case enjoyed being on the road, he enjoyed that first night home more.

"Do you still sense the gate?" Litha asked. "Because Jessie and I didn't see anything."

Tegan shifted and Case could almost watch the convoy leader re-center and open per senses to the forest and everything in it.

Chickadees peeped and called, and a jay shrieked. Tegan didn't flinch, brows drawn together in focus. All the knights held their peace. Drinking water. Eating a mouthful or two of field rations. Waiting.

So much of battle was about waiting. So much of scouting was about listening or sensing. Every single one of them had been trained to this, just as they were trained to uncoil and strike within seconds when under attack.

"It's due west," Tegan finally said, blinking, and twisting a couple of the tightly wound knots on per head. That was Tegan's main tell, a thing per did when worried about something. Otherwise, the hair knots only got twisted when Tegan was completely relaxed in one of the big, bathhouse soaker tubs. A sight Case was looking forward to as much as seeing his son.

"Let's go, then," he said. Might as well get this over with.

Litha nodded to Jessie, and the younger woman took the lead, helmet tucked beneath her right arm, long braid shining whenever the watery sun broke through the clouds to shine through the branches. A breeze moved through, shaking the fir needles and washing over Case's face. He had to admit, dealing with the elf queen and all the elfland shit left a bad taste in his mouth.

Give him a good clean physical fight any day. More and more lately, the Steel Clan had to engage with magical opposition. He kept hoping they'd catch a break.

But he knew there were rumblings on the spokescouncil about the fact that the princess was still trapped and likely dying. Now that the queen's access to human souls had been cut off…

Or had it?

He caught up with Tegan.

"Does this mean we're back to where we started?"

Tegan shrugged, shaking per head in annoyance.

"Fuck if I know. These pig-fucking elves can kiss my ass."

Case grinned. "Or I could do that for you."

"So you can." Tegan said, elbowing him in the side.

"Ouch! You been sharpening your elbows?"

Tegan laughed softly, then turned per attention back to the trail. Litha and the Wasco apprentice moved stealthily on ahead, which was a reminder to Case to lighten his own steps.

Not that traipsing through the forest with a dozen knights in leather, chains, and carrying steel was going to be anything actually quiet.

Tegan inhaled sharply. Case jerked his head around, and there it was.

"Fuck a fucking pig," he whispered. A shimmering seam of magic. A silvery gash between two enormous firs. A portal to a sideways world. A world that just under sixty years ago had been its own separate place.

The unchanging realm, people used to call it. The place of eternal twilight and endless spring.

He shivered as if a cold hand had traced a pathway up his spine. Nope. He didn't like this kind of magic. Not one bit.

Litha and Jessie had stopped just up ahead, scanning the perimeter, hurrying between trees. They looked both up and down, as well as in all four directions, the way a good scout did.

Litha's blond hair gleamed in the overcast light where it stuck out from beneath her helmet. A flash of white gold that complimented her pale eyes.

"It's your call," she said, looking at Tegan.

Though the Steel Clan worked on consensus, they had also discovered it was easier to appoint temporary leadership for each expedition or for specific tasks. Though anyone could always block or disagree, sometimes it was simpler to have one or two voices working in the best interests of the group.

They all traded off, though that burden lay more heavily on Tegan, Bocan, and Jenny's shoulders overall, with Case and Jerrod close behind.

Tegan looked at him, brow furrowed.

"What do you think?"

Case spat out the foul taste in his mouth. It tasted of bile. Of the memory of corpses marked with the queen's seal. It smelled of souls sucked from their bodies, leaving behind vacant husks. It tasted of Bocan's mother, still not recovered, and of all the dead left in Silverhair's wake.

He looked back at his comrade; mouth set in a grimace.

"We go home," he said. "Litha and Jessie can blaze the trail so we can find our way back here. But the council needs to know about this."

Tegan nodded, looking up at the patch of darkening sky above the tree-tops.

"You're right," per said. "We either camp out one more night and investigate more tomorrow, or we head back home..."

"And bring back a fucking mage," Case finished.

"All right!" Tegan raised per voice. "We're heading out. You two, you need help marking trees?"

Litha shook her head.

"We got this, Tegan," Jessie replied.

"Steel Clan, let's ride."

Case was happy to turn his boots back towards the shiny metal of his bike, and those last klicks that would take him home.

CHAPTER 3

ELZABETTA

Golden sunlight filtered through the apple branches. White blossoms drifted down to a carpet of green, and bees buzzed around, legs growing fat with golden pollen.

Elzabetta's white teeth crunched through the shining red surface of the perfectly ripe apple, sticky juice running across her tongue. Her back was propped against the smooth trunk of the tree, her eyes half closed as her mind drifted in and out, following the pathways of the white petals.

Apples here were always ripe. Flowers always bloomed and fell and bloomed again. The sky was unchanging. The air always a perfect temperature, with just a hint of gentle breeze.

At least, that was what her mother, Queen Silverhair, told her. That was the true nature of Faery. Of Elfland. Of the Shining Silver Realm of Underhill.

But now? Fissures marred the unchanging magical foundation. A few windfall apples lay rotting on the ground, mobbed by yellowjackets and the more vicious sprites. Some fey creatures had always lusted after blood and rot. This aftermath of the human Reckoning seemed to suit them just fine.

It would have suited Elzabetta fine, too, if it were not for the truth unwinding like a long worm inside her bones: as the realm changed and death entered through the gates, so she was dying, too.

Elzabetta lived in a time outside of time. A space between life and death. Her souls were not whole. Her days—unlike other fey royalty—were not a long, unlimited unspooling of endless spring and autumn days.

Queen Silverhair had done everything within her power to stop the change. She had harvested untold scores of human souls to feed Elzabetta's own. But part of Elzabetta still wandered between the realms, lost to this time, drifting in a time that seemed all its own. Traces of this strange world appeared in her dreams, haunting her with ghostly, laughing figures. Strange knights who rode machines instead of horses. Knights who wore rich red instead of the green of leaves.

Knights who roamed the human realms, swords strapped to their backs, feral grins lighting their many-hued faces.

A large purple drake also visited her mind, in those liminal times between fitful sleep and waking. It whispered of her destiny, and the life she could have were she not tethered to this place.

Such talk was treason. For a princess to abandon her realm was a death sentence more final than this slow disintegration of her souls. The executioner's axe hovered above her, always threatening, despite how much Silverhair proclaimed her love.

"My lady?"

She blinked her eyes at the figure standing at a respectful distance away. A fine figure of an elf, with sharp, pale cheekbones and delicately pointed ears, his pale green hair held a golden sheen and pulled back to fall in a long queue down his back. The knight wore the standard green leather tunic over green leather trews and boots. A quiver was strapped to his back, and a sword hung from his hip. The fingers of his right hand loosely held a curved bow.

"Sir Tarioc."

The current head of her entourage, Tarioc was Elzabetta's primary protector, elevated to the position after the defection of the alchemist, Carondel. He was kind to her, which she appreciated, though he watched her too closely for comfort sometimes.

"Your mother requests that you join her in her solar for tea."

Elzabetta stifled a groan. She was tired. Less tired than the days where all she could do was drift in and out of slumber, true, but still too tired for whatever Mother wished to discuss. Like marriage. Or more harvesting of souls.

Elzabetta stood slowly, brushing off the back of her long, pale green skirts. She stifled a sigh. Such protests did no good, and she knew not how much Sir Tarioc would report back to her mother, the Queen.

"Lead on," she said. Tarioc sketched a bow and

turned, soft green boots barely leaving an imprint on the green grasses.

When her mother summoned, there was no resisting; that only made things worse the times she did. Elzabetta had learned that when she was a small child. As she followed Tarioc's long, straight back, she pondered her options. They felt slim these days, though the fact that the alchemist had escaped with her mother's signet ring during the Great Battle of New Salem gave Elzabetta hope. It made her believe for the first time in her life that she could be something other than her mother's toy, a pawn in the endless game of court politics. A game she was ill-suited for, and heartily sick of.

At least since the alchemist's disappearance she had not been forced to engage in the torture of other beings. The stripping of humans of their varied souls to feed her own, leaving them either dead or mad, or husks of their former selves. She had tried as many forms of resistance against her mother's deadly plan as possible over the years.

Not eating. Hiding. Not speaking. Shouting. None of them ever helped for long. Her mother always found a way to force her to do her bidding. But the alchemist... Carondel had defied all historic protocol, bucking all odds and the Queen. That meant things were possible that Elzabetta had not allowed herself to dream before.

She wondered if this knight would help her, or if his loyalty was only to her mother. Only time would tell. Time, patience, and planning. She needed all three.

But for now, she would play the dutiful daughter and pretend she was pleased to see the Queen and to hear whatever the icy-cold woman who was her mother had to say.

Her long skirts swished on the grass, and her slippered feet soon felt the hard slabs that made up the outside walkways around her mother's keep. She followed the knight past the open colonnades and archways that led to a room filled with windows and sheer white curtains that caught the breeze. The gracefully carved light wood furniture looked beautiful but was as uncomfortable as her mother.

Nothing the Queen did was about providing comfort. It was all about appearances. Oh, and the face that turned toward Elzabetta was as beautiful as the moon or the sun, and as cold as the winter that never touched these lands.

Her silver hair tumbled in a fall down her back, almost reaching the floor. Queen Silverhair's locks were a wintry contrast to Elzabetta's pale blond hair. Her mother's eyes were like chips of glacial ice, and her smile was just as cold.

"Hello, my darling," her mother said. "And thank you, Sir Tarioc."

The knight inclined his head and gave a correctly deep bow.

"My Queen," he said, voice mellifluous and grave. But as he turned, he gave Elzabetta a wink, then went to join the guards who graced the doorways, providing constant protection against a breach of the realm. They stood at attention, close enough to see if something went awry, but far enough away to give their liege and her daughter privacy.

"You look well, my child." The Queen gestured for her to sit on one of the green damask covered sofas across from a low table set with dainty treats, fruits, and a pot of steaming tea.

Elisabetta gave a nod of acknowledgement. She sat and arranged her skirts around her automatically but didn't speak. What was there to say?

"I have been in correspondence with the Holly King," Queen Silverhair began, pouring tea into delicate china cups decorated with roses.

Elzabetta's hands clutched at her skirts. The Queen's gaze sharpened. Elzabetta forced her fingers to release the silky cloth and willed herself to smile.

"Oh?" she said, putting just the right amount of interest into her voice as she accepted a cup of the pale green brew.

"His son has inquired after you. He was captured by your beauty at the last ball, and wishes to wed. He wishes for you to bear his child. The Holly King has tentatively agreed to the match. At least in principle. Nothing can be decided until we two meet."

The silver blood in Elzabetta's veins grew cold. She shivered despite the warmth of the solar.

Her mother's smile cracked like the snarl of a wolf. Elzabetta could not school her own face anymore. Could not keep the political smile turning up the edges of her mouth. Her heart beat wild as a bird in hand, seeking freedom.

"But the alchemist said..."

"I do not care what lies that traitor filled your head with. He has gone now and has betrayed the realm." The Queen's knuckles were white around the fragile cup. She turned her head to look out the windows at the gardens beyond. "But my hounds shall find him soon enough."

That was new information. That her mother had sent her most fearsome hunters after Carondel was information Elzabetta warranted the Queen had not meant to let slip.

The news should not have surprised her, but she wondered what else she had missed while wallowing in her gloom and enjoying the brief respite from the experiments, the poking and prodding and force-feeding of human souls into her own.

Elzabetta cheated her eyes toward Tarioc, who stood tall, face a mask of correct indifference. Was that a sheen of intelligence she saw in his eyes? Was he listening?

It mattered not. In this, Elzabetta was alone. She had no protector but herself.

"He said that I would die if I tried to bear a child!" Elzabetta insisted.

Her mother's face was set in stone. "You think I have not sacrificed? You think I don't know grief? We all must sacrifice, my child. But you know I love you and would not ask you to do anything that would bring you harm."

Silverhair paused to sip some tea then spoke, voice as cool and calm as a viper's tongue. "I shall meet with the Holly King, and you shall not cause trouble about it. Besides, nothing has been decided yet."

But clearly the decision making would not include Elzabetta, despite it being her life.

"Yes, Mother." Elzabetta forced the words out with a smile. "Of course." She swallowed her queasiness, and hoped the sudden dampness on her brow would remain unmarked.

Her mother smiled then, slightly more genuine than before. "You know that I love you, my child. I wish only the best for you. And I wish only the best for this realm."

Elzabetta could not help but wish that what was best for the realm was also something that would bring her heart happiness. Instead, the back of her tongue tasted the bitter herbs of more misery to come.

CHAPTER 4
JENNY

Bocan came at her with his massive battle-axe, pale blue face set in a grimace. He moved slowly, almost stutteringly. Her comrade was not the powerhouse she had known her whole life. It was a testament to Jimena's healing power—along with Anandita and Doc Warren's—that he could hold an axe at all. A wolf had ripped at his left arm, tearing flesh and nicking tendons. He wore a protective leather brace of pigskin to support the injured flesh, and might never be able to fight in battle again.

At least, not physically. His newly awakened combat magic was a different story.

If he had not been a Steel Clan knight, Bocan would probably still be taking it easy. But the drive to fight again stirred the halbtroll to push himself. It was Jenny's task to make certain he didn't push his injured flesh too far.

Time to end this sparring match.

She dodged beneath the big blue brute's arm and

whirled around, smacking the hollow behind his left knee with the flat of her broadsword. The halbtroll bellowed and dropped to one knee.

"By all the Gods of Earth and Stone, I shall crush you!"

"You and what troll army?" Jenny taunted, face split with a wild grin. She pushed an errant shock of red hair from her sweaty face and sketched a bow to the apprentices and townsfolk watching their sparring match.

Having hit her comrade in such a way that would have cut the tendons on the back of his leg had the fight been in earnest, it meant that either Bocan had to fight from the ground, or that the bout was over, just as she intended.

"Shall we call it?" she asked. "Or do you want to kill me from the ground?"

Bocan was massive, and as tall on his knees as many humans were standing. This, plus the fact that he had a grievous injury, meant it was a pretty fair fight. Jenny's mobility was the one thing she had working in her favor. That, and the fact that the big oaf seemed distracted. Probably with the pain.

Or perhaps he was thinking of his ma, who was doing better, but still strange and wandering in the head, the way anyone would be after the torture Queen Silverhair subjected her to.

Bocan's ma was lucky to be alive.

"I need a break," he growled. "But watch your back later, pig fucker."

"You know that I prefer a woman's charms!" Jenny

quipped back. One woman in particular. The love of her life, Anandita.

Anandita's son scurried across the large practice field now, dodging the other sparring pairs and the group of students who had been watching Bocan and Jenny's demonstration. The gleaming, dusky-skinned boy blessedly had a water skin in his hands.

He pulled up short and held the skin out without a word, just as all apprentices were taught to do. Never make a fighter waste breath unless you had to. Unless the fighter was a cocky halbtroll you'd just felled with what would have been a crippling injury had the weapons not been practice grade and had the fighters not been pulling back.

"Thank you, Hypatia," she said. The boy was rapidly becoming like a son to her, too. The more her relationship with Anandita deepened, the more time she spent with the curious thirteen-year-old and the more she liked him. Hypatia was named for an ancient woman scientist. Rather than gifting the child with the name from her own family line, Anandita had decided that she wanted to gift the tiny human she first thought of as her daughter with a name of a researcher, scientist, and knowledge-keeper.

Though not a girl, Hypatia had turned out to follow in the ancient's footsteps indeed. He studied with as many different clans in Go No More as would allow him to tag along, though he tended to gravitate toward the engineers.

Bocan lumbered to his feet, blue skin damp with sweat. He wore a sumac-red linen tunic over his leather trousers, much as Jenny and all the knights of the Steel Clan did. Even his arm brace had been dyed red.

"Do I get some of that water?"

"You shouldn't," Jenny replied, holding out the skin, "considering how I just beat that giant ass of yours."

Then she turned her attention to the gathered people. A mixed group, with the long-time denizens of Go No More obvious. Not only did Jenny know all of them, but they carried themselves with a sense of relaxed strength and comfort that the refugees from New Salem hadn't quite adopted yet. Too many years of being ground down by a self-styled warlord had made them either brittle and angry, or cowed, with lowered heads and rounded backs.

"All right!" Jenny shouted. "You saw how a smaller person can best a larger one. It isn't always about strength. It's also about cunning, and knowing how your body can move. Over time, we'll also home in on the proper weapons for your body type, physical ability, and temperament."

A woman with a pinched face and pale skin raised a tentative hand. She wore a blue tunic and trews over worn brown elk-hide boots and had tied her rich brown hair back into a long tail.

"Yes?" Jenny asked.

"Why do we have to learn to fight? Isn't that what you lot are for?"

Jenny straightened her spine and adjusted her shoulders back.

"You see my height, and my muscles, and my prowess..." She delivered that last word with a sideways smirk at Bocan, who snorted and drank some more water. "But we are all responsible for keeping each other safe. What happens if you and your family are gathering wood or mushrooms in the forest and a bandit comes out of nowhere? Or a hungry animal?"

The woman's face paled further.

"The knights can't be everywhere, and you wouldn't want us to be. Besides, everyone is required to cross-train. Not only so we understand and respect each other's skills and work, but in case we are needed. What if the head weaver breaks her hand? Or there's an accident at the water mill or glassworks? Or what happens when a storm is threatening and the Green Clan needs to get the harvest in quickly? We all share the burdens and gifts of living in community."

Jenny scanned the faces, looking for opposition or grumbling. No one stirred. Several people nodded their heads. They'd heard variations on this theme practically since they arrived, and saw all the ways in which it was true, even as the sounds of hammers rang softly from the edges of the township, where new structures were quickly going up to provide better shelter for the people here before winter set in in earnest.

The rumble of motorcycles filled the air. Every head turned toward the convoy of bikes heading toward the large garage structure next to the horse barn and paddock.

There was no use getting back to the demonstration while everyone's attention was drawn to the dragoons dismounting from bikes bristling with weaponry. Jenny looked at her comrades. Even at a distance she could tell from the set of their shoulders that they were tense, whereas they should have been relaxed and happy, slapping each other's backs, ready to head to the bathhouse and then the public house for a well-deserved beer or mug of mead.

Tegan glanced her way and gave her a stare, mouth set in a grimace.

Jenny's comrade jerked per head toward the garage. Jenny couldn't see it from this distance, but she bet Tegan's scarred eyebrow was quirked upward in question. Tegan wanted a meeting, and wanted it soon.

"Should I go?" Bocan's gravelly voice rumbled next to Jenny. She startled. She hadn't even noticed he had approached, though how one could miss such a mountain of a knight, she was unsure. *Not good, Jenny. Keep your wits about you.* The cardinal rule of every fighter: pay attention to everything around you at all times. No matter how safe you think you are.

Clearly, something had disturbed the knights, and Tegan especially. She saw Litha's blond hair next to Jessie's dark. The scout and the apprentice gestured at each other and then followed the rest of the Steel Clan into the garage.

"Go," Jenny said to Bocan. "I'll be there as soon as I finish up here."

"I shall await your arrival with bated breath, oh Magic's Bane."

Jenny feinted toward her comrade, but he just

laughed and grabbed a rough piece of toweling to mop off his skin. Then he took up his leather jacket and his actual battle-axe as opposed to the practice weapon he'd been using and headed toward the garage with a ground-eating stride.

Much as she worried about him, it was good to have the halbtroll on the practice field again.

Jenny clapped her hands. "All right, people! Let's keep this going. A trained township is a safe township. Right, Hypatia?"

"Right!" he said.

"Now, I'm going to have you pair off and practice in a moment, but first, I want to go through what Bocan and I were demonstrating, but this time on the opposite end. All right, Hypatia."

She raised an eyebrow at the boy, who smiled up at her adoringly. Crap. His bouts of adulation both warmed her and made her squirm.

"Ready to attack me?"

"Yes!" He ran to the rack of practice swords and chose one suited to his small frame, along with a wooden knife.

Florentine style, it was. Jenny grabbed a knife of her own and turned to face the boy. Until practice hour was over, whatever had Tegan in a bother would have to wait.

CHAPTER 5
TEGAN

Tegan's skin crawled with the need for a shower and a soak, but there was too much work to be done. The yard outside the long garage building boiled with knights, apprentices, and townspeople who had heard the news.

The news about the shimmering gate not five klicks from Go No More. A gate that should not have been there, yet clearly was.

The stink of Underhill filled Tegan's nostrils, though that was impossible. The dragoons hadn't gotten close enough to scent anything more than that smell of roses Case had picked up on in the forest. Yet still, the mingled notes of roses in full bloom and apples rotting in the grove clawed at the back of per throat, causing panic to coil beneath the tight muscles of Tegan's belly.

A permanent gate in the forest a short motorcycle ride from Go No More was a direct threat from Underhill. Temporary gates came and went all the time, used by single people. Scouts. Traders. The occasional wanderer or explorer. Oh, to create a temporary gate took more magical finesse than most humans had, but a mage could pop one up fairly simply. And the beings for whom magic was their core essence?

Making a temporary gate was child's play.

But a permanent gate? Those were a large undertaking and required multiple magic users, great skill, and no small amount of time. Permanent gates required intention. And it was the intention behind this new gate that Tegan did not trust.

You could move an army through a permanent gate. You could move enough people to create a new settlement, disrupting the peace the Sovereign and Confederated Tribes, Go No More, and the other settlements that dotted the valley had forged. They worked on consensus and in the spirit of mutual aid and cooperation. The last thing they wanted or needed was a group of authoritarians run by so-called royalty to move in.

That would mean a war much larger and more drawn out than the land had seen since before the Reckoning. The Battle of New Salem had been just that: a single battle. And look at the consequences from that?

The thought of actual war made Tegan want to disgorge per last meal. It brought the image of the terrible, icy queen to Tegan's mind.

Tegan had seen the Queen of Underhill. Had heard her voice. Had felt her magic.

Tegan never wanted to experience any of that again.

"What do you need?"

Per hand jerked at Bocan's deep, gravelly voice, and Tegan knocked per machete against a hipbone with a sharp crack.

"Damn it, you pig fucker! Give a person some warning!"

Bocan's enormous hand was gentle on Tegan's wiry shoulder. "Take a breath, comrade. You're back with family. That gilded-arsed Queen isn't here."

Tegan looked up at the big blue oaf. His black eyes were steady. Calm.

Tegan sheathed the machete, shook out per hands, and did as he suggested. Felt per body weight distributed over the boots that stood on the packed dirt ground. Breathed in the scent of bio fuel, warm metal, and knights who'd just spent too long on the road without a proper bath. Listened to the clamor of voices, and the whinnying of horses in the paddock, and the sharp clicking of per dad Angel's voice as he put horses and riders through their paces.

Tegan snaked per energy down into the earth, and felt Go No More rise to meet it.

The next breath came more easily. Some of the tension in per muscles eased.

"Thanks, comrade."

He nodded, then repeated himself. "What do you need?"

Tegan looked through the large open barn doors at the milling, excitable crowd outside. "Besides a big spliff of L'Ouverture's Finest? And a shower and a bowl of Porrac's autumn stew?"

"Besides all that."

"I need the mages and the council and probably the drakes, too."

Tegan should also make time to check in with Starlight, per bonded lynx. Though who knew where the cat was roaming? Tegan was too tired to broadcast a thought the beast's way. The animal would notice the commotion soon enough if she was close by.

If not, Starlight was likely on a mission of her own.

The big halbtroll nodded, running a hand across his bald blue head. "I've already sent runners to alert the council. You should probably report to them and the mages before we contact the drakes."

He sniffed ostentatiously. "And frankly, you should take the time to shower before the meeting. It will be more pleasant for all involved."

Tegan punched the solid rock of his bicep.

Jenny ran into the garage, red braids flying as she stomped her way across the packed dirt floor.

"What the fuck happened?"

Tegan's best mate was a tall, strapping, gorgeous beast of a woman. They'd been friends since childhood, all three of them, forming a bond the other knights sometimes groused about. Tegan got that people felt left out sometimes, but per wouldn't trade these friends for anyone. The other knights were comrades, and Tegan had plenty of family, but Bocan and Jenny were special and always would be.

"We found a gate." Tegan's throat was tight with

the worry that gnawed at per hungry belly. "But I need to talk with the council. Quickly. Is your mother around?"

Jenny's mother, Danika, was currently the council scribe. She had been a member of the Steel Clan, once upon a time, before her husband had been killed in a skirmish and the once great warrior had lost her heart. Lose your heart, you lose your fight. Everyone knew it, and so Danika had set aside her leathers. She was still greatly esteemed, and it was her ancestor, Molly, whose wheel and wings insignia every knight wore somewhere on their leathers. An outlaw back when some adversary called simply The Man had held the human world in thrall, back before that world had cracked, opening the gates for magic to flood back in.

Jenny shook her head, braids twining together, brow furrowed. "I haven't seen her. Did you send a runner?"

"Per did." The voice that answered was filled with shadows. A light wind whipped into the garage where there had been no breeze before.

Abyad the djinni stood before Tegan, black dog at his side, dressed head to toe in layer upon layer of flowing black that protected his ice-white skin from the sun. Some djinni were dark as night, or so Tegan had heard. Darker than Tegan perself. Those were the fire djinn. The air djinn were paler than Jenny's fish-white belly. Abyad's eyes were stark black and as cold as a pool of water high up on Wy'East's peak.

"Tell me what you saw." The djinni's voice sliced like an icy knife across Tegan's face, but Tegan held firm. Per was exhausted, annoyed, and yeah, still really wanting nothing more than a smoke and a soak.

Damn responsibility. Tegan had really hoped for a break after New Salem, but things had been nonstop since then. Building housing for the refugees. Tending to the wounded. Mourning the dead.

Tegan scrubbed a hand over per face and huffed out a sigh. "I really just want to tell the whole council everything all at once."

"Tell me now." The djinni was implacable. Immovable as Wy'East itself.

Tegan looked towards the towering Douglas fir in the center of the town. Listened again to the sounds that spelled home. The sound of horses and goats—and adult conversations—were joined by a steady clang from the forge and the shrieks and laughs of children on a break from the schoolroom. The school where per mother Winney taught. Per other mother was likely out in the fields with the Green Clan right now.

Per would love nothing more than a hug from both mothers right about now. But instead, there was this uncanny magical creature facing per down and the weight of the Steel Clan resting upon per shoulders. That damned responsibility again. Sometimes Tegan wished for the more top-down authoritarian structure that per had read about in Winney's books. Though the Clans loosely traded off leadership, each person was equal, and every person did their part.

Tegan sighed again, struggling to swallow around a suddenly dry throat.

Case passed a water skin. He was so attuned to per sometimes it felt as uncanny as the djinn. Per nodded thanks and sent a sluice of moisture down per throat. Coughing, per handed the skin back to Case, who looked as if he wanted to stop whatever it was Tegan was about to do. As if he wanted to protect Tegan. And wasn't that an unsettling thought? As if Tegan was not a fearsome warrior who could best almost any other, and kill when necessary, too.

Tegan shook the thoughts aside and faced the djinni again. He waited with preternatural stillness. Spooky as fuck. His black dog whined but held still at one gesture from the djinni's pale hand. The dog was as uncanny as the djinni.

"We were headed home and a flicker flew by. I tracked it and saw a shimmering seam."

"Where?" the djinni asked.

"About five klicks away."

"Show me."

Tegan scowled, shaking per head. "I don't have time for this."

"In your mind," Abyad said. "Show me a picture of where you were. Where you saw the gate."

The djinni's words were measured out as if speaking with a child. Perhaps the djinni saw humans as children. Who knew how old he was, anyway?

"Tegan." Abyad softened his voice until it felt less like a knife and more like a caress but caused Tegan to shiver all the same.

"Close your eyes. And show me."

Tegan grimaced, belly coiling with unease, but

closed per eyes all the same. Slowed down the breathing. Felt the feet in boots standing on familiar, comforting ground. As Tegan breathed, per felt the djinni gently probing at the edges of per mind. It was not a terrible feeling, though uncanny. It felt too intimate. Too personal.

Tegan never let in people in this way. Not even lovers...

"Tegan."

That soft voice again. A knife's edge in a velvet casing. "Let me in."

Tegan felt Case tense at per side. Per comrade gripped Tegan's right arm as if to stop per.

"Case," Tegan said. He dropped his hand and shifted away.

Tegan took a long, slow, shuddering breath, sending per attention through per whipcord-muscled body from the soles of per boots to the Bantu knots crowning per head.

Then Tegan opened and let Abyad in.

Let him dance through per mind, snaking through fold upon pink fold. Showing him the forest, and the dusky orange flicker's wing. Remembering the call of birds and animals. And farther in the forest, the shining seam of light that echoed the magic that was Underhill.

The djinni cursed in some ancient language Tegan did not know. It was not the Arabic the djinni sometimes spoke with Rafiq, the current council head. It was something else, perhaps a language only djinn knew. For the first time, Tegan wondered if Abyad was lonely. As soon as the thought crossed Tegan's mind, the djinni broke the connection, leaving Tegan gasping.

Eyes fluttering open, per turned to look at the djinni, but his head was turned away, as if embarrassed or shocked.

Tegan shrugged. There was no telling what went on inside a djinn. If he was human, Tegan would say that the djinni had felt the intimacy as keenly as Tegan had.

Case cleared his throat. "Did you get what you needed?"

The djinni's head snapped towards Tegan's comrade, but his pale lips remained pursed. The two stared at each other as if in a standoff. Finally, Abyad gave a sharp nod.

"I did."

And then a wind rose around the djinni, and in a furling flurry of black cloth, he and his black dog disappeared.

"What the actual fuck?" Jenny said.

Tegan couldn't help but agree.

CHAPTER 6
BOCAN

Bocan had the information he needed from Tegan and his other comrades, so he skipped the council meeting. There was somewhere else he needed to be. Someone else he needed to see.

His arm was throbbing, and right now? He could not bear the crush of the public house or the clamor of argument and discussion sure to come. He could not bear decisions coldly made about the future. About the danger once again stalking their gates. Bocan knew the danger. He felt it in his bones, and tasted it on his tongue. Felt it in his abused muscles and flesh.

Serena the snowy owl flew just overhead as they headed out of the township toward the forest.

It had been too much to hope that Go No More would have time to get the refugees settled in their new life, and folded into the township and surrounding areas. It had been too much to hope that his mother would have time and space to continue healing without further interference from Underhill. It had taken everything Bocan had to get her out of that rotting realm. And then the Battle of New Salem had taken even more.

Bocan followed a deer path deep into the woods that lay just outside the township. That's where Da had built Ma a home. There was no safe place for either of them anymore. Not really. Underhill had done terrible things to Ma, and the human realms? Well, they had failed to save her.

Bocan had failed to save her.

But he could go and visit her now. He needed to, the way a baby animal needed its mother and her den. He needed the comforting rumble of Da's voice and he needed to make sure that Ma was still alive. She had been fine last he saw her, three days ago, but he was also never certain which visit would become his last.

As he approached, Bocan heard the *tock-pause-tock* of wood being split for the fire. He came upon a clearing, and sure enough, there was his massive father, axe in hand. His skin was a richer, darker blue than Bocan's, and he was half a torso taller and broader. A true troll his da, a metal worker. An artisan. At least, he had been until his heart was ripped from his chest with grief and anger.

It was this same grief and anger Bocan carried, buried deep inside his chest. His father paused in his labor to wipe his brow with an enormous linen kerchief. He wore rough-spun hemp trousers in dark gray and an undyed hemp shirt, despite the cold in the air, his body warmed by labor and the natural, internal heat all trolls had. As if he'd heard his son's thoughts,

Bocan's father stooped and picked up a heavy hemp jacket, donning it in silence as his son made his way between the trees and into the clearing itself.

Serena circled once, then perched on a spruce tree just at the edge of the forest. The owl must be worried about him, to have accompanied him here. A night hunter, she used a goodly portion of daylight hours to rest. Perhaps she would nap while he conferred with his da.

Past his da stood a humble wooden dwelling, that Bocan knew led to a large cavern carved out of the mountain behind it. But Bocan barely saw the tidy troll-sized cottage. All he saw was his blue-skinned father with a head as bald as Bocan's own, a sad smile on his broad and craggy face. Every scar on Da's skin was as familiar as the ache in Bocan's own arm from an injury that would never fully heal.

"Son." His father's voice, deep and steady as the mountain itself, brought the prickle of tears to his eyes, and then Bocan was in his father's embrace, being held by the only someone he knew who was larger than himself. Broader. Sturdier. Taller than himself. Body made of glorious muscle and fat. The smell of woodsmoke and the tang of metal. The scents that called out safety. Spelled out home. Bocan swallowed back the tears threatening to erupt like one of the valley volcanoes.

His da gripped the back of his neck for a moment, like a mother cat did to her kits. And then the troll and halbtroll released each other, and took a step apart.

"How is she?" Bocan asked.

Da shrugged. "Much the same."

Father and son paused on the porch to undo their boots. As his da had built the home, the porch was broad, and the door was tall and wide. Both set their boots neatly on the woven mat to the right of the carved wood door. The metalwork hinges and latch were elaborate and beautiful. Da's work, of course.

Da's hands could build just about anything as far as Bocan could tell. Bocan could build, too, though not as well. Only simple things. He looked down at his broad, pale blue fingers and felt the battle axe strapped to his back. His hands were mostly used for killing, he supposed, though Da—and Ma herself once upon a time—would have said his hands were used for protection. And that was a noble thing.

Bocan was not so certain how much protection his hands could offer anymore. He was still uneasy with the magic that had rolled through him, too, shaking the foundations of New Salem as he lay delirious with fever, his comrades fighting down below.

He shook the thoughts aside as they entered the pale light filtering through the wavy glass of new windows, casting strange shapes on the sturdy table and chairs.

Next to the woodstove, with its small fire banked and glowing, sat a human woman. His ma. A pale shadow of her former self, she sat, not in the rocker Da had made for her, but tucked into a troll-sized over-stuffed chair with a blanket wrapped around her too-thin frame. Her once lustrous, acorn-brown hair lay lank and brittle across the woven plaid. Her eyes, once bright and shining, had grown dim.

But she breathed more easily now than when he rescued her from Underhill, and her eyes had more life than even a few moon cycles before.

She seemed content staring at the small flicker of flames through tempered glass. Da washed his hands at the large sink and filled the iron kettle before setting it carefully on top of the woodstove he had built with his own hands.

It was a cunningly crafted stove, with woodland scenes around the sides. A thing of beauty, like everything made by Da.

By all the Gods of earth and stone, a powerful wish to be back in his childhood gripped Bocan's chest, sharp with the keen sense of all that he had lost.

You have some good things now, too, he chided himself. Like his comrades and best friends. Like Jimena, the healer he had slowly courted over many years, who had finally moved to Go No More with her brother and cousins, the horse breeders and ranchers working with the Wasco just south of Go No More, and with their relative, Angel, here in town.

Jimena had already been put to work, and found a place in Go No More. Her skills at mind healing were unmatched by anyone already living there.

But she had not been able to heal his mother. At least not yet, though he knew Jimena came to visit Ma and Da every few days or so, sometimes bringing herbal unguents made by Anandita and her apprentice Tokki.

He crouched at his mother's knees, still looming over her, and gently clasped one of her pale, cold hands.

"Ma," he said. "It's me, Bocan. I've come to visit."

She turned her head and gave a soft smile.

"Come to visit," she repeated. "How nice. Who are you?"

"Ma, I am your son." And the tears he had been holding back trailed in rivulets down his broad face.

His mother reached out a gentle hand and wiped them away.

"Now, why would a strapping man like yourself need to cry?"

He looked up at Da, who had settled into a second chair, a mate to the one cradling his ma.

Da looked pained, but steady, as he shook some herbs into a glazed teapot, waiting for the water on the hob to boil.

"We all need to cry sometimes, my love," he said, keeping his voice gentle. A voice that could boom like a thunderstorm, a voice that could crack stones, now sounded like the warmth of a rising loaf of good brown bread.

That only made Bocan wish to cry all the more. But now was not the time. The time for crying was on his walk home to Jimena's arms.

"Why have you come, son?" his father asked. "And won't you sit?"

Bocan nodded and gave Ma's hand another squeeze before settling into a large chair of his own with a sigh. He clenched and released his fist, trying to ease the aching in his injured arm. He should have put some liniment on it after practice, but had not wished to take the time.

Jimena would scold him for it later, but it would be worth it. Worth just having her there to scold him.

"Tegan and the others…"

He waited as Da filled the teapot from the now-rattling iron kettle and replaced the ceramic lid.

Bocan cleared his throat.

"They found another gate."

Da's hands held their place for a moment, hovering as if frozen in midair.

"Permanent?"

"They think so."

His father shook his broad blue head, brow creased and mouth turned down at the edges.

"We need to move back into town?"

"I know you don't want to, but…"

Bocan followed his father's gaze to where it rested on Ma's face. She was off in her own world again, but seemed content enough. She no longer made the horrible mewling sounds she used to make when he first rescued her from Underhill. That was good.

Bocan's da looked his way. "You see how much better she is now. She feels comfortable here. Moving her again…"

Could undo the delicate balance that kept his ma alive.

"We can build fortifications, then, if you want to. I'll help, and so will the other knights, plus the carpenters and engineers."

"No, son. They'll be too busy protecting the township and are already stretched making spaces for the refugees. Your ma and I? We can retreat deep into the cave if need be. Or move to rooms in the public house."

"All right," Bocan replied, though he felt uneasy with his da's decision. "But if things change..."

"If things change, you can tell us where to go and what to do."

That would have to be enough for now. But it wasn't good enough to calm the disquiet making a home inside of Bocan's heart.

CHAPTER 7

SILVERHAIR

It was another beautiful day in Underhill, though the Queen could sense the slow rot around the edges of what was once a realm unchanging. The humans, in their greed and lust for power, had ruined everything. They had laid waste to their own realm, bringing about the Reckoning that had rocked all the worlds, and sown slow death into the Faery realms.

Seelie and Unseelie alike, elf, sprite, fae, gnome, and troll. The other magic realms had also been affected thus, opening the gates once more, until manitou, chaneques, nagini, and drakes all traversed the human realms openly, whereas once their realms had lived side by side, much as the realm Underhill.

Once upon a time, elven royalty could be killed only by direct assault. A silver-tipped arrow. Certain types of poison. Otherwise, they were as immortal as magic itself.

Until the Reckoning had seeded the soul sickness

into the royal court. This sickness infected the Queen's womb and the babe within. Elzabetta, her shining child. The rare offspring of the royal line. The one foretold. Her daughter with the shimmering fall of hair, tinged green, yet pale as the sunlight that warmed the floorboards beneath the Queen's delicate silk slippers.

Her daughter, whose souls wandered that realm, dividing her mind, her heart, her body. Her daughter, sickly where she should be strong. Her daughter...who had begun refusing the only treatment the Queen had found that just might save her. That just might save the realm itself.

Ungrateful girl.

Silverhair paced the room, two guards patiently at the double doors beneath the gracefully arched lintel. Two more guards were stationed near the long, tall windows.

She ignored the sweating elf on his knees in the middle of the room, though each sweep of her skirts caught his slightly acrid scent. No elf should smell that way. He was tainted from his time in the human realms.

Silverhair was not pleased. She was not pleased at her rebellious daughter. She was not pleased that her pet alchemist had fled, taking her seal with him. She was even not pleased at the sniveling sycophant who moments ago had groveled at her feet.

Peridot. Named for a precious gem. He was not so precious anymore. The elf had been her trusted spy to the township with a ridiculous name. Go No More. As if not traversing their stinking lands had any merit. As if the place they had stopped their horses and weary feet was of any consequence. As if it were a sheltered spot. As if there was safety to be had there.

There was no safety anywhere, not if the inviolable realm of Underhill had been rocked and sent to slow ruin.

The elf kneeling in the center of the sunwashed wood floors was still beautiful, as all elves were. Long, pale green hair. Eyes once as bright as the gemstone of his name, now slightly dulled from pain and fear.

A traitor to all sides, he was. Untrustworthy. Compromised. And yet, right now he was all the Queen had at her disposal.

She made another turn that swept her flowing, lichen-green skirts across the polished wood floors. As she paced, delicate, her long fingers tapped at her arms, her hair a silver waterfall down her back.

"What information have you?" she finally asked.

"I told you, my Queen." Peridot's voice was weak. Querulous. The sound of it grated, filling her with anger.

"Nothing? Nothing? Why should I keep you alive, fool?"

"Your Majesty, it isn't my fault!"

"No, it never is. Nothing is ever your fault. Nothing is ever anyone's fault. And yet, no one ever does as I ask, do they?"

She glared at her subject, whose eyes flashed with defiance before dimming once more. Well. Perhaps the sniveler still had some backbone after all.

"You were supposed to have remained in Go No

More. You were supposed to have been my eyes and ears there!"

"Your Majesty, I was compromised!"

She continued in her tirade as if he had not said a word. "...and yet you could not take it. You weak coward. You fled. Just like that fool alchemist fled and where is he now? Can you tell me that?"

Peridot's skin was white as alabaster. He looked gaunt. Too thin. As if he had not been eating or perhaps he had the same sickness her daughter had. The wasting sickness. The wandering souls leaching the life from the body until nothing was left.

"They tortured me..." The elf licked at dry lips.

"Torture. What do you know of torture?"

The Queen shot out a hand, and with a flick of her finger pierced his left shoulder blade with an elf dart filled with magic. He screamed, clutching his shoulder, and dropped to his knees. As he writhed on the floor, she caught the disgusting sweet scent of urine. The elf had pissed himself.

"Stand up," she said.

"Your Majesty," he gasped out, looking as if he were about to faint.

"Stand up. You rise in my presence. You do not kneel or sit unless I tell you so."

The two guards flanking the double doors beneath the archway flinched as if trying to figure out whether or not to help the elf. But they knew better than to move without her say, so just stood in their soft green boots, faces stoic once again.

Peridot pushed himself up and staggered to his feet.

"I need you to return to the human realms," she said. "I need you to tell me what is happening."

"But Your Majesty...they know who I am."

"Disguise yourself," she said, "or hide. I care not how you do it. But it must be done."

"Yes, your Majesty," he said.

"Leave me," she said, "and be ready to cross through the gate before night falls again on human lands."

"Yes, your Majesty. It shall be done."

"Yes," she said. "It shall."

She waved her right hand and the guards swung the doors open.

Bowing and scraping, Peridot backed out of the room, taking his sickly scent with him.

The Queen felt the threads she had woven so carefully begin to unravel and fray. She needed a new plan. She didn't trust that Peridot would bring her anything useful. She just wanted him out of her sight.

The Queen whirled to her guards. "Send for Tarioc."

"Yes, my Queen." The guard bowed and exited.

At least there was still someone she could trust. Tarioc would tell her of her daughter.

She loved her daughter, but the child had not lived up to the promise of her birth. Her souls were beyond saving now, and her usefulness to the realm diminished. But there had to be another way, to use Elzabetta as a pawn in the great game of keeping the power of this realm alive.

Yes. If Elzabetta could not be saved, perhaps the Queen's shining child could be made into a weapon of war.

CHAPTER 8
ABYAD

Abyad stepped through the temporary gate he'd sketched with his mind, into a green place filled with trees and shadows, dripping with moisture. His dog, Dukhan, followed. Abyad inhaled deeply, drawing in the fresh air of this place, so different from his home. A home he had not seen in more years than he cared to count.

The dog snuffled and scratched at the roots of trees, scenting the creatures who lived in this dense forest.

It was a strange thing, being in this place of green and damp. Not that djinn did not travel; they did and always had. But like most elemental beings, they grew familiar with certain pockets of water, air, and soil. They grew used to the way the sun cast its light, and the heat of it. But Abyad had made his choices long ago, traveling far and wide to distant places, planning to return to the desert. To undulating waves of sand.

To the fertile places of oasis. To a wide sky and punishing sun.

Abyad had travelled to this place hundreds of years ago by human estimation, off on an adventure. And now, though he could once travel with the blink of an eye, he was also trapped, for the same gates that opened the realms between magic and human had also made other pathways much more difficult and complex to navigate.

The air currents were uncertain. The waters muddied. The fiery pathways splintered.

And so, he made arrows and thumb rings for bowyers, and worked fine leather to pass the time, yoking his lot with these humans who worked together to try to make a better place.

He admired them for that. Admired, that in all the brevity of their lives, they had courage enough to live their lives to the fullest. To not hoard goods, power, or time, and to not weep overlong when calamity befell them.

Resilient creatures, humans. Some of the strongest ones he knew.

Even the Reckoning could not take that away; coming with fire and the shaking of earth, it changed everything. It had rocked all the worlds, sundering some pathways permanently, and drawing other spaces much closer than they had ever been.

To return to his home now would have taken more magic than he had at his disposal. Perhaps someday....

And, though his heart sometimes longed for the shifting desert winds, the air in this place welcomed him. They had come to an agreement, and he found he had grown to love the softer qualities of both air and sun in this part of the human realm. Though he still wore the traditional swathes of black to protect the bone-white skin that covered his muscles and his flesh, most days he likely did not need them.

But, like the glowing orb he wore on a thong around his neck, the black garments were a reminder, a piece of the home he had left behind. A comfort to him in this strange, beautiful land.

Abyad tilted his head back, staring up at the tall, majestic trees of this once alien landscape. Spruce. Western Hemlock. Douglas fir. Underscoring the earthy smell of slowly composting plant matter, he caught the scent of roses. A scent that should not be in such a place. No roses grew beneath these trees. Not unless willed there by magic.

There were none of the usual forest sounds. The animals and birds were silent, possibly at his use of portal magic. The djinni tried to use the transportation magic as little as possible. He knew that it spooked the humans, and animals as well. Making temporary portals also tapped some reserve that Abyad was yet uncertain how to replenish in these human realms.

It took a goodly amount of rest and sustenance for him to be able to do several feats of complex magic in a row. Once upon a time, in his old home, he could command the forces of magic with a thought. These days? Only the magic of air was consistently his friend.

He paused. Breathed. Tasted the damp and green.

And, despite the lack of ordinary sounds, Abyad listened.

He was good at listening. And at standing very, very, still. Reading his energy, Dukhan ceased his snuffling as well.

Tilting his head, Abyad heard the scurry of mice through the fallen needles and carpeting of leaves. And there, in the distance, the cry of a hunting falcon. Slowly, the other forest sounds returned, along with a variety of scents his keen nose had missed before. A skunk. A fox. A trio of deer.

Sniffing at the air, Abyad took in the citrusy balsam scent of hemlock spruce and yes, that undernote of roses lingered. It was coupled now with the throat-coating smells of rotting fruit. The scent of Underhill.

Underhill's signature had always been roses, sometimes roses and amber, mixed. The decaying apple scent was new, increasing over the past few years. Post-Reckoning, so much had changed.

Abyad knew this, as he knew so many magical things.

Abyad was wise, though he kept his own counsel most of the time.

It was easier to keep one's counsel when one was solitary, and Abyad had been alone for too long. Too many years in this place far from his windswept home. Too many years living in a human settlement, yet never quite part of their rituals and ways.

The djinn make a home everywhere they go, said his mentor. But his mentor was gone to the winds of time as well.

As he woolgathered in the forest, Abyad paced, black shod feet tracing the forest floor, eyes seeking out clues, information, magical traces.

He tasted magic on the wind. Underhill magic.

He missed djinn magic, though, be they comrades of fire or of air.

Abyad stopped, expanding his field of awareness. Seeking out that which still felt wrong.

The shining, shimmering seam was only several paces away, but Abyad did not approach. Not yet.

He needed to get the lay of the land first. See what he could see. Sense what he could sense. Figure out who had been here. Who had opened this gate at great expense to their magical stores.

Dukhan barked, alerting Abyad to pay attention. His black eyes followed the black gaze of his companion and saw a curious thing. In the midst of this mixed-wood forest was a tree that did not belong, a mighty oak, spreading its branches gracefully outward as if reaching for the heart of the forest itself.

It was not that oaks did not grow in this part of the human world. They did. But generally oaks liked more space to spread. They did not wish to be crowded in by other trees, particularly not trees of their own kind.

They were a bit like djinn in that way.

Abyad strode toward the tree, black garments flowing about him.

He could unwrap himself, for the sun was weak this time of year and did not reach far into dense forest. But the voluminous robes and pants and shawls and all the black accoutrement that made him a djinni of the air? Yes. They gave him comfort in the strange, uncanny land.

When Abyad was a shorter distance from the tree, he bowed.

"Greetings, friend oak."

The tree responded slowly, as trees always did. If they responded at all.

"Greetings, magic one," it said, voice low and sweet as honey.

"I wish to know of any interesting magic or other things you may wish to impart that you have sensed here recently."

There was a long pause.

Abyad waited. Patience was nothing to djinn. Or rather, patience was everything. He let the wind ruffle his robes, and inhaled deeply, enjoying the ability to simply stand and be for a moment.

"Big magic," the old oak finally said. "Not of this place. Old magic."

"Old magic," Abyad repeated. "How much? And how many magic users?"

The tree did not answer the first question, and Abyad cursed himself for asking. It was a foolish question. Extraneous. Like asking a fish how much water was around.

"Elf," the oak replied after long silence.

That could have meant the kind of magic or could have meant that there was but one magician at play. Abyad thought long and hard what other questions he could ask the tree, as the breeze played with his robes and a shy fox darted by between two trees.

"One elf? You sense one elf?"

The oak remained silent, the few remaining leaves upon its branches softly rustling. It began to sing in a counterpoint to the whistle of the breeze. Clearly, the conversation was closed.

Abyad moved closer to the shining seam in the middle of the forest.

The gate looked permanent, not the quick opener and closer Abyad had used to get here, and not a temporary gate that might last for a few days, up to one cycle of the moon. To build a gate such as this took time and the effort of several beings.

So, when the oak had simply replied elf, did it mean the type of magic that had built the gate? Or that one elf had traveled through?

If the latter was the case—and Abyad suspected it was so—who was that elf, and where were they now?

He deepened his attention, and tried to tune into the singing tree, hoping to glean more information from its slow, woody thoughts.

He saw the sheen of sun upon pale hair. A tall creature whose face the djinni recognized.

"Peridot," he murmured to himself. The elf that had betrayed the township of Go No More. The djinni was not surprised.

Wrapping his black clothing more firmly around his limbs, he clicked his tongue at the black dog, and set about tracking the rogue.

CHAPTER 9
TEGAN

The tall, beamed ceilings towered overhead, and a fire crackled and spat in the enormous fieldstone hearth. The public house was packed, though Tegan was not there for revelry. Per was upstairs in a room that should have been relatively quiet, and was, compared to the rest of the place, but nonetheless, Tegan's head pounded. The sounds of the boisterous crowd drinking and carousing down below wafted up and through the open door. The noise was not helping matters.

Along with drunk and stoned laughter there were arguments that cut off suddenly, hushed murmurs, and the whispers of people huddled together. Waiting.

Waiting for the council to share with the rest of the township word of what Tegan and the dragoons had brought back. The townspeople knew better than to spread much speculation—unfounded rumors were a good way to sow panic—but that didn't keep curiosity and worry at bay.

And the New Salem refugees? Well, speculation and rumor were all they had to go on, wasn't it? Having lived beneath a petty despot's thumb, they were unused to the free flow of actual information. Tegan hoped the folks from Go No More could calm their fears.

The council met upstairs in the large, spacious room around a long table set aside for these sorts of meetings. The door was open because Jenny had yet to arrive, likely getting beer and snacks from Porrac, curse the toothsome knight.

The council did not usually meet upstairs these days, not since Anandita had joined in on rotation. Her wheelchair would not make it up the stairs.

But Anandita had other business to attend to this evening. There was so much work to be done with the New Salem refugees, all the healers were run ragged. She and her apprentice Tokki were working with Doc Warren and Jimena, the mind healer from the ranchero down south. The woman that had stolen Bocan's heart.

The healers were busy taking care of some of the trauma left from the years of abuse by that warlord Wulf and the aftermath—psychological, magical, and physical—from the Battle of New Salem itself.

At least Tegan had clean skin and a scrubbed scalp. Per belly was filled with pork stew, and a cup of Jamie's finest ale sat sweating in a ceramic mug at per right hand. All of this helped, as did the occasional press of Case's muscular thigh against per own.

Tegan shot per comrade a look. He winked at her,

eyes shining above those always ruddy cheeks. Damn, the man was sexy. Tegan looked up and caught Litha the scout stifling a grin. Great. Just great. That meant Tegan was going to get shit later. But maybe it would be worth it.

These days, Tegan grew ever closer to saying fuck it and grabbing Case by the cock. Per had also been intrigued by the black eyes of the djinn, Abyad, of late. Per wondered where the black-clad djinni had gone off to. Tegan's thoughts wandered for a moment, wondering what it would be like to tumble into a large bed with both of them, a concept per entertained now and then.

One night in a town far away—when per had smoked one bowl too many—per had fallen into bed for quite a sporting time. Two buxom women had enjoyed Tegan's prowess and the sheen that came from bedding a Steel Clan Knight.

Tegan grinned at the memory. Case cocked an eyebrow in question. Tegan shook per head and tried to pay attention. Rafiq had many questions yet again, and was arguing with Charles Wong and Aphrodite. The Go No More mages disagreed with the current council head about what needed to be done.

Tegan was bored and jittery and did not understand how the council members sat through such tedious meetings all the time. Tegan had given per report. Now all per wanted was to smoke a bowl, crawl into bed, and sleep for three days...and then actually *do* something. This was why Tegan was a Knight and, per supposed, why all the clan heads rotated on and off the council. The town charter said the council rotation was to keep any one clan or faction from consolidating power, but really? The reason had to be to stave off boredom.

Tegan hoped to never have to do that sort of service to the town, but knew per day would come. Preferably when Tegan was getting too old to be first on the lines of skirmish.

For now, give Tegan per kpingas and machete close to hand, a horse or bike between per thighs, and scouting to be done. Tegan would even take dispatching smelly bandits or fighting a protracted battle over sitting around this thrice-damned table.

Two sets of boots shook the stairs outside the room and in barreled red-haired Jenny, also known as Magic's Bane, much to her chagrine. Jenny was followed by a slower halbtroll who looked to be in pain. Bocan was always in pain these days. He ducked to enter and carried a steaming mug of foul-smelling brew in his good hand. Willow bark and who knows what else? Tegan glanced down at the sweating mug of beer, wishing per had been wise enough to opt for the vile tea. That likely would have taken care of per pounding head, at least, making this meeting more pleasant.

Jenny scraped a chair along the wood planks of the floor. Tegan winced at the sound as per comrade plopped her strapping frame down next to Tegan. Bocan sat on a sturdy bench against the wall. He'd sat on a council chair one time. Neither he nor the chair had had a very good time of things that day.

"What news?" John, the current head of the Dairy and Husbandry Clan, spoke to Jenny. He was a white man with a kind, round face and a steady nature. Tegan respected him. He didn't speak much, but when he did, it was usually worth listening to.

Jenny shook her head. "No news. I just came to report on the township's training program."

Rafiq gestured for Jenny to go ahead. Tegan's mind wandered as per comrade spoke of the township's readiness for random incursions and others chimed in on the refugees. The conversation went on and on, until Tegan's head was fit to burst.

"You have our reports," Tegan snapped, "and now you lot need to decide what exactly we're going to do about the gate."

And let the rest of us be about our business.

Case leaned over the table, looking directly at Rafiq. "The only reason we came back so quickly was because we needed to consult Aphrodite and Charles. I'd really like to hear what they have to say."

The mages shared a look. Aphrodite made a "go ahead" hand motion to Charles Wong, who tugged at the neck of his robes.

"Yes," he said, "we've been trying to ascertain if there's a difference in the winds. We've consulted the runes and the crystal ball and have even considered inquiring with the drakes."

"But it does not seem to be the time for that yet," Aphrodite added. "Nothing feels urgent as of yet. At least one of us should go with the Knights and do further reconnaissance. See if we can pick up on any traces."

The blond-haired, voluptuous mage looked around the table, a slight frown on her face. "I truly wish Abyad was here. We could use his expertise."

"Where did he go?" Bocan rumbled.

Tegan turned to the weary halbtroll, surprised. "We don't quite know. You were there. You saw. He simply just disappeared."

Bocan shook his head slowly, like an injured bear.

"Yes," Jenny said. "He opened a temporary gate and walked through."

Her words hung over the table like a pall. Everyone fell silent for a moment. Taking it in. Weighing the implications.

"You think the djinni...?" John, the dairyman, began.

"Of course not," Charles Wong snapped out. "That is ridiculous. Abyad would not betray us in that way."

But, Tegan thought, *Peridot betrayed us.* And if an elf known to the township and considered a friend could do such a thing, why not the djinn?

Tegan did not want to believe it. But as attractive as she found Abyad, per could not deny his uncanny nature. Which meant per did not really know who exactly he was. Tegan shrugged.

The only words per spoke out loud were, "How well do any of us know each other? Yet we have to trust as best we can."

Or the world they had built would fall to pieces.

"Trust Allah, and tether your camel," Rafiq replied. An old, PR reference. Tegan had only seen a picture of the strange beast in one of Winney's books.

Per looked at the council head. "Indeed. Trust, but remain on guard. Now let's figure out what exactly we're going to do about the new gate."

CHAPTER 10

PERIDOT

It was raining again. Not a deluge, thank the elements, but a soft pattering on the dense fir-needle canopy above.

It always seemed to rain in this human realm except for the bursts of heat during summer that caused everything to ripen and grow to enormous proportions.

Peridot like neither extreme heat nor cold, but he also did not like the barely changing landscape of Underhill. The elf was dissatisfied with everything about his life.

Sick of being at the Queen's beck and call. Weary of being a spy. Tired to death of growing to like people, only to have friendships snatched from his fingertips. He had been comfortable in Go No More. He had grown to appreciate the technologies of the humans. The way they adapted and changed. The way they looked out for one another, rather than stabbing each other in the back constantly like the upper caste elves did in Underhill.

Politics, politics, politics. His mind buzzed with it like a swarm of hornets, and Peridot wanted nothing more than to be free. But here he was, trapped in between yet again. Still in thrall to the Queen and her wishes, yet banished from the human spaces.

He had also lost his closest friend, Damson, unutterably ruining their relationship. They had grown to trust each other. Their bond was deepening even toward—dare he say it?—love. Peridot's heart yearned for love, but it was not to be his. Not if things continued thus.

Instead, here he was, having poured sweat, concentration, and magic together with the Underhill mages and sorcerers to build this new gate.

A gate that could spell the ruin of this realm. And the saving of Underhill.

So here he was in these woods, staring up at the tall trees with green needles dripping wet onto the dun-brown cloak he used to cover his green leathers.

He'd also tasked the shoe-making gnomes Underhill to fashion him sturdy brown boots. As long as he kept his hair covered, he was passable at a distance. In close proximity, of course, the fine bones of his face and arched peaks of his eyebrows would give him away, even if they never saw the tilted tips of his ears.

He would just have to not let anyone get that close now, wouldn't he?

He didn't want anyone to get that close. He didn't deserve for anyone to get that close. Peridot's life was forfeit to the stupid chess game he was but a rook in. Or he had been a rook, once upon a time, with real power to affect things. Time and chance seemed to have relegated him to a mere pawn.

His boots squelched into a pile of moldering leaves. By all the gold in the mountains, this place was disgusting. Everything was dying all the time. Dying, or being born in a bloody, fluid-soaked mess.

Yet his heart longed for all this too. Though he'd built a gate to the Queen's specifications, knowing that she had a plan, he actually was not certain...what would destroy or save this place or Underhill? Stealing souls and the mounting human dead were a strategy, to be sure, though that had stopped for now. Though short term? Elzabetta was not improved and Underhill still showed signs of this selfsame rot around the edges. Apples growing brown and soft on green grass as flies swarmed the fallen fruit.

Such things were anathema to Underhill, and yet, they were now part of Underhill all the same.

So no, Peridot was not certain what the fate of Underhill would be. Nor was he certain what the Queen wanted anymore, other than that he was to track down the alchemist. To bring him back or kill him. Peridot also had the sense that Silverhair grew tired of the whole charade.

He had heard her muttering to herself one day when she thought no one was listening. She swore that if her ungrateful daughter wanted to die, the queen would let her...but not until there was a baby quickening in her daughter's womb. Not until after the forced birth of royalty. Though how exactly the Queen expected this to happen when elvish babes were rare to begin with, and her daughter was so sick, Peridot did not know.

Probably more necromantic nonsense. He shuddered beneath his brown wool cloak.

Peridot had thought that magic wrought by the alchemist was evil, but then he saw the necromancers at work at Silverhair's behest. A stomach-churning sight he hoped to never witness again. In the back of his brain was a thrumming, disquieting sense that the evil at Queen Silverhair's disposal knew no bounds.

His boots squelched on something that he hoped was simply rotting leaves.

Peridot looked up toward the tangled branches and dark gray sky, rain washing his face.

He wished he could be free of it. Wished he could hang himself from one of these mighty trees and be done with it. Or perhaps he could fling himself from the top of the high, snow-peaked mountain where the purple dragon lived.

But Peridot knew he never would. He was weak. Too weak to do what must be done. Too weak to kill the queen. Too weak to kill himself.

So, he continued in limbo. Pushing forward. Always wondering what was next.

CHAPTER II
CASE

Case was glad to be working on something simple with his son. The council meeting the night before—and his discussions with the Knights—had left his head as sore as if he'd drunk half a barrel of mead. He'd sparred a bit that morning after making Jason breakfast, and though that did his body good, his heart hadn't been in it.

Winney had declared school out for the day, so Jason was able to join Case in the shop, working on his bike. There was always tinkering to be done after a long trip. The engineers and mechanics had done a beautiful job forming the machine he lovingly cared for, but with the uncertain PR roads, the bikes needed diligent maintenance.

Jason handed him a wrench, towhead even more rumpled than usual, his rough hemp work shirt already stained with the brassica oil used to power the metal beasts.

"Thanks, son. How are you doing today?"

Jason was a pensive child. A strong boy with a big heart, he often felt things keenly. Case knew he was concerned, and who wouldn't be? Everyone who was paying attention was concerned.

"I'm okay." His son shrugged. "You know?"

"Well, I don't know. That's why I'm asking." Case probed gently, not wanting to upset his son, but also wanting to teach him that a person who evaded their emotions was a person who ended up with long-term trouble.

"It's okay to talk about it, you know," he said.

Jason shrugged again and bent his head, hands already at work cleaning some of the parts Case had lifted out of the bike earlier. The bike didn't really need to be disassembled so thoroughly, though it didn't hurt. Some of the other Steel Clan members were at the same task, and the gentle sounds of conversation, the clank of tools and the scent of biofuel and grease filled the air. It was a combination that soothed Case's souls.

He and his growing-too-rapidly son worked in companionable silence for a while.

"I just..." Jason finally spoke, voice faltering. "I just don't understand. What do they want from us?"

His son looked up, suddenly fierce, hazel green eyes flashing with anger. His creamy skin flushed to almost Case-levels of ruddiness, and his shoulders were stiff with tension.

Case looked at his son with respect. He understood that anger. It was a natural anger that any person would seek to harm another without good cause. It sent a kindling of pride through his chest that he had raised to son to think that way.

Swan, too, he thought grudgingly. In line with their arrangement, the bowyer who had carried his child had never really acted as a mother. Case wanted a child, and Swan had been willing to bear the baby if he took on the brunt of parenting.

I'm not cut out for it, she had said. Case could not fault or blame her for it, because every human was different, but the swell of love he felt while looking at his son made it harder to understand. He wanted and loved his son so much that Swan's cheerful indifference seemed strange.

Almost as strange and inexplicable as the cruelty of Underhill seemed to his son.

"Not sure, son," Case replied, tinkering with the small plugs that lent a spark to power the engine. He was always amazed at what the machinists could make, cutting forged metal in such a fine, intricate fashion. The large tools used to power the mills and help with harvest made sense to him. But these finely wrought parts were amazing. As astounding to him as the human heart.

"You remember I talked to you about Wulf from New Salem? And the reason so many people live here now, and we're building more homes just outside the gates?"

Jason nodded.

"Well, Wulf cared more about power than he cared about the people. More than he cared about the animals, and the land, and the river, even. More than he cared about the magical beings who make the Willamette Valley their home. The only reason he cared about magic at all was that he could use it. And he used it in the worst way and for the worst reasons possible."

Jason's hands were still. He leaned toward Case, waiting. "What reasons?"

Case looked out the big bay doors out toward the towering fir at the center of town. He took in the sounds of industry, and thought about all that had been built in this place, and all that would be built in time.

"Magic gave Wulf more power over other people, to manipulate and control their spirits. Their lives."

And wasn't that a bitter thing? As bitter as anything the silver-haired queen had wrought.

Jason frowned. "I don't get it. It doesn't make any sense."

"It doesn't to us," Case replied, keeping his voice steady, "because we were raised to share things, and to think of the good of community before the good of ourselves. Not everyone is like that. And Underhill? Well, they're worse than most. They have an ingrained hierarchy that has gone on for longer than we can even imagine. Kings and Queens and princesses and all the like...."

"That sounds stupid. Like a dumb old book."

"Well," Case said with a laugh. "I can't really disagree with you there. I find it foolish, too. It's a dangerous sort of foolishness, though, and one we need to keep on guard against. That's why we have the council, and the members change out every few years or so. This gives them enough time to get good at what they're doing, but doesn't give them enough time to become entrenched and think they can lord it over the rest of us. And they always report back to their Clans and get consensus on any major, long term decisions. The Clans have opted to trust the council members for decisions that must be made during crisis, though."

This time his son nodded. "That makes sense."

Good, Case thought. Lessons imparted.

A slender, wiry, shadow fell across the shop floor. Case knew that shadow anywhere.

"Tegan," he said, looking up. And there per was, whipcord slim, wearing a ratty old sumac-dyed sweater, per leathers and boots, hair freshly twisted after the bath they'd all enjoyed. A bath in which Case had done his damnedest to not stare at the slight breasts and the muscular arms and shoulders of the person who was probably one of his best friends besides his son. A person who was his comrade, and had had his back in so many battles and skirmishes.

He owed Tegan a lot. Tegan would reply that they all owed each other. And that was true. It was the way things should be among comrades and friends.

He'd always been attracted to Tegan. To per strength and concentrated power, to per insightfulness, and even per impulsiveness. Neither of them was in any way celibate. Tegan had bedded as many people as Case, yet the two of them had never bedded one another.

"Case," Tegan said, "and Jason."

His heart lurched at per voice, and he realized he'd been staring at per lips.

Right. There were two reasons Case had never rolled in the blankets with Tegan. His friendship with Tegan was too important to him for a mere dalliance, and he didn't want to mess things up. And his son needed to remain the most important person in his life, at least for a few more precious years.

But damn, didn't those slim muscles fill out a pair of leather pants nicely?

"More meetings this morning?" Case asked. Tegan nodded, face pinched.

"Yes. That's why I never want to join the thrice-damned council. If they ever try to rope me in...hold me back, okay?"

"You got it," he said. Tegan stalked over to per own hog and started working on a tune-up. They worked in silence. Jason moved to help both Tegan and Case, the trio falling into a natural rhythm.

Jason and Tegan never talked much to each other but seemed to have some sort of understanding. It was funny. Case never would have said that Tegan was particularly good with children, but for a certain type of child like his son? That was perfect. Tegan treated everyone with the same respect—or scorn—so per treated Jason as if he were an adult, and Jason responded to that just fine.

Tegan shot him a grin and Case smiled back, heart lifting.

This was good. This was the life they were meant to build in the township. Camaraderie and honest work.

A shout came up from outside. Jason dropped the wire scrub brush he'd been using and ran out to see what the commotion was. Tegan and Case both rose, wiping their hands on greasy shop rags.

"Dad! Tegan! You better come!"

Case and Tegan and all the other Knights reached for whatever weapons were to hand and boiled out the garage doors, aimed toward the paddock and the training ground.

CHAPTER 12

JENNY

Jenny was hot with anger, not only that Tegan and per comrades found another permanent gate, but now Jenny suspected just who had made it. It was the pig fucker stumbling in front of her, roughly pulled along by two angry refugees from New Salem.

Apparently, the two had found him staggering half delirious in the woods. Jenny was also angry that Anandita pushed her chair beside Jenny, shouting like a swarm of bees. Jenny half listened, and half tuned her out. Which she knew would piss off her lover even more.

"Are you listening to me?" Anandita shouted. "He needs a healer! Not a tribunal!"

Jenny kept walking, face set in a grimace, ignoring her partner's huffed-out breath that telegraphed that Jenny was walking a bit too fast.

"Maybe he needs a tribunal, then a healer," Jenny replied, cutting off each word as if biting through a hard trail ration. By the time Jenny got to Tegan, they had amassed a small crowd of interested townspeople wondering what was going on.

Bocan came walking up from the opposite direction, Serena flying just behind. Jenny noticed he'd been absent a bit lately, and looked as if he still had a lot on his mind. She'd have to talk to her comrade later and figure out what was happening with him. But right now, there was something much more urgent at stake.

"What do we have here?" Tegan asked, machete strapped at per hip, that scarred right eyebrow raised and arms crossed over per narrow chest. Haryath and Amarpal stood at per side, faces looking grim.

"The alchemist." Jenny practically spat the words out. "And probably the person who made that gate."

"I didn't." The alchemist's voice was weak and dry, the protest feeble, as if he knew he would not be believed.

"I don't believe you," Jenny said. "Who else would have made a gate like that, and why?"

"The Queen…"

"Quiet!" Tegan said. The alchemist sagged between his two captors. "Bring him to the bench."

Tegan jerked per head toward the ell of sturdy benches outside the garage, then stared at Jenny.

"He looks like he's about to fall over."

Jenny knew that explanation wasn't compassion on her comrade's part, but simple expediency. The alchemist would be easier to question if the two new townspeople didn't have to keep him on his feet the entire time. Jenny didn't like giving the pig fucker any measure of comfort, but Tegan was right.

The New Salem refugees did as Tegan asked, and headed toward the benches.

"Where did they find him?" Tegan asked quietly.

"Apparently, staggering through the woods, half out of his mind with delirium, which is why he needs a healer," Anandita remarked, tapping her fingers on the push rims of her chair. "Just look at the man!"

Jenny finally looked down at her partner. "He's an elf. Look, I know you're angry, Anandita. And I know the Healing Clan has their own ways. But right now, you need to trust the Steel Clan to do our job."

Anandita started to protest again, but Jenny raised one hand.

"Our job is keeping the township safe. And right now this man is a major security breach and we have to find out what he knows, and why he's here."

Now it was Anandita's turn to cross arms over her ample, curvaceous chest. If Jenny hadn't been so focused on the alchemist, that alone would have been a distraction. As it was, she filed the image away for later. Maybe there would be some makeup sex in her future.

"Are we going to do this?" Case asked, just as Rafiq and John the dairyman and Jenny's mother, Danica, came bustling over.

"What in the world is going on here?" Rafiq demanded.

"These two found the alchemist wandering in our woods," Jenny replied.

"Gods of Earth and Stone," Bocan muttered. The big halbtroll had taken up position near the benches, and was looking very much as if he wanted to sit down himself.

He held his left arm with his right, and Jenny could tell he didn't even realize he was doing it, which meant he was in pain, and which also meant they'd overdone it during sparring practice. Great, another reason for Anandita to to be pissed at her. The Knights were going to have to force their comrade into more rest, because Bocan needed to heal and not do foolish things. But getting a Knight to not spar was tricky. Ego got in the way. The halbtroll's pride would be wounded, and Jenny was sure he'd end up acting like a cow with a sore head. But she'd deal with that later.

Right now, her attention needed to be focused on the alchemist, who was sipping water from a skin Case's son, Jason, had brought him. Anandita was right, the elf did look terrible. He was gaunt looking, and filthy, as if he hadn't eaten or slept properly in who knew how long.

And that didn't make any sense. If he had just come from Underhill, he should look better cared for.

"I did not fashion the gate," he insisted. "I don't have the wherewithal to do that. Not on my own. I haven't been Underhill since the battle..."

That stopped Jenny's protests in her mouth. "What do you mean?"

"I escaped," he said wearily. "With this."

He held up Queen Silverhair's seal. The sundered triangle with three oak leaves.

"What does that mean," Tegan muttered, "that he has the seal?"

Jenny shook her head. She didn't know enough about Underhill politics to be able to say. Bocan looked troubled, but kept his counsel, most likely because Aphrodite and Charles Wong arrived in a swirl of cloaks and arcanely embroidered robes.

Jenny breathed a sigh of relief at seeing the two mages. Charles Wong, slight-framed, with olive-gold skin and the elaborately embroidered robes that were his signature, and her former sometimes-lover Aphrodite with her shock of short blond hair and her sumptuous curves.

Today, Aphrodite wore a purple tunic over dark knee-high boots, topped with a navy cloak.

Anandita jabbed Jenny in the side.

"What was that for?" Jenny startled, rubbing where her partner's finger had poked. Hard.

"Don't think I didn't see you looking." Anandita scowled.

Jenny grinned. "Jealous, lover?"

Anandita huffed and crossed her arms over her chest, settling her goldenrod cloak around her shoulders. The cloak was pinned on her left shoulder with a beautiful brooch made by Dita's husband, Long. He had died of the same soul sickness that took too many. The same soul sickness that this pig fucker had brought about.

Jenny glared at the elf.

"I'm not inclined to trust you," she said. "I'm not

inclined to trust anything you say or do. Not after the havoc you've wreaked on this realm."

Carondel shook his head and rubbed his eyes.

"I do not blame you," he said. "All I can do is tell you that the princess is in danger. And if the princess is in danger, Underhill is in danger."

"And if Underhill is in danger," Aphrodite interjected, "our realm might be, too. We just don't know enough about the interdependence of all the realms. Anything can upset the balance again, for good or ill."

Well, shit, Jenny thought.

"So what do we do?" She gestured toward the slumped figure on the bench. "With him?"

"As I said," Anandita said, voice bristling with irritation, "the elf needs a healer."

"Also needs a good washing," said one of the New Salemites, wrinkling their nose. Jenny didn't blame them. She could smell the man from where she stood.

"All right," Jenny conceded. "He needs to be guarded day and night. But for now, get him cleaned up and fed. And yes," she turned to Anandita, "I suppose the healers should look after him as well."

"Where should we put him?" asked one of the New Salemites. "You all don't have a jail, do you?"

Jenny shuddered. Such things were anathema in Go No More, and yet sometimes people did need to be held safely until an issue got figured out.

"He can stay in one of the rooms in the public house." That would be easy to guard. There would be food on hand, one room with one locking door and one window high above the ground. One guard outside, one guard by the door. Two Steel Clan members.

Jenny pointed to the two Sikhs. "Haryath and Amarpal, you two are on first watch. Help get him to the bathhouse, then take him to the public house ...get him some food, and whatever the healers need. Jason?"

"Yes!" The towheaded boy practically bristled with excitement.

"Send word to Jamie and Porrac. They're about to have a guest, and we'll need a secure room and some hot food."

Case's son ran off.

Jenny looked at the small crowd gathered near the garage bays.

"The rest of you? Show's over. We'll know more when we know more. And trust me, there will be a public house meeting about it."

The one trouble with the founder's insistence that Go No More remain an egalitarian-run township? Meetings.

And in the meantime, it looked as if they really needed to do something about that damn gate. At least that meant a road trip. Jenny could stand to have some wind in her hair about now.

CHAPTER 13

BOCAN

Bocan's arm was on fire again, but he knew better than to let it show on his face. Not with Anandita around. The healer had been commiserating with his partner, Jimena, who was already angry enough with him for sparring with Jenny. He gotten quite the earful when he arrived home afterwards, and was frankly surprised she hadn't thrown him out. It was only her healer's code that had made her give him the medicine he needed. She had grumbled and cursed the entire time she was rubbing Anandita's special liniment into his tortured flesh.

At least he knew that she loved him, otherwise she wouldn't have gotten as angry as she had. But that didn't mean she wouldn't get a report from Anandita later if he so much as scratched his arm. Not that Jimena would ask Anandita to spy on him, it was just that healers talked. Especially healers that were new friends.

It was one surprise after another with Jimena. Not

only had she finally moved to Go No More, but their relationship seemed to be deepening. Bocan's heart swelled at the thought. He'd loved the crotchety mind-healer for so long, he'd grown used to thinking it would never really happen for them. That they would have their occasional bed sport when Bocan traveled southwest...but that Jimena would remain as she always was: an isolated woman living alone on the edges of community.

Turned out she wasn't as much of a loner as he'd always thought. Her friendship with Anandita was just more proof of that.

But right now? That friendship gave him a pain in the head to match the pain in his arm.

Bocan pulled his attention back to the meeting. It was mostly the current council, most of the Steel Clan, two of the trolls, and Go No More's remaining elf, Damson. Beneath the coiled green braids piled on her head, her moon-pale face looked weary. Beaten down. Peridot's betrayal had been hard on her. It also could not have been easy to have to torture her heart friend.

Anandita sat in her chair, arms crossed over her chest, next to the large river stone fireplace. He sat on a bench next to her, his own arms crossed—right gently supporting the throbbing left—watching the proceedings across the room.

Tegan was practically bursting from per skin. His comrade's whipcord body vibrated with tension.

Jenny leaned down, saying something in per ear. Tegan scowled. Bocan felt a pang of regret, seeing them. He knew that soon they would both likely be off with the mages and the scouts, investigating the gate. Even he had to admit that the foolish sparring session had proven that he was unfit for a long motorcycle ride. If his arm seized up mid-journey, there was no way he could control his bike.

He could take Bodie, his Percheron, but with everyone else on their hogs, that would be too slow. The only way to get to the gate site in good enough time was by motorcycle. So Bocan was getting stuck with township duty, which was all right, he supposed. Someone had to do it, and a cadre of other Steel Clan Knights had already been picked to stay behind. They would continue training the New Salem refugees while keeping the township under a watchful guard. There were too many variables at play. Always. An attack could come from everywhere or nowhere. Gates appearing and disappearing. The djinni gone some-where. Peridot the elf on the loose...And here, Caron-del, looking much cleaner and a little less ragged, but still a ghost of his former self. Who knew what the pig fucker was up to? Bocan had no sympathy for the elvish alchemist though, not since he had been the one to experiment on Bocan's ma.

"Can I rip his head off from his neck?" Bocan asked.

"Hush," Anandita said.

He shrugged. "I get that you're annoyed with me on Jimena's behalf, but that pig fucker ruined my ma."

Ripping Carondel's head from his neck was prob-ably too kind, given the havoc and destruction the elf was party to.

"I know," Anandita said, relenting slightly. "I know

this is hard on you. But it's hard on us all. And beating him to a pulp isn't going to help matters. For one thing, we need more information."

The healer was right.

Bocan grimaced, but settled down to listen and ignored the throbbing from his left arm.

"Will you agree to this?" Aphrodite was saying. The mage leaned over the alchemist. Her short blond hair stuck out around her head like a baby chick's down, but did nothing to soften the grave look on her round face. Apparently the mages wanted to use some sort of psychic coercion on Carondel. That was serious business. It would go better for everyone if he agreed. If not, it would be hour upon hour of questioning, and they might end up using coercion anyway, if it was deemed necessary.

The matter made humans squeamish, Bocan knew. As a halbtroll whose parents had fled the evil machinations Underhill? And as the son of a human woman missing whole swathes of her soul because of this elf? Bocan had far more stomach for the process. Not that this made him any better or worse than the humans gathered here. His sense of ethics was just slightly different.

Every person in the room was silent now, leaning toward the two mages and the elf. The door opened and Arrow snuck in, looking around the room. She caught Bocan looking at her, and her eyes skittered away. A strange one, Arrow was. A dark-skinned elf with pale green hair, and the gray leathers she favored, Arrow had come to Go No More a prisoner. Although she'd been integrating into the township, Bocan and the other Knights did not quite trust her.

"What is she doing here?" Anandita hissed.

Well, that was interesting. Apparently the Knights weren't the only ones lacking trust in Arrow's integrity.

Bocan caught Amarpal's eye. The turbaned Knight had propped herself against one of the massive pillars holding up the mezzanine above. She raised a dark eyebrow in question and he jerked his head toward Arrow.

Amarpal's eyes grew wide. She nodded, then began weaving her way toward the elf, stopping Arrow before she could fade into a spot against the wall under the shadows of the second floor. The Sikh gestured sharply, pointing a finger from the elf to the door. Arrow shook her head and crossed her arms in refusal. Jerrod joined them, face grim.

Bocan shifted his attention back to the center of the room. Charles Wong and Aphrodite were carving gestures in the air around the alchemist's head. Carondel's body jerked, and he took in a massive breath, then coughed, closing his eyes.

When his eyes opened again, they looked strange. As if he had taken one of Anandita's sleeping draughts. All of a sudden, Bocan wondered why the mages had not asked Jimena here. As a mind healer, she should be able to also probe past people's defenses to get to the truth, and do so without whatever magic was causing the alchemist to change in this way.

Although, she had seemed extra grumpy over breakfast. He had chalked it up to his own foolishness at re-injuring his wounded arm. But perhaps there was more to it than that. Had the mages asked for her assistance? Had she refused?

A tap on the shoulder brought him back.

"Bocan." Jerrod leaned toward his ear. "We need you outside."

Bocan nodded and rose, following the tall Knight through the large double doors, leaving the disturbing sight of the ensorcelled alchemist behind. He would get a report back later.

For now, Amarpal and her brother, Haryath, flanked Arrow on the broad Douglas fir planks of the covered porch.

"What is wrong?" Bocan asked.

"This one should not be here," Amarpal spat.

The right edge of Arrow's mouth quirked, though whether in annoyance or amusement, Bocan could not tell.

"I am part of this township, am I not?" the elf replied. "Therefore, I have a right to attend township meetings."

"Except this is not an open meeting," Bocan said, keeping his voice calm. "This is a meeting for the Knights, the council, the healers, and the mages. The township meeting will occur once we have more information. You are part of none of these groups, and therefore I, too, would like to know why you are here."

Arrow shifted her weight over her boots, and looked down for a moment. Ah. The first sign of discomfort.

The three Knights waited.

"I know something," Arrow finally admitted, just as Damson ran up the porch steps and smacked the elf on the cheek.

"You!" The pale, slender elf practically vibrated with anger. Arrow's hand shot to her cheek, as if she couldn't believe the other elf had struck her.

"What is going on?" asked Haryath.

Damson's face contorted. She looked about to spit. It was almost funny to see two elves face off like this. Both wearing soft leathers and hemp shirts. One smaller, slender, and pale. The other much taller, equally as slender, and dark. Both with matching pale green hair.

Almost funny. Except clearly the situation was deadly serious.

"She stole my spyglass. She's up to something nefarious again. I *told* you all to not trust this one!"

Arrow lowered her hand and spoke clearly. "That is what I was trying to tell you all. I saw something through the spyglass. I came to the meeting to tell someone, but decided to wait until..."

"What did you see?" Jerrod asked.

"Wolves, running through the forest."

"And what concern is the wildlife to you?" Amarpal asked. The Sikh really did not like Arrow, and was clearly not backing down.

"These were the magic wolves."

And they all knew what that meant, but Bocan was the only one to speak the words aloud.

"The Raven Priestess is back."

CHAPTER 14
ELZABETTA

In her bower, in a bed hung with white drapery, Elzabetta dreamed.

She dreamed of drakes with purple wings. She dreamed of snow-peaked mountains and fertile green fields. She dreamed of towering dark trees and rain-streaked skies. She dreamed of places she had never seen, but only heard of. She dreamed of a large blue Knight, neither troll nor man but some strange in between.

She dreamed of a human warrior with dark skin, fierce eyes, and strangely knotted hair. The human stood at a river's edge, weapons raised, shouting something Elzabetta could not hear.

Elzabetta turned, fitful on the soft sheets, pale hair tangled about her delicate face. Elzabetta dreamed of herself, laughing, surrounded by humans. Children playing, shrieking with laughter. She dreamed of humans who seemed not so different than herself.

She dreamed of exploring in the woods, and splashing at the stream that tumbled down from the great mountain.

Elzabetta woke, face wet with tears, chest heaving with strangled sobs that, had she not been in that unguarded state between slumber and wakefulness, she would never have released.

It did not do to show weakness in Underhill. Especially not to the Queen.

Her mother had once held her close, but was a stranger to Elzabetta now. A viper in the hallowed Underhill. A poison in the realm. She was old enough to see it now. She had been tortured by her mother in the name of love.

But that was not love. It was coercion and a desperate attempt to shore up her power. Her mother was a terrible, terrible, person and now that Elzabetta knew, she would not forget.

She had to find a way to stop her mother's mad campaign. But who would help her?

She scrubbed at her face with pale hands, the dreams still dancing through her head. Taunting her. Calling her. Filling her breast with a longing for a world she did not know.

The world the alchemist had disappeared into, fleeing during the great battle. The court had been abuzz with it for days, until they tired of talking of things they knew nothing about and went back to sniping at each other. Their usual sport.

Elzabetta sighed, then rose and washed her face in

the basin of scented water in the corner of her chamber. Orange blossoms today.

Her mother would tell her how fortunate she was, to live the pampered life she did. Except Elzabetta knew it was only half a life. The beautiful room with its high, soft bed and carved posts that looked like dancing trees. The soft coverlets in shades of green and gold...she supposed that yes, she was fortunate in her own way. But she hated this place, nonetheless. It was nothing more than a gilded prison.

She hated her mother, too.

Perhaps it was her wandering souls that caused Elzabetta to feel this way. All the other elves seemed happy enough to live in this place of roses, and apple blossoms, and sweet fruit.

She wandered to a small table set by one of the large, arched windows looking out onto the apple grove. The table was set a carafe of cool, clear water, and a cup to drink it in.

Elzabetta poured herself some water and drank it thoughtfully.

The alchemist and her mother had told her that breathing in the souls of humans would heal her and make her strong. They would call her own souls back home from their wandering. But so far, it had not worked. Nothing had worked. It had only caused her pain, a sharp agony pulsing at her temples and aching in her belly. And how many scores of humans were now dead on her account?

"I cannot abide this anymore," she murmured to

the apple trees outside. But what to do? A soft rap came on her doorway.

She slid her feet into soft slippers and wrapped a robe of shimmering blue around herself and opened the door.

The tall, straight-backed elvish knight peered down at her with silver eyes. Was he her protector, or her jailer? Elzabetta could never decide.

"Sir Tarioc," she said, "what is it that you wish?"

He bowed. "My lady Elzabetta. Good day to you. I wondered if you wish to go for a ride."

"A ride?" she asked, furrowing her delicate brow. That was passing strange. Generally, if Elzabetta wished to ride, she had to request it specifically, and get permission, and at least three knights in entourage.

"Indeed," he said, "my horse could use the exercise, and I thought perhaps that you could too."

He kept his face a neutral mask, and his melodious voice was steady and calm. But there was something interesting in his eyes. A spark. A mild intensity. It was almost as if he were trying to convey something to her without words. She stared at him a moment, then nodded.

"Give me time to break my fast and dress properly, and I should quite enjoy that ride."

"Yes, my lady. Ah," he said, poking his head back into the hallway. "And here is your food now, and your maid to help you dress."

Elzabetta tilted her head.

"You planned this?" She thought she had not

spoken the words aloud, but Tarioc nodded, all the same, as if he had heard her loud and clear.

"I shall return shortly, after I get the horses ready."

"You do that," she replied, moving slightly to one side to allow the maid entry to her chambers. Elzabetta paid the bustling servant no mind, watching Tarioc's proud back as he walked down the long, bright hallway.

CHAPTER 15

KARAKTILLA

The purple drake paced the high walled space of her cavern, up near the peak of the majestic Wy'East.

A fire crackled on a hearth large enough to roast an elk or bison, should Karaktilla wish a change from raw meat. Sometimes she did, even adding herbs the troll Recoana brought her to the succulent, roasting flesh.

Towering shelves held her most precious treasures, the books and scrolls she had collected over hundreds of years. Some drakes liked shiny things. Karaktilla preferred knowledge. Jewel-like carpets and piles of cushions were arrayed along the floor near the hearth and in the corner, and the table with her great crystal orb sat near a narrow tunnel shaft that let in light and air to the depths of the room.

Resting on the cushions near the fire was her nearest neighbor and sometime lover, Daraktal. A handsome drake with shimmering red scales, Daraktal was smaller than herself. He smoked a pipe, some clever human creation made of carved wood. Fragrant smoke wound in lazy loops around his long snout. He gazed at her, the film across one dark, nictating eye shuttering and opening, as he waited for her to say something sensible. But she had nothing sensible to say. He was here because she needed help thinking.

"Would you like some tea?" she asked, teeth and jaws clicking and clattering out the words. He huffed, then clicked and clattered back.

"You have asked me that thrice now, my dear."

Oh. Indeed she had. And what an embarrassment that was, offering further proof that Karktilla was not herself these days.

"Damn that Queen, anyway," she said, shaking her shoulders and slamming her tail against the stone beneath the carpets.

"Surely you did not think the Battle of New Salem was the end of her?" He let free a mighty puff of smoke. Karaktilla coughed.

"Of course I didn't," she snapped out, jaws clacking her mighty teeth together, "but I wish she would remain in her own realm and leave the rest of us alone! A rank nuisance she is. I trust her not, and I scent her plotting on the wind."

"And what have you seen in the orb?"

She heaved her bulk down on a pile of cushions near the fire opposite Daraktal.

"The Queen, traveling to the Unseelie realms. And why would she wish to do that?" Neither drake spoke for a moment, pondering the strangeness of a Seelie Queen treating with Unseelie. It was a disturbing thought indeed, and one that signaled greater change to the realms than anticipated.

"Mostly I see the princess," Karaktilla resumed the thread, "and strangely, she seems better than she was. Healthier somehow."

Daraktal sat up, eyes alight with interest. "Do you think the Queen's experiments were harming the child?"

Karaktilla shook her head. "I know not, but I do know that should we wish things to turn around, the princess may need our help."

Daraktal grumbled, and shook the large triangular wedge of his head, setting the fine scales around his neck to tinkling like bells.

"The princess is a pawn," he clacked out. "And dangerous to meddle with. Unless that crystal orb of yours shows us something with greater clarity, I dislike the thought of riding in to rescue a Seelie elf that just may spell our doom."

Karaktilla swung the large, iron arm that held the well blackened-kettle over the fire. This conversation needed tea.

"The princess may be a pawn, but that does not mean she cannot play on our side of the board."

She gathered two small pots of dried herbs from the niche carved into the side of the fireplace and dropped them into a second iron kettle with a fat belly designed for brewing. It was made by one of the Seelie trolls, and besides her books and crystal orb, was Karaktilla's favorite possession. The troll had fashioned a cunning drake in flight around the pot, with its head and open mouth forming the spout. Clever people, trolls.

"But how much in Silverhair's thrall is her daughter?" Karaktilla mused. "And would she be willing to leave Underhill?"

"There is one way to find out," Daraktal replied.

Karaktilla looked at her friend, startled.

"How?"

He grinned a toothsome grin.

"We send an envoy to ask."

"And that is a task easier spoken of than done," Karaktilla replied.

Daraktal shrugged and re-lit his pipe.

The iron pot was steaming and water rumbled inside. Time to brew some tea.

Time to think some more.

CHAPTER 16
TEGAN

Tegan breathed slowly through per mouth. In, two, three, four. Pause, two, three, four. Out through per nose, two, three, four. Pause... As per breathed, Tegan throttled per mind and senses down toward the calm that rested in the belly. A calm per could barely reach but insisted upon by sheer force of will. Tegan's pulse still raced, verging on panic.

Tegan never panicked, but the ancestors were knocking on per head and invading per dreams. Dreams that were also haunted alternately by the black eyes of the djinni and the pale green eyes of an elvish princess sleeping in her bower.

What in the ancestor's names had gotten into per? Nothing got to Tegan. Not the scent of blood and battle. Not seeing per comrades cut down, never to rise again. Not sex. Not love. Not rage or grief.

Not until now.

What had changed? Tegan wasn't certain. All per knew was the very fabric of per magic was changing.

And Tegan didn't know how or why or what it meant. But there was no time to deal with that. Not when per comrades were staring. Waiting. Not when Jerrod shifted uncomfortably on his boots, as if trying to decide whether or not to broach an uncomfortable subject or not, the big oaf.

Tegan cracked half a smile as Case sidled over, though per didn't really feel it. Per appreciated Case's presence, though, even if the damn Knight had yet to agree to share per bed.

"You all right there, comrade?" he said, bumping per shoulder with his own.

Tegan took in another long breath. "Just assessing the situation."

Case gave Tegan a look that said he knew exactly what sort of cow shit Tegan was feeding him. But in the way of all good comrades, he knew when to speak and when to shut the fuck up. Now was definitely shut the fuck up time.

Luckily, all those eyes Tegan thought were staring at per were actually trained on Aphrodite. And the thing that was causing Tegan the sense of panic was the shining, shimmering gate just beyond the curvaceous mage. The gate that had been haunting Tegan ever since per caught sight of it a week ago. Too much had transpired since then. Conflict brewing within the refugees. Arguments with the council. Questioning that damn alchemist... Tegan swore the stink of weird magic on the elf made her skin crawl.

He claimed that the princess was in grave danger, and that Silverhair was planning something worse than what had come before. The mages said the alchemist told the truth.

Or at least he thought he did. For all Tegan knew, Silverhair's necromancers had found a way to implant false memories inside a person's head, so any probing would come up with only lies.

Tegan sighed, and looked around, peering through the towering trees, seeking the elegant tipped ears of the lynx. Starlight had gone sniffing around the forest, doing scouting of her own. That was how they usually worked, but all of a sudden, Tegan needed Starlight. Needed her calming, sometimes cranky presence. Tegan wished Starlight would hurry back already.

Tegan also wished Bocan was here. Or the djinn, or even Damson. Or any of the trolls...

One human mage didn't feel like enough. Aphrodite was good, and well trained, but her magic was not enough. Not here. Not now.

The magic pulsing from the gate felt bad. Worse than the magic of the warlord Wulf and his sick ties to Queen Silverhair. Tegan's gorge rose.

Memories flashed through per mind. Chanting necromancers and the animated head of the Elven King.

Per swallowed hard and stepped away from the gate.

"Tegan." Case's voice cracked through the vile churn of images, low and urgent. "What do you need?"

Tegan shook per head.

"I need to away from here," per muttered, and stumbled toward a deer path, heading farther into the deep green forest, pausing to retch next to a hemlock spruce.

As per bent, braced against the rough trunk, the bile flooded per mouth, acrid and sour. Per spat, stomach clenching once more as bread and cheese clawed their way up from Tegan's belly, spattering onto the forest floor.

Tegan's body wracked and shuddered with the force of it. Per coughed, then retched again, emptying per guts onto the ground for the carrion eaters who were sure to come by, as soon as the humans left.

Per was aware of movement behind per. Case.

"Here." Case was next to her then, holding out a water skin. "Rinse your mouth."

Tegan spilled some water onto a kerchief dragged from per leathers, and wiped per face before doing as instructed, swishing and spitting three times before finally taking a cautious sip.

The water was spiked with a small amount of last year's wine to keep away the bugs that made people sick.

"Thanks, comrade," Tegan said, shoving the skin back at Case without looking up to meet his eyes.

"Two more sips," he instructed, "and there's nothing to be ashamed of."

Tegan's laugh was harsh, rasping through the forest like a calling crow.

"Oh, no? Losing my breakfast in the forest for no reason? A badass Knight like me?"

Case chuckled. "It's happened to all of us, Tegan,

and you know it. You're still worthy of the wheel and wings."

The wheel and wings. The emblem of the Steel Clan, passed down from Jenny's great-gran Molly. The emblem of strength and freedom.

Tegan felt neither of those things now.

Case stood in silence as Tegan took in more long, slow breaths, trying to compose perself again.

"Where's Starlight?" he asked, looking around. The lynx had disappeared, off on her own business.

Tegan shrugged, starting to feel better. It was nice here in the woods. Peaceful, once away from the magic hum of the gate. For a moment, Tegan wished they were just out on a jaunt together. Comrades exploring the land. Fuck, even friends out on a picnic...anything but working, always working, trying to foil whatever fucked-up plans that thrice-damned Silverhair had put into play.

Tegan wished down to per boots that things were simpler. Fuck. Fight. Eat. Sleep. Have a nice long soak in the bathhouse. Share a bowl with per comrades. This magic shit? Tegan didn't need it anymore. Didn't want it. But the image of her ancestor's dark eyes stared beneath a gleaming sun, so orange and bright and different from the sun here.

Those eyes would not let Tegan go.

"Let's go for a walk," Case said.

"Don't we need to get back to the gate?"

"Aphrodite will take who knows how long to figure anything out, and there are already too many people crowded around that damn thing. They won't miss us if we're gone a bit longer."

Tegan slitted per eyes, but Case kept his face neutral, as if he wasn't lying in order to make per feel better. Well, per would take the out, anyway, because something about this gate in particular made per skin crawl.

So per followed Case deeper into the woods, toward the sound of running water, until they came upon a small clearing around a bubbling stream. Tegan inhaled the fresh scent of running water and green forest. The knocking was still there, at the base of per skull, but was eased by the sound of burbling water.

Walking past a cluster of large rocks, through a gateway made of branches reaching out toward one another, Tegan walked until per boots were at the water's edge. Per knelt, patting the surface of the stream with per bare hands.

Tegan sent up a brief prayer, one per had not recited since childhood. "Mboli, thank you for the gift of water, and the flow of life. Ease my spirit in this place. Bless my ancestors and bless those I walk with on my journey. So be it."

Tegan heard Case shifting behind per, but paid the Knight no mind. Every person in Go No More was pledged to respect and honor the ways of every other, except for those who used their beliefs to conquer or enslave. Go No More was having trouble with that of late, with some of the New Salemites. But the township had been clear: honor our ways or go.

Why someone would not respect the variety of

spirit-honoring a person did was as foreign to Tegan as forcing a person into sex or labor. Coercion made no rational sense, not when the whole world was alive with spirits, and a drop of Mboli's cleansing water dwelled inside each soul. Mboli was part of all that existed.

Always honor the ancestors and the spirits that dwell in each place, and when you encounter a stream, remember Mboli, he who is the fountain of all things. Per mother Inaya instructed Tegan at her knee when Tegan was small. She had taught per only child the scant ancestral ways that her own family had passed to her from days long before the Reckoning came. Ways that were almost lost, per mother said, by the coming of new religions to a vast land far away from Go No More.

The land of endless sun, per mother called it.

Abyad once told per that his own home was not far from that place where Tegan's ancestors had once walked, barefoot, upon the earth. To Tegan, mostly this was all the stuff of legend. At least, per had always thought them so.

But the dreams of late…and the increased sense of magic in per bones?

Was all too real.

And the waters of Mboli flowed in Tegan's veins, his voice whispering in per ears at night.

The gift of flowing water is the gift of life itself.

And what was the opposite of that?

Tegan's churning gut offered a warning. They were all going to find out, and far too soon.

CHAPTER 17

JENNY

Jenny felt as useless as tits on a bull. She had come to the gate along with several comrades, leaving Bocan behind—along with Haryath and Amarpal—to keep Go No More protected, and continue the much-needed training of the New Salem refugees. There was also some disgruntlement from those parties. Despite the Battle of New Salem having been over for months now, acclimating the refugees was a larger feat than anyone had guessed. Some people were still having trouble adjusting to the egalitarian, everyone-pitches-in nature of Go No More. Others were closed-mouthed about it all, but Jenny had caught flashes of wariness in their eyes.

Anandita told Jenny she needed to be patient. That people were still traumatized. And Jenny got that. But heck, who hadn't been traumatized lately? Though she supposed she would be wary, too, if she had lived for years beneath a so-called warlord's thumb.

Nonetheless, there was trauma aplenty. Whole

towns were gone because of Queen Silverhair and her terrible soul-stealing campaign, trying to save that daughter of hers. Jenny snorted, causing Jerrod to send an inquiring look her way. She shook her head at the tall, dark-skinned Knight, and pretended to pay attention to what was happening at the gate.

Silverhair's daughter was some pampered princess Jenny hoped to never meet. She'd had enough dealings with Underhill to have a permanently bad taste in her mouth from it all. And if she forgot? All she had to do was pay a visit to Bocan's ma, a woman she remembered as being vibrant, strong, and filled with life. Now she sat in a rocker by the woodstove, barely speaking more than a word or two throughout the day.

So Jenny had little use for Elvish princesses. Especially since the alchemist seemed to think they needed to mount some sort of rescue mission. Jenny was none too pleased with that. They had enough problems as it was, including the fact that Bocan was injured, both in body and soul, and who knew how long it would take him to recover? And Tegan?

Jenny looked toward the pathway her comrade had taken. Per and Case had gone deep enough into the woods that she could no longer see the dull flash of sumac-dyed leather.

Yeah. Something was up with Tegan, Jenny could tell. Tegan was being tight-lipped about it as usual. But things had shifted for her comrade in a way that felt big. Also, Jenny was less and less able to read her comrade. Despite their years of friendship, and all the shit they'd been through, Tegan had become a closed book, and Jenny didn't know why.

She was starting to suspect it had something to do with magic.

Why else would her comrade disappear from Jenny's senses half the time? It made Jenny wonder if Tegan wasn't having flares of magic per couldn't control…. Like just now, she had just left the gate and wandered off. Jenny and Case had conferred and decided he was the better one to go deal with Tegan.

So here Jenny was, waiting like an apprentice to be told what to do, watching her former lover Aphrodite do her woo-woo thing at the gate. Magic. The realm was filled with it, and all Jenny could do was break it when necessary. Bah. Give her a skull to crack or a child to save. Leave the rest to those who liked this shit.

At least this sort of permanent gate was the kind of magic even magically dense people like Jenny could see. To her untrained eyes, it looked like a strange rift in the forest. More than that, it felt just *wrong*, as if earth and sky had been disturbed, cloven in two, never to be put together again.

"How long is this going to take?" she muttered. Jerrod snorted at her side.

"It really bugs you not to be able to do anything about magic, doesn't it?"

"It would bug you, too," Jenny grumped, shifting on her feet. She was tired of standing around and wished she'd gone off with Jessie and Litha to scout the area. At least she could have looked for things that were out of place in the physical world, instead of standing around doing nothing while the mages worked.

"It wouldn't bug me if I was Jenny Magic's Bane and one of my powers was cracking the shit out of magic that shouldn't be there."

She smacked Jerrod's arm and got a wicked grin in return.

"Pig fucker," she muttered.

"Maybe Aphrodite will let you bust this one, too."

Jenny just shook her head. They both knew the toll that breaking the gate at Wimal falls had taken on her. And they both remembered their comrades who died there. She would do it again in a heartbeat, but only if she had to. A Knight did their best to avoid a fight at all costs, but once committed to the fight? A Knight went all in. This was not an all-in situation yet, and she could only hope and pray it never became one.

"What do you think of the alchemist wanting to do this rescue mission?" she asked. Aphrodite had switched from one side of the gate to the other, and was sketching symbols into the air. Jenny supposed those glyphs she could not see must have been doing something, because the Steel Clan Knights standing closest to the gate suddenly backed up three paces.

Jenny and Jerrod backed up, too, to give their comrades room. And to get farther away from whatever the fuck the mage was up to. There was no telling what might happen.

Of course, they backed right up beneath a dripping Douglas fir. Jenny swiped at the fat drops trailing down her neck, looked up, and got a drop straight in her eye. Great.

"Can we move over there?"

Without waiting for an answer, she stomped over toward the slender pathway that first Tegan, then Case had taken what now felt like too long ago. Jerrod followed. The forest was more dense here, and the trees less likely to drip, though if a storm rolled through in earnest, everyone would get truly wet. But that's what their oiled canvas cloaks were for. Too bad Jenny had left hers rolled up on her bike.

Jerrod pulled a fruit and nut bar from his belt pouch and took a hefty bite. "Want some?"

Jenny shook her head. She should eat something while they waited, but her stomach was in knots, wondering what the fuck was going on with Tegan. Case really should have hauled per back by now.

Jerrod chewed and swallowed. "I don't relish heading Underhill again, that's for sure. Especially not to rescue some elf we've never met before. Plus, it's the Queen's daughter? Does he really think we're going to trust her?"

"He has to get us to trust him, first."

"That's right."

Litha and Jessie entered the copse from the left. Jessie had a streak of mud on her face, and Litha's blond hair was marred by the same mud. They were followed by a stealthy figure, shrouded in black robes.

The djinn.

"What in Bright Brigid's name is he doing here?" Jenny asked.

"Guess we're about to find out."

The djinni's black eyes scanned the forest, finally resting on Jenny and Jerrod. He studied the gate for a moment, and Jenny assumed he would follow the two scouts who were clearly headed toward the mages to report their findings. Jenny was about to head that way herself, when Abyad's eyes found hers.

The black-clad djinni headed her way, sliding his way among the rocks, bushes, and trees, as if he were the wind itself.

BOCAN

Bocan gritted his teeth against the pain. His arm had begun to worry him again, but he couldn't tell Jimena because she'd already given him quite the verbal thrashing for overdoing it while sparring, likely setting back his recovery. And she was right. This current pain flare was his own fracked-earth fault.

You damn fool.

Turns out, recovering from a wolf chewing on your arm took longer than he wanted. Go figure. The whispering voice in the back of his head feared that he might never recover. He did his best to push that voice away.

Besides, he really didn't have time to deal with the pain. There was no time off for a Knight. Especially now. There was too much to do. Between keeping the township safe, getting the refugees trained and up to speed, and breaking up fights among people who were used to resources being scarce? He shook his head. Too many of the New Salemites were used to living in a world where it was every person for their own self.

The man sulking in front of him right now was the latest example. A white man in a much-patched wool jacket and pale hair that needed trimming, his body posture managed to look both petulant and aggressive, as if he were a child just growing into their powers, and uncertain of the world.

"James," Bocan said, "you can't hoard your eggs."

"Why not?" There was a mulish scowl on James's weather-beaten face. "My chickens, my eggs."

"Well," Bocan said, "we could just as easily say, 'our township, get out.'"

James's hands bunched into fists and a red flush stained his creased face.

"You kicking out my family? You'll kick out a man and a woman and their child? Damned trolls. What do you know? Not even human." A fleck of spittle flew from the man's mouth. Blessedly, Bocan stood far enough back from the man to miss being sprayed. And James wasn't done yet. "What do you know what it's like to struggle and get along?"

Bocan didn't rise to the bait. He'd been called worse, plus lived through many actually dangerous situations. The man in front of him held no immediate threat. Though long term? If Bocan couldn't get James calmed down, it could continue to spell trouble for Go No More.

"I'm not threatening you. I'm just explaining how things work here. You're not in New Salem anymore...."

The man scoffed. "Yeah, well, you all made sure of that, didn't you?"

Bocan throttled down a flash of anger, shaking his head. James and his family could have stayed. Some folks did.

"All we've done is offer you a space to live in freedom. If you don't want it, we'll make certain you and your family have what's needed to get you back to the city."

The man's wife put a hand on his arm. Named Rosa, she was a dark-skinned, beautiful woman with long plaits of thick hair running down her back.

"James, you know there's nothing for us there. And I think things are better here." She raised her eyes to Bocan. "I'm grateful. To the Knights. To the township. Grateful to you all. Forgive my husband. Living in New Salem was... Well. You tell us we can live free here, and from the looks of things so far, I think that's true."

Rosa turned her gaze back to James, eyes set, mouth firm. "Look at how much they've shared with us already. Don't be a fool. We'll be sharing our eggs."

Her husband jerked away from her and stalked off.

Rosa's eyes followed James. She threw her hands up, then dropped them in resignation. "Just tell me what we need to do."

Bocan breathed a sigh of relief inside and smiled at the woman.

"John the Dairyman." He jerked his head towards the portly white farmer talking with some others near the town center. "You talk to him. He's part of the

Dairy and Husbandry Clan. That includes eggs from chickens and ducks. He'll get you set up properly."

The woman nodded and moved to walk toward the cluster around John. Bocan stopped her, one hand on her arm.

"Ma'am? You do realize you and your family are welcome here. Right?"

"Yes." She nodded.

"There's a place for you here as long as you make a place for us."

"Understood," she said, then walked away. He watched her back for a while, wondering if she and her children would remain while the husband struck off on his own. Not that there was anywhere for the man to go. Oh, he could return to the husk of New Salem and help with rebuilding there. Or be captured by bandits en route.

Bocan sighed. Why couldn't the man understand how good he had it here? But you couldn't force a person's heart to change. They had to do that for themselves. All Bocan could do was make it clear how things operated in the township, and make certain people abided by the agreements that kept things running.

Bocan had done his best. So, that problem taken care of—for the moment at least—Bocan looked around, satisfied with what he saw. The carpenters were hard at work putting up more buildings both inside and outside the gates. The Town Council and the Sovereign and Confederated Tribes were still negotiating for more space, trying to figure out where exactly they should put new walls. It wouldn't do just to give people places to sleep without also offering them protection, which was why Haryath and Amarpal were once again drilling townspeople on the practice field next to the horse paddock, and Swan the bowyer had a group of children on the archery range. In Go No More, as soon as your little arm muscles could draw the lightest bow string, you learned to shoot.

Tall, blond-haired Swan, despite not wanting to be a parent, and despite saying she was not good with children? Luckily, she actually was great with children, and patient as the summer days were long. All it took was doing one of her favorite things with the children: shooting arrows at targets with bows made to her own design.

Bocan turned, ready to go check in with the head of the carpenters on this particular job to see if they needed more assistance from the Knights that were left. On his roster after that was checking in with the patrols, making certain there wasn't anything he should be paying attention to.

"Bocan!" Hypatia, Andandita's son ran toward him, dark hair sticking up around his head. "The healers need you!"

"Why is that?"

The boy scuffed his toe on the ground.

"Not sure," he said. "I think that elf wants to talk to you."

The boy had to mean the alchemist.

"Thank you, Hypatia. I'll be there directly."

Bocan wasn't sure if what he felt inside himself was excitement or dread.

He didn't trust the alchemist, and with very good reason. Mainly, the vacant look in his mother's eyes, and the whimpering noises she'd made when he first found her Underhill. Those sounds would stay with him forever.

He would like nothing more than to throttle the elf and make him pay. But as long as the alchemist might be of use to Go No More or the human realms, Bocan stayed his hand.

Community health is better than revenge. He kept reminding himself of that, though his heart didn't always feel that way. He was trying to learn though. Especially since the Gods of Earth and Stone had cracked open his magic in such a way that he was far more powerful, and thrice as dangerous as he used to be. A Knight always needed to modulate their power, and these days Bocan had more power than most.

He had to learn to dance with it. And, well, if he wasn't quite graceful? That was just the way things were for now.

Bocan walked through the town, appreciating the buzz of activity. The acrid scents from the glass blowers... The rhythmic pounding from the forge... The squeals of delight and the *tung* of arrows from the archery range... Angel and his crew working with the horses...

And he knew that farther outside the gates Tegan's mother Inaya, Hakim L'Ouverture, and the rest of the Green Clan were working hard to store and process this year's crops.

Soon enough, he approached the giant, ragged fir

in the center of town. Just beyond it was the massive building that was the public house. It was a PR building and as such, had several intact panes of clear smooth glass. The broken panes had been replaced by pocked and wavy contemporary glass. Go No More's glass blowers were good, but large, clear panes were the trickiest thing to do.

The building had broad planks and waving corrugated metal on its rooftop, another PR technology. Luckily, the engineers had figured out how to approximate those panels for repairs. It was a nice blend of the old and new and very pleasing to Bocan's eye. What was less pleasing, though, was the prospect of walking across that broad porch into the public house, and climbing the interior stairs to face the alchemist again.

"Everyone has a part of their job they dislike," he muttered. Turns out, facing his mother's torturer was one of them. He took in a deep breath, centered himself, and then climbed the steps to the porch, heading for the large, double doors.

TEGAN

Saying some prayers and making an offering at the water had soothed Tegan somewhat, though per was still agitated. The sense of magic crawled beneath per skin, increasing in intensity, causing per scalp to itch again. Tegan did per best to slowly exhale and push the energy fields around the edges of per skin outward, hoping to give the magic more room. That helped a bit.

Thank the ancestors for Steel Clan training. It was good to be able to fall back on some of the basics Tegan had learned during per apprenticeship.

Case seemed thoughtful as they walked back towards the gate, but he didn't say anything. They were good at companionable silence, which was just as well, because whatever questions Case had? Tegan was afraid per had no answers for.

The pair picked their way along the small deer trail, shoving through undergrowth and catching tree limbs. The scent of earth warming up after a long winter filled the forest, along with the balsam citrus of hemlock spruce and the woodier scent of the towering firs. Tegan took a moment to breathe in and simply enjoy being out in the woods. If only per could pretend that the two of them were simply out on a friendly walk rather than tracking down the latest cow shit Queen Silverhair was concocting.

As they entered the clearing once again, Tegan was surprised to see that not only had the scouts returned with Starlight, they brought the djinni with them, a black-garbed presence amidst the sumac-red leathers. His black dog, Dukhan, stalked at his side.

Starlight caught per eyes and padded over to join Tegan, who nodded at the lynx, but kept walking.

::You look like squirrel shit,:: the lynx said.

::Thanks, oh furry one.::

Starlight swiped at per playfully, claws sheathed, then bumped her head against Tegan's leg.

::What happened?::

"Later," Tegan said out loud. Per had to admit, it felt better having the bonded animal close again.

"Abyad," Tegan said on approach to the gate and the cluster of Knights. The djinn's head whipped around, and those beautiful black eyes were trained upon per once more.

Tegan shivered at his gaze. Case grunted. Tegan had no idea what that grunt meant, but there was no time to assess. Abyad did not move to greet the pair, but remained where he stood, conferring with the scouts and Aphrodite as his black dog paced forward to touch noses with Starlight.

Conversation grew silent as the Knights waited for Tegan and Case to approach. From another corner of the small clearing, Jenny spotted them and stomped over, followed by Jerrod. The lanky Knight look bored while Jenny's brow was furrowed with concern.

Tegan didn't have time for Jenny's questions or coddling.

"You disappeared," Tegan said, looking at the djinn. "From Go No More. And now you're here."

What the fuck? was the unspoken question that seemed to signal loud and clear.

Abyad nodded slowly. "I did."

Starlight gave a low growl, signaling annoyance. Dukhan growled back, but there was little warning in the sound.

The djinni flashed a grin, showing gleaming white teeth in that unnaturally white face of his. How someone who looked as if he had come from the land of Rafiq's ancestors was pale as the snows on Wy'East instead of golden brown of the desert sands was a mystery. But then, all the creatures made of magic were strange, and to hold them to human standards was impossible.

The djinni was made of magic. Tegan felt the magic inside per breast rise to meet his. Abyad's eyes widened slightly, feeling the connection.

"And now I am here," he continued. They simply stared at each other for a moment, not speaking, before Tegan turned to Aphrodite.

"Any news about the gate?"

Aphrodite shook her head and squirted some water into her mouth.

"Not much of use. It was definitely formed Underhill," she said, wiping the back of her hand across her mouth. Her blue tunic was damp with the sweat of exertion despite the cold air. "And there are at least five different magical signatures woven into it...but I couldn't get much more than that."

"I hooked in near the end," said Litha, "and could definitely feel more than one signature, though I wasn't able to parse out five."

"But more than one means it couldn't have been made by the alchemist? Or not him alone?" Case asked.

"I don't see how," Aphrodite continued. "I think the elf was telling the truth. Besides, with the state he was in? He wouldn't have the power to make a gate."

Or he'd used all his power making one. But that wouldn't account for the extra magic woven into the gate. Aphrodite was right.

"So, we're back at the beginning?" Tegan asked, frustration rising in per voice.

Aphrodite gave Tegan a strange look. "Not exactly. Knowing the permanent gate was made by several magic users, coupled with the state the alchemist was in? It means that Silverhair is plotting something, and we need to be on guard against it. I wouldn't be surprised if temporary gates don't start popping up here and there, too. I sense disruption in the air. But meanwhile, we still need to decide whether we shut this gate down, or leave it, buying time while awaiting more information."

Tegan looked toward Jenny, whose shoulders hunched, mouth set in a mulish line. Magic's Bane was not happy with the conversation of closing gates again, and Tegan could not blame her. It had taken Jenny longer to recover from closing the Wimal Falls gate than per comrade ever fully admitted.

Tegan nodded at per comrade, and Jenny relaxed slightly.

Turning back to the djinn, per quirked an eyebrow. "And you? What have you been up to?"

"Tracking," the djinni said.

"Tracking? Who or what?" Case asked.

"Peridot."

The traitor elf.

"Then why are you here?" Jenny burst out, face flashing with anger.

"Because I lost him." The djinn's mouth twisted, and his voice was tinged with disgust, clearly directed at himself.

"Where exactly did you lose him?" Tegan asked, keeping per voice carefully neutral.

"He was heading toward Wy'East."

"Did you tag him?" Aphrodite asked.

Abyad grinned that predator grin again.

"I did. Why do you think I came to get you?"

Tegan looked to the mage and scouts. "Anything else to be done here?"

"Not for the moment, no," Aphrodite replied. "But we need to reassess and decide whether or not we need to try to shut this thing down sooner rather than later."

All eyes flicked to Jenny again, though no one spoke the words out loud. Jenny pushed her shoulders up around her ears and scowled, looking down at her boots.

"All right, then," Tegan said, turning attention away from per comrade, "let's track this pig fucker."

Aphrodite cleared her throat. "With the djinni here, I'm not needed. I should head back to Go No More with news of the gate."

Tegan scanned the group. "Who shall take the mage?"

Jenny stepped forward. "I will. I want to check on the big blue oaf, anyway. Make sure he hasn't hurt himself again."

"Pig fucker," one of the Knights cheerfully quipped. Every single Knight understood injury just as they understood what a pain in the ass recovery was. And sitting on a comrade to keep them from further injury? Well, they'd all done some of that, as well.

Everyone started toward their bikes, mood temporarily lightened.

"Abyad," Tegan said. "You ride with me. Starlight? You're with Case, please."

Starlight glared. Tegan glared back.

::I do not want to ride with someone else.::

::I wouldn't ask if it was not important. I need the djinn's help to navigate.::

Starlight gave a low growl, then stalked toward Case. The djinni was already at Tegan's bike, winding his black clothing more tightly about his body. He had sent his uncanny dog to ride on the supply trailer.

Tegan noticed the djinni had arranged for a blanket to cushion the beast as they rode. Good. A person should always treat their animal companions with respect, even when they were a pain, like Starlight was sometimes.

"Steel Clan!" Jenny shouted. "Move out!"

"Why do we ride?" Tegan shouted back.

"We ride for Go No More!"

CHAPTER 20
PERIDOT

eridot's cover was blown. He knew the djinni followed him.

And though he had given Abyad the slip, Peridot was under no illusion that the djinni could not find him again. Uncanny creatures, djinn, from a realm far away from both Underhill and this dripping wet human place.

A person would think after living Underhill and interacting with all the manner of creatures there—especially the Queen and her necromancers—that such as a djinni would not disquiet him so, and yet the tang of unfamiliar magic troubled the elf's heart, mind, and souls.

Peridot paused and leaned against a mighty oak tree to rest for a moment. His body was unused to walking for such long distances over unfamiliar terrain. He drank some water from the skin strapped across his chest and pondered what to do. Two ravens quokked softly overhead.

He glanced up and saw two large, handsome birds, heads canted sideways, beady black eyes staring down at him through branches just beginning to leaf.

Shit. He should have known better than to pause beneath an oak, and he should have known there were spies everywhere.

Though ravens were not uncommon in this place, this pair carried a spark of magic that disturbed him. He shivered, wondering whether he would live to a ripe age of several hundred before fading gently into eternal bliss in the Summerlands...or whether someday soon an arrow would pierce his heart.

The ravens quokked once more.

"Go away, you," Peridot muttered. "Leave me here in peace."

But peace was not to be, not with a cloaked figure heading his way.

His burdens were heavy enough without dealing with the figure who strode calmly toward him through the forest, two silvery beasts trotting alongside. Wolves.

The human was dark-skinned with elaborate coils of braids wound around a fine face. The black feathers woven into her hair fluttered as she walked, and long ocher skirts skimmed just above booted ankles. In her right hand was a staff festooned with more black feathers and softly chiming bells.

The human's gaze was calm yet determined. *The Raven Priestess,* he thought with a shudder of recognition. No human should hold such strong, uncanny power. Every fiber of Peridot's being screamed at him to run, but there was no escaping now. Fleet as foot as he was, there was no outrunning wolves, and he had no time to spare to fashion a temporary gate, not with five sets of eyes trained on his face. Two wolves, two ravens, and one woman who looked as if she knew everything held in his souls.

"Why have you come to my forest, traitor elf?" she said, voice as mellow as honey from happy, dozing bees. If the bee's stingers were trapped inside the amber liquid.

Traitor elf. Peridot had been called worse, and traitor he was, to both humankind and Underhill, destined now to walk between the realms for the rest of his days, friendless and alone.

The Raven Priestess snapped her fingers, shaking him out of his self-pitying reverie. What had he become?

"I believe I asked you a question, elf."

He studied her dark, implacable face, mind churning, wondering. He knew he should trust no one, and yet he wished desperately he could trust this priestess with eyes as dark as the ravens that now graced each of her shoulders, having fluttered down from the tree above his head. There was no doubt in his mind that the birds had called to her, giving away his position, so now six beings knew exactly where he was. The djinn, the ravens, the wolves, and this woman whose magic he failed to understand.

He had thought himself so clever. So wise, even. And yet, it turned out that—for all his machinations and maneuvering—Peridot knew very little at all.

"I was looking for you," he quickly dissembled. The priestess arched one eyebrow at that but did not speak. "I thought that we could strike a deal, you and I."

The words tumbled out with barely a thought behind them. He was simply trying to buy time.

The larger of the two wolves slinked forward. Peridot forced himself to hold very still as it sniffed at his boots.

"Is that a warning?" Peridot asked out loud.

The Raven Priestess smiled. "The wolves do as they wish. Until I tell them otherwise."

"Your words give me no comfort, priestess."

"They are not meant to," she replied. "Why come you here, stinking of Underhill? You were banished, were you not? Or ran away? It's funny. I don't quite recall."

If she truly did not recall, Peridot did not care to enlighten her.

She gazed up at the bare branches of the mighty oak he stood beneath, as if communing with her God. He knew she followed the ways of the Gray Man. The poet. The warrior. She closed her eyes for the space of one long breath, and he wondered what messages she received.

"What is this deal you wish to strike?" she said, dark eyes snapping open to hold his gaze with her own.

"Power," he said. "I wish to share power."

She scoffed. "I have power enough."

"Not this kind," he replied.

"And what kind is that?"

"The power to take down Underhill. To crack its gates and smash its thrones." And suddenly, the lies he was spouting felt true. The words filled his whole being, and he realized there was nothing he wanted more. But how to go about it? How to do this thing, when he had no trust from human or elf alike? When he had been tasked to spy once again? A job he no longer had a belly for. He had never had such a strong stomach anyway. Had he?

The second wolf paced forward now to join its friend. Both animals sat a scant meter away, staring up at him with sober, measuring eyes. A line of sweat ran down his neck into his tunic, despite the chill spring air.

The priestess stirred once more.

"Come with me," she said, then turned with a swirl of cloak and skirts, as if expecting him to follow. One of the great gray beasts snapped its jaws his way, and a raven flew circled over his head.

"All right. Your message is clear." There was no escaping now, despite the priestess walking away, staff in hand, as if she had not a care in all the worlds.

He had walked directly into a trap.

Two traps.

First, the djinn, and now this human priestess, and he an elf with loyalties to no one but himself. And no desire any deeper than keeping himself alive.

Well, he had played both sides before. He could play two sides again, or more if he had to. There was nothing to be done for it.

"Lead on," he said to the wolves. One trotted

ahead, while the other beast stayed at his side. The ravens flew overhead, and the forest—so strangely quiet before—burst back into life.

Funny he had not realized the absence of sounds, so captured was he by the priestess's gaze and his own tumbling thoughts.

If he were going to get out of this alive, he needed to pay better attention.

CHAPTER 21

KARAKTILLA

Flying was one of life's greatest pleasures.

The feel of the wind beneath the long stretch of her wings. The push and flex of muscles. The taste of the air. Some days, there was also the thrill of the hunt. Scoping out a herd of bison or elk, or dive-bombing the local condor pair just because she could.

Today was not one of those days, though. Today's flight was a necessary attempt to clear her head and seek perspective. As she did so, she veered toward the verdant fields that marked the edge of Go No More.

Karaktilla's mind still worried at the visions from the orb, and the discussions with Daraktal had not helped matters. The questions raised by her sometime companion only served to make her worry more, and brought more questions winging their way, buffeting her thoughts.

When would Underhill cease its grabs for power? When would the Queen realize that trying to save her realm at the expense of other realms spelled doom for them all?

Karaktilla banked her wings, sliding into an updraft that held her aloft for a few moments. Soon would come the slow descent to the horse field of the human settlement.

There were too many loose threads these days. The careful weaving of the worlds quickly unraveled. Karaktilla needed to speak with one of the humans she trusted most, the herbalist and healer Anandita.

And so, she flew from the high, snow-peaked mountain top, over the valleys wet with spring rain.

The most pressingly urgent matter, which she must discuss with the human healer, was Elzabetta's power.

As Karaktilla and Daraktal had dug through scrolls and ancient books, they had discovered a troubling thing. If Elzabetta was not saved and her souls were not allowed to return home on their own, all the realms could perish.

Elzabetta must be rescued not only for herself, but also for the good of all.

Because it had become abundantly clear to Karaktilla that Queen Silverhair no longer wanted to save her only child. She simply wanted to shore up her power. The sacrifice of souls to reweave her daughter's fate and the fate of Underhill had failed, time and again. It was natural that Silverhair would try another path.

But the humans of Go No More must not fail. The Reckoning had done its worst on the human realms, but it had also opened the door to change.

And change—though Underhill feared it—was the only way toward a future that might accommodate them all.

Even if it meant the fall of elven hierarchy. Karaktilla would not mourn the loss.

She beat her wings again, drawing closer to the township, soaring above the vast fields of human cultivation. A herd of elk running free. And yes, the pair of condors hunting just below.

And there was the brown and gray of the new structures outside the human settlement. The refugees from the great battle Karaktilla had fought, with the Knights of Go No More at her side.

She and a mass of dragons had worked together in an unprecedented act of solidarity. They had hoped their work in New Salem spelled an end to the current strife. That had proven untrue. The once-peaceful valley was now marred by noise and clamor as the humans made more dwellings for the influx of their kind.

The Battle of New Salem had reshaped the landscape in more ways than one, and her visions intimated that the battle—though several moon cycles in the past—was not over.

And Karaktilla feared that she would call upon the other drakes yet again. She just was not certain when.

She made a slow, lazy loop around the township, not searching for anything in particular, but eyes opened for whatever it was she might see.

There was nothing of note, and she did not know whether to be relieved or dismayed. Nothing of note was usually good. It meant no immediate trouble. But it also meant no new information for her hoard.

Karaktilla traded on information. Her massive collection of books and scrolls were legendary in the area, with trolls traversing mountains, and drakes flying in from far distances to consult her vast library with the understanding that no books or scrolls would ever leave her lair.

A treasure, her books. And one she guarded jealously.

Finally, she saw the great paddock on the edge of town. Some humans worked with horses there, running them through their paces, training them to work in concert with humans, to serve human needs. In exchange, they were well treated, with warm dry places to rest during harsh winter.

The horses did not seem to mind the bargain.

Karaktilla snorted, emitting a puff of smoke as she lowered towards the ground with a mighty beat of her wings.

Some of the faces looked upward. Arms waved in greeting. A smaller figure took off running, likely to alert the township she was here.

Karaktilla banked her wings once more, heading into a slow descent. She pulled up short just before reaching the ground. The horses and humans had cleared the way for her as they always did. No one wanted to take the risk of being crushed. Karaktilla was skilled at both flying and landing, but a beast could never be too careful, could they?

Not when they are as small and fragile as a human

or a horse. Not when to stand against a drake would take a whole phalanx of warriors, and still, some of them would die.

There would be no blood shed this day. Not if Karaktilla had any say in the matter.

CHAPTER 22
BOCAN

Bocan nodded to the Knight outside the alchemist's door. Jade was a young Steel Clan apprentice who was proving to be stable and trustworthy so far.

"How are things?"

"It's been quiet in there, other than some moaning," the guard replied. She was a small, wiry Knight with golden brown skin, but strongly muscled. Bocan knew that Jade could throw a knife from a far distance and kill a person as quickly as a hummingbird could buzz your head. She was also a dab hand with a pole arm, which was good, because she needed everything she could get to increase her reach.

Bocan exhaled and rapped on the door three times. The door was opened by Doc Warren, a middle-aged white woman with sandy brown hair wearing her usual uniform of an undyed hemp shirt tucked into dark canvas trousers.

"Bocan." She blinked up at him as if surprised to see him standing there. Must be preoccupied.

"You needed me?" he said.

Doc Warren grimaced. "Well, he does."

She jerked her head over her shoulder.

"He says he needed to talk to you, and you alone."

Bocan steeled himself but did not reply. He simply ducked his head and stepped into a room that felt claustrophobic to him, though spacious enough for a human, he supposed. And palatial for one being held for punishment.

"I'll be on my way then," Doc Warren said, grabbing her bag of instruments and shutting the door behind her. Bocan barely noticed, because there he was. The alchemist.

The elf looked slightly better than he had when he arrived, yet still gaunt around the face and undernourished of the body. The elf's eyes alternated between looking wide with distress, then calm and clear. Rational even.

Bocan wondered what was going on inside the elf and what toll his vile work had taken on his own souls.

This was not something Bocan ever thought he would care about, yet here he was...though even one ounce of sympathy towards this torturer felt like a betrayal of his ma.

There were no chairs in the room sturdy enough to hold a halbtroll's weight, so he stood, arms crossed, glaring down at the alchemist.

"Carondel," he said, "what do you want?"

"I want to apologize..." the alchemist began.

Bocan held up a hand to stop him, suffused with sudden anger. "You think you can just apologize for what you did to my mother? You think that is enough? You think you can apologize for whole villages gone? Parents, grandparents, babes in arm, all dead? Souls stolen away?"

His voice grew louder, vibrating his chest.

"You think you can *apologize*?" Bocan's heart raced and his hands formed themselves into fists, ready to strike.

The alchemist blanched and leaned backwards. But still, he held Bocan's gaze, even though Bocan knew it cost Carondel, and the elf likely wanted to piss his trews.

"I know that apology is not enough," he stammered, "but it is the only place I have to begin."

Bocan willed his hands to unclenched themselves and rolled his head on his neck, inhaling deeply, before looking at the trembling elf once more.

"And?"

The alchemist licked his lips. "And I want to figure out—with your help—what our next steps..."

"*Our* next steps? Our next steps to what?" Bocan asked, crossing his arms over his chest. The nerve of this elf. Thinking that Bocan would have anything to do with his fracked-earth plans.

"Next steps to saving the princess and saving the realm."

Bocan's hackles raised with suspicion.

"Why should we save Silverhair's brat? And save Underhill? Why should I care?"

Carondel's face blanched.

"Ask the mages! Ask them what they pulled out of my mind!"

Bocan had been called away to deal with Arrow's news before the mages had finished. The sighting of the Raven Priestess gave him no disquiet. She was an ally, as far as he was concerned.

By the time he had finished with that, his arm hurt so badly he had sought out his bed, and then—since his comrades returned to assess the gate—his day had been busy from sunup. He never found out exactly what had been pulled from the alchemist's mind.

"The princess is in grave danger. I have sensed it for a long time. And yes—" He held up a hand to stave off the objections warring with each other on the tip of Bocan's tongue. "I know that I had a part in putting her at risk. But I did not know then what I know now."

Bocan frowned.

"And what is that?"

"The Queen is in league with worse and worse types. I once trusted her to guide the realm and set things to rights, but as our plan failed, she reached for further, and less savory, sources of power."

"Less savory that stealing human souls?"

The alchemist hung his head in shame, then took in a heaving breath.

"I have much to pay for. Please, allow me to try."

Bocan paced the narrow confines of the room. The space was far too small for his liking, and this conversation was making his head hurt all over again. Jimena said that, just as his arm would take time to heal, so would his head.

He was impatient with both and would rather throw this sniveling elf from the window than listen to any more blather.

"Let us say we choose to believe your story. That the princess is in danger, and Underhill at risk. Do you actually think you can save her? I don't care much about the fate of Underhill. It has caused my family nothing but grief. But the princess? I am willing to believe for a moment that she is an unwitting innocent, and worth saving. Do you think such a thing can actually be done? And that you are the one to do it?"

Most likely this was some elaborate ruse to free Carondel from his confinement, enabling him to make his way back to his liege. But Bocan was here and might as well listen.

The alchemist shrugged slightly. "With your help, and the Steel Clan and the mages, I believe we have a good chance for more than that. I also firmly believe we have to try."

Bocan waited, not saying anything. Let the elf sweat a bit. He stared across the sparely furnished room toward the window. Serena flew past, a white and tawny blur. Bocan wondered where the owl was off to. Usually, she would be napping at this time of day. He could use a nap himself. Not that he would allow it, despite Jimena's prodding for him to rest more.

He had rested enough.

When he finally looked back, the alchemist licked

his lips nervously, as if frightened to say the words clearly crowding up against his teeth.

Bocan widened his stance and drew his spine up. Ignoring the throbbing pain in his injured arm, he made himself look as large and intimidating as possible.

"Is there something else?"

Carondel nodded, head jerking like a child's puppet on a string. But the elf said nothing.

Bocan heard the guard talking with someone outside the door. They might not have much more time.

"Well?" Bocan said, scowling at the elf.

"I want to take the bitch Queen down."

Bocan grinned, feeling a sharp spike of angry glee pierce his chest.

"Alchemist, I do not yet know if I can trust you, or whether your plan is sound. But taking the bitch Queen down? If you have a plan for that, it is a thing I wish to hear."

CHAPTER 23
TEGAN

Tegan usually did not like people riding pillion on per bike, Starlight the lynx being the one exception. But needs must.

Fortunately, the djinni was a surprisingly good rider. He tucked his many black layers around his body and held on, remaining perfectly still. Abyad leaned when Tegan and the bike leaned and straightened when Tegan and the bike straightened. Tegan could not have asked for a better passenger. As a matter of fact, per suspected the djinni of making the ride easier than usual.

"Are you pushing us?" Tegan shouted into the wind over per shoulder. Per felt the djinni chuckle at per back and took that as a yes. Tegan shook per head but smiled a bit beneath per kerchief. The djinni was a creature of air, after all; if he wanted to give the bikes a tailwind to push them faster without using more fuel, Tegan was all for it.

Per settled in to enjoy the ride, knowing that the djinni would tap out where to turn and when to stop.

As the green rolled by, dotted with the blues, yellows, and purples of early flowers, Tegan's thoughts wandered back to standing at the waters, deep in the sheltering forest. Per could still feel the spirit of Mboli dancing in per blood.

Tegan really needed to consult with the elders once back in Go No More. Per needed to talk with her mothers, particularly Inaya. And perhaps to Hakim L'Ouverture and some of the other elders descended from those who came from the great continent of Africa.

Africa—like Europe, India, or China—was a place of legend. A place Tegan had only seen in pictures in the schoolhouse books in strange silvery images called photographs, the technology lost long ago.

The amulet Tegan's breastbone buzzed, alerting per to magic being used. Tegan jerked per head to the left, just as the djinni tapped per shoulder and pointed that direction. Well, and wasn't that interesting? Was the amulet picking up on the djinn's magical tracker? Or was the djinni engaged in some magical operation as they rode? Whatever the case, Tegan raised a fist and signaled that they would be turning left at the next cutoff.

The dragoons turned at a small tributary road half as wide as the cracking black ribbon they were on, but wide enough to still be useful enough that the Go No More clans and other humans kept them clear for use. So many of the roads were now choked by forest and wild vegetation. *Gone to green*, as the elders called it.

Gone to green was just as well. Choked pathways meant fewer routes for attack. Fewer ways for roving bandits to access the area around Go No More.

More room for animals, insects, and birds, let alone the spirits and magical beings that liked wild spaces best. The area was filled with nagini, chaneques, and entities like the Sasquatch and Deer Woman. Tegan hoped to never meet most of these beings, and luckily, they preferred their own spaces. While some of the magical creatures deigned to work with humans, most —it was said—found humans to be curiosities at best, and untrustworthy at worst.

Having been raised on stories of the Pre-Reckoning passed down from the distant ancestors, Tegan could not blame them. Long lived, these beings' memories were equally as long.

The dragoons rumbled behind Tegan. Jenny positioned her bike beside Tegan's, her red braids whipping out from beneath her helmet. Case was at per back. Tegan found she missed Bocan, though it was wise for the halbtroll to stay at home. He needed to heal further and Go No More needed his experienced assistance. Nonetheless, it was strange going on a mission like this without him. Tegan had come to rely not only on the Steel Clan itself, but on the tighter network of per closer friends and comrades.

Large, outstretched shadows dappled the road ahead, shifting with the wind. Condors. The mighty birds must be hunting carcasses of some of the larger beasts that roamed the area. Buffalo and elk and deer. Or they were hunting rabbits or foxes. None of the smaller animals were safe when the massive birds flew. The condors put Tegan in mind of small drakes, and per wondered if they were some sort of cousins to the ancient magical drakes?

The djinni tapped per shoulder once more and signaled to the left. Tegan held up a closed fist, signaling the convoy to stop, and found a place to pull off to the side of the road. There was a small, paved place choked around the edges with bushes leading into dense trees.

Tegan stopped and kicked down the stand that kept the bike upright before cutting power to the machine. Before the rumbling of the bike cut off completely, the djinni leapt nimbly from the bike and was stalking into the forest, black cloth floating around his graceful frame.

Tegan unsheathed the machete from its case on the bike and readied a kpinga on per back. Satisfied that the weapons were easily within reach, per followed the djinn, not bothering to wait for per comrades, and not removing per pigskin-lined helmet. A person never knew when attack might come, or from where.

Per hurried as the djinni disappeared between two trees with spreading branches. It was a strange bit of forest, not the usual. Those were oak trees, and large ones. A veritable grove of them, all reaching out as if to hug the ground below.

Tegan realized per had never been in this place before, though it was near enough to the township on horseback or hog.

The place felt uncanny, and at per breastbone, the

amulet pinged and buzzed and bit, increasing Tegan's agitation. Per forced perself to walk lightly and carefully, to slow per breathing down and calm per rapidly beating heart.

"Fire," Tegan said, the word leaving per mouth almost as quickly as the scent of burning wood reached per nostrils.

"Indeed," the djinni said from just up ahead.

"What the fuck is this place?" per heard Jerrod say further back on the path.

"Stay the course, comrade," Case replied.

So, it turned out Tegan was not the only one feeling antsy at what lay ahead.

The djinni walked on, seemingly unconcerned, black clothes billowing around him, dog at his side, both walking as silent as the night. Talk about uncanny. Uncanny yet strangely compelling at the same time. Abyad intrigued Tegan. Per attraction to Case was simple, that of comrade to comrade, the bond of friendship grown deeper over time. And of course, bare, brutal, physical lust as well. Tegan had no shortage of that.

But the djinni was a puzzle Tegan did not think per would ever put together.

A squirrel chattered overhead, flinging down a nut that bounced off Tegan's helmet. Per grinned, flipping off the small rodent, but kept moving on ahead.

The sky that had been light gray just moments before now boiled with black clouds, and the wind whipped through, shaking the oak trees, setting the fresh young leaves just budding on the branches to shiver and shake. Tegan did not know if the djinni had called the storm, or if it was a natural storm of early spring.

The temperature dropped. Tegan shivered in per leathers, feeling a frisson of fear, wondering what awaited them.

Much as Tegan enjoyed being on the road with per comrades, per hoped that someday soon per would have several uninterrupted months at home to sit by the fire. Wouldn't that be something? To smoke a bowl with per friends, spar with per comrades, and bed whomever was willing and fun. Perhaps even—finally—Case. But those days were not to be. Likely not for a long time.

For now, Tegan straightened per spine, adjusted the grip on per machete, and followed the djinni more deeply into the oak grove, toward the scent of burning.

ANANDITA

The workspace in Anandita's cottage was controlled chaos. Herbs drying overhead. A few precious jars of last year's stores, now run low from winter's illnesses, a battle that had left too many injured, and the influx of refugees from New Salem. Baskets of fresh herbs, waiting to be sorted and dried, or steeped into tinctures.

Most of the herbs they needed were not yet ready for harvest, but it would not do to wait. Anandita was determined to get ahead of her usual distilling and drying schedule, because one never knew what was coming. She could make specific blends later, but for now? Processing raw materials was the driving force.

Her apprentice Tokki ground herbs with the large wooden mortar and pestle at the large table in the center of the room. Jars and tincture bottles boiled in a large pot on the wood stove.

Anandita's father had been in and out all day, dropping off Ayurvedic plants he grew in his greenhouses, and praise God and thank the Asvini for his insistence on that first greenhouse, and the two more he had built since. It meant that they did not have to wait on the weather to cooperate, plus, he was able to grow plants from a different climate, which simply did not grow well in the rain and cold of the Willamette Valley.

Meanwhile, her parttime apprentice, the troll Recoana, was gathering still more plants and herbs from the forest outside the township. These were for the other types of medicine Anandita made, that she, Doc Warren, and the townspeople used regularly.

Anandita had never been busier. Not only were she and her apprentices working to replenish depleted stores, but everyone in Go No More still worked at getting the new people settled. That was a tricky process, and not always easy.

Anandita worked with Doc Warren and Jimena to treat the trauma of the refugees, and some of the Knights who had come back from the Battle of New Salem with nightmares. Ordinary battle was rough. Magical battle? That seemed even more difficult for humans to process. It was just going to take time. Time Anandita was no longer certain they had.

The whole township needed a pause to take a breath. But that was not going to happen. At least more small houses had been built, freeing up the over-crowded rooms in the public house and giving the refugee families proper places to call home.

On top of that, Jenny was busy, too. It seemed the two of them barely had any time together, and, only months into their relationship, that grated. Too often, they fell into bed exhausted, and that was when Jenny wasn't on the road. Anandita looked forward to more time with her lover; she just wasn't sure when.

She shook her head. The two of them would just need to make time.

Even her son, Hypatia, was busy. Everyone in Go No More had too much to do. Much more than they were used to.

So today, she had taken time out from getting the alchemist settled, leaving him to Jimena the mind healer from the ranchero outside New Salem.

It was good to be back in her own space, checking in with Tokki and her father. His diligent work on cultivating rarer strains of herbs in his greenhouse was finally showing good result, and the proof was on her table. Tulsi, ginger root, and feverfew all waited to be sorted. The scents were rich and heady. Anandita inhaled deeply, pausing a moment to let the sense of satisfaction fill her, body and soul.

Working with family was a boon. Anandita cherished her aunties, her mother, her father, her child, and now Jenny. They all made Anandita's life feel stable and good, even in the midst of the current chaos.

She wheeled her chair toward the worktable where Tokki, dark hair like a cloud around her head, ground herbs using the big carved mortar and pestle. The teen was becoming quite the herbalist in her own right. Tokki's father, Jerrod, was a Steel Clan Knight, and her mother was a weaver of great renown in the township.

But Tokki followed in neither parent's footsteps,

having discovered she had an affinity with plants from a young age, when she'd first toddled around Anandita's garden, happily smelling things, and grabbing at herbs and flowers with chubby fists. Her apprenticeship revealed an instinct and talent for blending herbs together. She was taking a break from processing to blend together a few mixtures they relied on and had run out of.

"Is that the new winter blend?" Anandita asked. Though early spring, winter ailments were still common.

"It is," Tokki replied. "Want to smell?"

Anandita leaned toward the mortar, and inhaled mint, comfrey, horehound, and some of the rarer mushrooms Recoana had found.

"I have thoughts for another," Tokki said, moving a stray lock of hair from her face with the back of a hand stained with turmeric root. She tilted her head toward a thick, rich gold root broken into three large pieces. "I want to make a year-round blend for general health using some of the spices your father cultivated. By the way, he said to tell you that your auntie invited you to dinner tonight. You, Hypatia, and Jenny, if you have the time."

Anandita nodded, mind rapidly ticking over her long to-do list. It was endless, really, but she had to eat. Jenny too. And she had not made enough time for her family recently, though Hypatia had been spending extra hours with his Nani and nana. Speaking of which, there was movement outside the window. Her son, racing towards her cottage, skirting his way through the planted vegetable beds and pausing briefly to greet the yakshini, the spirits who took care of the plants.

Anandita smiled at her son. She had first thought he was a girl who would follow in her footsteps as a healer. He had turned out to be a boy, and to be taking on some of the other qualities of the ancient woman scientist he'd been named for. Anandita loved him with all her heart.

He was a curious child, not so young anymore. Thirteen, going on fourteen years. For a long time, they had thought he would apprentice with the engineers, and he would likely end up there before long, but for now, Hypatia had an ad hoc agreement with several of the clans to get training in as many different crafts as possible.

Smart as a whip, he was. This blended apprenticeship gave him the freedom to run about town and deliver messages as needed. Clearly, Hypatia was on his way to deliver a message to her now.

Either that, or he was hungry for an early lunch.

The door burst open, but her son did not come in. Clearly, he was in too big a hurry to take off his boots.

"Maan!"

"Yes, beti? What is it?"

Hypatia vibrated with excitement, his brown face alight.

"The drake is here. And she wishes to speak with you!"

Tokki and Anandita looked at each other, and then both looked back at Hypatia.

"Karaktilla is here?" How had she missed the sound of those massive, beating wings?

Hypatia nodded, grinning broadly enough to show his white teeth. He loved the drakes and wanted nothing more than to travel drake-back the way Anandita had. She could not blame him. Terrified as she had been that first flight, it was the most thrilling thing she had ever experienced. She also appreciated consulting the drake's great library. Recoana was also a great friend to the drake, and Anandita wondered if the troll was already in the horse paddock, greeting her old friend.

"Tokki? Are you content to stay here and work, or do you wish to come with us?"

The teen's face broke into a smile.

"Really? I can come? You can spare me?"

Anandita shrugged. "We don't know what Karaktilla wants, and I may need help depending on what she says, so if both of you can come with me, I would appreciate it."

Tokki nodded and carefully put her herbs away, then brushed off her hands.

Anandita wrapped her goldenrod cloak around her shoulders and pinned it with the brooch made by her husband, Long. She looked down at the knotted silver and kissed it in his memory.

He had fallen to the silver queen long before they knew what was happening. And long before Anandita—who had thought she would never fall in love again—gave in to Jenny's courtship.

"I'll tell her you're coming!" Hypatia said, and ran

off again. Anandita waved him off, then rolled out to the porch to join Tokki as she pulled her boots back on.

The air was cool, with the soft kiss of coming rain. Anandita looked forward to seeing Karaktilla again, though she hoped the visit did not bode ill.

Tokki stood and wiped her hands on her brown canvas trousers. Anandita smiled.

"Let's go see the drake," she said, and wheeled her chair down the ramp, following the wake of her fast-running son. Uneasiness settled into Anandita's heart.

The drake would not be here if there was not some urgent need.

CHAPTER 25

SILVERHAIR

Through one of the arched windows of her private chamber, she watched her daughter ride off with her guard, beneath the apple trees, off to who knows where.

Silverhair's meeting with Tarioc was less than satisfactory. The elf's manner was perfectly correct, and he had said all the correct things, but the encounter had left her restless.

She needed to do something.

Taking a deep draught of apple juice and nectar from her favorite silver cup, she pondered.

On a small table at her side rested a heavy book, bound in softest doeskin leather, stained a royal blue. It was the legends passed down from Queen to Queen, and King to King. In it were stories often told, and others barely remembered.

Others still were forgotten. Had they not been written down in oak-boll ink on the fine vellum pages, they would have been lost to time.

She set down her cup and opened the heavy tome on her silk clad lap, flipping through the thick pages until she found the one she wanted. The one she needed.

An illustration of intertwined holly and oak branches filled the page. It was beautiful to behold, the pattern picked out in shades of gold, green, brown, and berry-red.

Arresting as the image was, it was the story held in the few scant pages beyond that held her eye. "Once upon a time," the tale began, "Holly battled Oak."

It was an old, familiar tale. A tale of night and day, winter and spring, and the eternal battle of time itself. A battle that barely touched these realms, unless you counted one day as many years, and one season as aeons passing by.

But then the tale changed from one of battle, shifting instead to one of courtship and love.

Holly and Oak twined themselves together, growing strong.

She tugged on the embroidered pull and moments later, a guard opened the large double doors onto the courtier on duty.

"My Queen?" The courtier bowed, his green hair cut short in a new fashion Silverhair did not care for.

"Fetch my maids and tell them to pack for one week's journey."

"My liege?" The courtier's dark brow furrowed in confusion.

"Tell them!" she snapped. The courtier bowed again and backed away, leaving her alone again.

Alone to plan her journey to the Unseelie realms. A place she had seldom been since before her husband had been taken from her arms.

After much correspondence, she would finally meet with the Holly King, liege of the Unseelie Court.

Queen Silverhair closed the heavy book and smiled. Yes, the Unseelie King had a son who might marry her daughter, forming an alliance. Her realm would grow strong once again.

But she had not ruled out other options. Not just yet. Elzabetta was right to quail at the thought of childbearing. Perhaps her daughter was too weak. Perhaps Silverhair would marry the Holly King himself. Or wed his handsome son.

After all, what did age matter to almost-immortals? And an alliance of Seelie and Unseelie would be one that had never been seen in thousands upon thousands of years.

Who knew what power would rise should Holly and Oak join together once again?

Perhaps, the Queen thought, it was time for legends to be born again.

CHAPTER 26

PERIDOT

Peridot did not know whether to be terrified or grateful. The Raven Priestess was a strange one, to be sure. And those birds were unsettling, staring at him with their black eyes, as if they knew something about him. More than he knew himself.

He still was not sure where the priestess's allegiances lay, other than with her one-eyed God. A beautiful human with skin as dark as her elaborate coils of hair, she spoke with the other realms with ease. It was almost as if she had a portal gate inside her head with a direct connection to whatever Gods and spirits she communed with.

Dark tunic and long skirt swaying softly, she brewed tea at her woodstove as Peridot watched. He sat, one ankle crossed over his knee, seated on a comfortable chair, with a small wood table at his side. Another chair sat opposite, a carved wooden rocker. They were the only two chairs in the small place, besides a stool tucked against one wall that currently served to hold a bowl of water. For the ravens? Clearly, she did not get many guests, though the cozy, small cabin on the edge of an oak grove sat not half a day's walk from Go No More.

"Why don't you live in the township?" he asked.

The priestess grunted and softly shook her head, setting the feathers and bells that nested among the dark coils to fluttering and chiming.

"I like to live among the trees," she said simply, and left it at that.

Peridot knew there had to be more to it than that simple phrase, but clearly the priestess kept her own counsel, and he would do well to do the same.

Except he needed help. He was undecided as of yet how much to help Queen Silverhair, and how much to go his own way. All his planning had come to naught, and he was in a worse position than when he had begun. Why had he succumbed to the wish for power within the Seelie Court?

It was better than the alternative, he thought. But was it, really? He could have done what Damson, the trolls, and the others had done: learned to live simply among humankind. To share their lives, in sorrow and in joy. To defend their freedom.

Instead? He had followed the allure of fitting into a society that scorned him until they discovered he might be of use. If only he had figured that out before everything went to shit.

Peridot felt a pang of regret at his betrayal of his

human friends. And more than that, regret and anger about his friend and sometimes lover, Damson.

She had tortured him, and though he knew she had held back from the worst of it, that was nonetheless a thing he might never forgive her for. Just as she might never forgive him for the lies and betrayal that had led to the coercion.

He watched the Raven Priestess pour steaming water from a copper kettle into an earthenware pot. She seemed unruffled. Unbothered. He wished to have her sense of grace and ease.

"Why did you stop me?" he said.

"Because you are a threat," she replied.

"Then why have you not bound me?"

She didn't speak for a moment, gathering cups and pouring the fragrant brew from the round-bellied pot. She handed him a brown earthenware mug with no handle. The warmth felt good in his hands. He sniffed at the tea. Some nutty combination of toasted grains and herbs he only half recognized.

"Will you poison me?" he asked.

She smirked, dark lips twitching upward.

"I could," she replied. "But I won't."

"And why is that?"

He watched her face carefully as she settled herself into into a carved wooden rocking chair. One raven perched on each side of the chair's back, swaying comfortably back and forth as the chair began to rock.

The smaller of the wolves sat at her side, head on its large silvery paws. The second lay crosswise, blocking the door. Message received.

"Because I am not done with you yet," she said. "You have information to give, do you not?"

The large birds turned their heads and trained beady eyes upon him.

Peridot throttled down a shiver. He was an elf, damn it. An elf with his own magic. An elf on a mission from Queen Silverhair herself. At least he had been.

But is that what you want? he asked himself. *Is that the life you want to live for the rest of your days? As a syco-phant and toadie?* For that was the truth of the matter, wasn't it? He would never become more than a spy. A servant to the Queen. When a person was looking at eternity, these were powerful questions, and ones he had not often pondered. Not until recently.

Not until this tangled mess.

Perhaps an elf like him could be more. Could have a home. And friends. Perhaps an elf like him could contribute something good to life.

But he could say none of this to the woman who sat across from him, guarded by her ravens and her wolves.

"What do you want from me?" he finally said.

She simply rocked and sipped her tea, signaling that it was safe for him to drink his own. It tasted of roasted barley and thyme. He liked it.

He liked sitting here. It was the most companion-able moment he had had in many months.

There was something about the Raven Priestess's home that lulled Peridot into a false sense of comfort and ease. He should have been wary, terrified even. After all, she had basically threatened him with dismemberment by those damn wolves of hers to get him to come here. As he sipped the tea, his thoughts scrambled themselves, trying to work out how many ways he could use the situation to his advantage.

How could he placate Queen Silverhair, while still breaking his vows to serve her? How could he keep from getting killed by some Go No More Knights with a vendetta, and warn Damson that both Underhill and the human realms were in grave danger if they didn't do something to help the princess, and soon?

Peridot wished he had a crystal ball or some way to see the future. Something to help him measure which path was correct. Which action would offer the best outcome for him? And for everyone? He honestly did not know. The destruction of the Reckoning had altered time and space in all the realms forever, it seemed, and this thing that might be needed? Rescuing the princess?

Well, that was treason, and taking her away from Underhill could very well destroy that realm too, and then what would the world be like?

Would there be any more sitting by fires, sipping tea with strange, magic-working witchy women dedicated to ancient Gods? Would it all be obliterated? Would the hierarchy of Underhill disappear? Would elves themselves disappear without the steady pulse of the magic from Underhill?

He gulped his tea too quickly and coughed.

"What are you thinking of, you scheming one?" the Raven Priestess asked, dark eyes shrewd.

Peridot licked his lips. "Nothing I care to share."

"Oh, you'll share soon enough if I require it." Her voice sent a shard of ice to pierce his heart. Peridot recognized that he walked a knife's edge over a chasm buffeted by harsh wind. A wind he could hear moving outside. A spring storm rolled in again, the wind snatching at the edges of the wooden shutters outside and setting the handle of the well pump to creak.

He returned the Raven Priestess's gaze. The wolf at her side sat up and licked its chops.

Right. He was a captive here. A prisoner.

But he had to make this work. He had to find a way to get out of here alive without ruining everything he had ever worked for in his life.

CASE

Case had mixed feelings about the djinni riding pillion with Tegan and him getting stuck with per bonded lynx. On one hand, both Tegan and Abyad were scorching hot and made his groin tight. And the steady hum of the motorcycle hadn't helped matters.

He was glad to be on foot again, just so the fracked-earth taint vibration would stop.

On the other hand, Case had been inching closer and closer to being Tegan's bedmate for two years now. Ever since Jason was old enough to take care of himself most of the time, Case found that he wanted more than just occasional bed sport with whatever hotness caught his fancy and was up for a fuck.

He wanted a person, if not to come home to, at least someone he could count on to be around day to day. Someone who understood him. Shared that intangible quality he saw between Jenny and Anandita, Winney and Inaya.

Oh, he had that with his comrades to be sure. And he appreciated his friends more than anything. He loved them almost as much as he loved his son.

But these days? He had to admit that for his heart, it no longer felt like enough. His heart *longed*, and he hated that feeling. It was like an itch on his back that he couldn't reach beneath the layers of hemp and leather.

And no other person captured and held his attention and imagination the way Tegan did. His finest comrade. The person who always had his back.

Tegan was closer with Jenny and Bocan, to be sure, but in the past year, Tegan had also opened more to Case. They began spending more time together. Sparring and joking, planning, and plotting. Flirting. Working on the plan to free New Salem, and then helping all the people and animals displaced from their homes.

Case watched Tegan walk ahead of him now, burgundy leather trousers snug around that tight ass, shoulders slim, back straight, weapons to hand, looking fierce and tasty. The djinni strode next to per, black clothing swirling about him with each step, as if it were the wind itself.

Yeah, Abyad was tasty, too, but Case needed to keep his head on a swivel and his cock in his pants. It wouldn't do right now to be mooning over his comrade and the djinn, both of whom yes, he would take to his bed in an instant. Preferably together.

Get your shit clear, he thought to himself, and put his head on a swivel for real, scanning the strangely placed oak grove on the edge of the forest that bordered Go No More.

He wished they'd brought more of the animals along to do some scouting. They could use Flex and Serena along with Starlight, Tegan's bonded lynx. Starlight walked stiff-legged, still angry at Tegan for bumping her off pillion and forcing her to ride with Case. It wasn't that Case and the lynx didn't get along, they did, but Case could see why the lynx felt insulted. Though it was made clear to everyone that the djinni was helping Tegan navigate, it clearly still stung.

The lynx looked back at him, as if she had heard his thoughts. He grinned and gave Starlight a thumbs-up. She sneezed, which set her whiskers quivering, and then padded off, likely seeking out the djinni's black dog who had ridden on the supply trailer.

Their small group followed whatever tracker the djinni had put on Peridot the elf, but also the scent of woodsmoke that hung rich in the rainy, fir and oak scented air.

The smell of smoke had alarmed Case at first, until he realized it didn't carry the acrid stink of a forest on fire, but rather the homely scent of a woodstove burning merrily away. He wouldn't mind sitting by a woodstove himself since the rain had started up again. The *drip drip drip* from the trees didn't bother him much, not in his waxed canvas hood and cloak, and his leathers kept the rest of him protected well enough. Besides, the life of a warrior was largely spent dealing with a combination of the elements, discomfort, and exhaustion along with the camaraderie that came from long hours of reconnaissance punctuated by smashing heads.

Tegan held up a fist, signaling *stop*. Case and the other Knights moved to cluster around per, along with the two scouts.

Litha's blond hair poked out from beneath her own waxed hood, and Jessie's face was damp.

"What did you find?" Tegan asked.

"There's a small house just up ahead—more of a hut, really—smoke coming out of the chimney. Protected by magic."

Huh.

"What sort of magic?" Case asked.

"Not one hundred percent sure, though it felt familiar," Litha said.

"And I found this." Jessie held up a dark, iridescent feather.

"Crow?" Tegan asked.

The scouts both looked at each other.

"Raven," Jessie replied. "At least I think so. It's a bit large to have come from a crow."

Oh shit, right. The Raven Priestess. The uncanny witch had disappeared between the Battle of New Salem and the journey back to Go No More with the masses of refugees.

"So, this was where she ended up," Jerrod mused.

"You still feel the elf?" Tegan asked, turning to Abyad.

The djinni sniffed the air, closed his eyes, and then did something that caused the hairs on the back of Case's neck to stand on end.

A light breeze whipped through the grove, spinning raindrops directly into Case's face. He sputtered.

Then the djinni opened his eyes again, and those black circles stared right at him as if he knew something about Case that Case didn't even know about himself.

Fuck. He didn't know what to do with that look. At all.

Tegan raised that scarred eyebrow and glanced between the two of them. Per looked interested, as if Tegan was Starlight, hungry and on the prowl.

Abyad slowly smiled. "The elf is here, and I think you need to go in after him."

"What?" Case protested. "Why me?"

"Because you are the one he trusts the most."

Case scoffed. "How is that even possible? I don't know what you think you see, but..."

The djinni just shrugged.

"So, what's the plan?" Jerrod asked.

Tegan looked up at the oaks, then back down the path. Assessing.

"We split up. Three of us head to the door. The rest of you? Fan out around the building because we don't know if there are other routes of escape. Scouts? Keep eyes on the path."

Tegan ran a hand over per mouth, clearly still thinking, then returned per gaze to Case.

"Even though the Raven Priestess helped us in New Salem doesn't mean I trust her."

Case nodded. He wasn't sure he trusted her either. But then, it took him a long time to trust anyone.

"Let's do this," he replied. Then winked at Tegan, who stifled a smile.

The moment only lasted a few seconds but was enough to warm Case inside. Then he took a breath, recentered himself, and started walking forward, towards the smell of fire.

CHAPTER 28

ELZABETTA

The white pony rocked gently beneath Elzabetta. Her pale green skirts were arrayed around the horse, and her gloved hands gripped the reins. As the pony clopped through an apple grove, the light and shadow shifted and changed as if dancing.

Elzabetta had not been riding in far too long and was pleasantly surprised—though mildly wary—at Tarioc's invitation. Clearly, her guard and protector had something on his mind. The invitation had not come out of nowhere, but was it under his own volition? Or was this another way her mother was trying to lull her into complacency? To persuade her to confide in Tarioc the way she would no longer confide in the Queen?

Or was it something else?

The graceful sweep of Tarioc's long, straight spine gave nothing away, though his face was thoughtful. But every time he caught Elzabetta looking, he schooled it into a bland, blank slate. As if he was doing nothing more than riding his bay horse next to her, enjoying the soft air and the fall of apple blossoms in the dappled light.

They passed Mother's rose garden and headed toward a copse of wood, a dense green place that Elzabetta had not visited since she was a child. She had been too weak of late. Too overwrought and wrung out by the alchemist's treatments and her mother's constant pushing.

It was almost amusing: since they had ceased to strap her to a chair, struggling and fighting...since they had ceased to force Elzabetta through their vile rite of ingesting human souls...she felt better. Stronger. Oh, her mind still drifted and fought to come back to focus, and something was still missing from her, she could tell. Shards of her soul still seemed to wander, the way the alchemist had said.

But the struggle was gone.

Despite the occasional fog, her mind felt clear for the first time in a long while. Perhaps that was why Tarioc had invited her to the ride. She was no longer a frail puppet with barely enough energy to fight for herself. She was stronger now, she felt with some amount of satisfaction.

So, if there were plans afoot...

He most certainly seemed to have something he wished to speak with her about. She wondered when he would broach whatever caused that thoughtful look to crease his unmarked brow.

They entered the woods, sunlight barely reaching

the ground shadowed by leaves of oak and ash and hawthorn.

This was the Sacred Grove. The place the more religiously inclined courtiers, and even servants, gathered. Elzabetta could understand why. The place was beautiful, and the trees immediately made her feel at ease. It felt as if all her cares slowly lifted from her shoulders. Her mind and heart felt lighter, more at peace.

Small birds flitted to and fro. They were bright things in shades of brilliant yellow and rich blue.

One tiny bird, no larger than her thumb, buzzed nearby, wings and breast flashing iridescent green. She laughed.

Tarioc smiled. "It is good as music to hear you laugh, princess."

"That bird's livery is almost the same as your own," she replied.

"And so it is."

They shared a fleeting smile, then continued their ride in silence, enjoying the calls of the birds, the rustling of small creatures, and the soft clop of hooves.

"Are you weary, princess?" Tarioc broke the pleasant quiet.

"No," Elzabetta replied, surprised to find that it was true. "I think the exercise is doing me good."

Tarioc nodded.

"I had hoped it would be so."

Elzabetta frowned. "But how did you know? How did you know I was strong enough?"

"I have eyes in my head, princess. You have a bloom in your cheeks that was not there before and a brightness in your eyes. Not that you were not always beautiful," he hastened to amend, "but you are more..."

He paused as if searching for a word, body gently rocking with the cadence of his horse.

"More what?"

He looked keenly at her, piercing her with a steady gaze.

"Present," he finally said. "You are present."

Well, and was not that a funny thing for a person to say? Had Elzabetta not been present before?

She pondered this as they rode and found that it was true. As her souls had wandered, so to had the rest of her, it seemed. Her body may have remained in one place Underhill, but in between bouts of fighting off her mother or Carondel? Once she was strapped firmly to the chair for the terrible experiments—the "saving grace" her mother called it, as if the process was anything other than vile murder and torture—she had indeed flown off somewhere. The scraps of her soul would leave the alchemist's laboratory, leave behind the torture and the grave knowledge that because of her, people had died.

She felt it fully now, those scores of people. A whole host by now, and yet around her, Elzabetta saw the signs that Underhill was crumbling and changing. In the orchard, a few ripe apples had taken to falling on the grass, beginning the slow, sweet stink of rot, as butterflies gathered in some macabre dance.

There were other things, too. A new crack at the very edge of the throne room entryway. A servant who had suddenly developed a limp, then disappeared....

Even the sun overhead seemed to have shifted, though Elzabetta could not detail how or why.

Tarioc pulled his horse up, pausing next to a small, burbling stream in which silver fish swam happily. A brown, slender dryad startled, disappearing into her willow tree, whose long green fronds dangled in the water like a fine lady's skirts.

Elzabetta smiled. The dryad was a beautiful creature, to be sure. As beautiful as people said Elzabetta was, when they tried to curry favor.

"Shall I help you down?" Tarioc asked, dismounting from his bay. The horse was already hard at work, cropping the grasses that grew at the base of a gracious hawthorn tree.

"Yes, please," she said, gathering the reins about the saddle pommel and reaching out her hands.

Tarioc took a hand in one of his, while his other grasped her waist. She could feel his fingers firm on her side. It felt pleasant. She was so rarely touched by anyone other than her maidservant, that it was a novelty. She wished that it might happen again.

Elzabetta slid off her pony and soon stood on the springy green of the ground.

The sounds of the woodland filtered through the trill of birdsong. The rustle of leaves. The chatter and buzz of two sprites arguing over a flowering bush. She turned to the knight, who was contemplating her. There was that thoughtful look again.

She set her feet and tilted up her chin.

"Why did you bring me here, Tarioc? Though I appreciate it to be sure. It is a pleasant day, and the exercise has done me good, but I think that is not the only reason you have brought me to this place."

This place outside of the eyes and ears of her mother's spies, she did not say, though they both knew that she meant it.

He looked uncomfortable for a moment, which was strange for such a confident elf. Looking at the hawthorn as if wondering at its thorns, he spoke again.

"Princess, I wonder, are you happy?"

A shocked laugh burst from her lungs.

"Happy? Is anyone Underhill happy?"

Tarioc's lips turned down and his brow furrowed once again. "Perhaps that was the wrong question. And I...I'm not sure how to ask what I need to."

"Just speak. I will not report you to my mother. Though I probably should." And the old Elzabetta certainly would have done.

Her words did not seem to set him at ease, but she was in no mood to do so. *Trust no one* had been the last words her nursemaid-cum-tutor had said to her before she disappeared. That elf had been her only true confidant and safe haven. But the tutor had balked when the experiments began.

Elzabetta had been confused, those first mornings that Marian had failed to appear.

But now she understood. Marian had become a threat to Queen Silverhair's plans. After that, Elzabetta had learned to guard her heart.

"Have you ever longed to see someplace besides this?" Tarioc spoke as she pondered.

"Some place besides the unchanging beauty and wonder of Underhill, you mean?"

Though change was slowly creeping in, wasn't it?

"Precisely."

"All the time." Her voice was sharp as a crow's. Her vehemence surprised even her. "I dream of it, Tarioc. I dream of it constantly."

"Well, then," Tarioc replied, flashing her a true smile for the first time ever. "Would you care to hear my plan?"

CHAPTER 29
JENNY

What a strange and glorious world she lived in.

Jenny and Bocan hurried towards the horse paddock. Jenny's eyes were trained on the massive purple drake. Even seated, it was taller than the large old apple trees in the corner of the field. Karaktilla's scales shimmered and shifted, changing color from the richest plum to an iridescent purple tinged with green.

Angel and the Horse Clan were stabling the beasts that usually roamed the paddock, running and playing or placidly cropping grass. They were restive today, not placid. Horses bucked and snorted, shaking their heads and rolling their eyes. All except Angel's own black beast, a horse named Stone. Stone was as solid as his name, and Angel relied on him to help calm the others.

Jenny couldn't blame the beasts for expressing their displeasure. Karaktilla was massive and smelled slightly of burning forests, even at this distance. Closer in, Jenny knew there would also be a whiff of death around her from the latest buffalo or elk she had consumed.

But the drake was also beautiful.

"Magnificent," Jenny murmured. Bocan glanced at her but said nothing. It was only recently that the drakes of legend had come down to visit the humans of Go No More. Oh, the various Indigenous tribes had spoken of contact, but the drakes mostly kept to themselves on their mountain peaks, high at the eternally snowcapped peaks where most people did not venture except for a few like Recoana the troll. She loved to gather wild herbs in the mountains and had been the first from the township to befriend the purple drake.

The troll stood at the drake's side. Taller and broader than Bocan, and with darker blue skin, Recoana cut an imposing figure. The troll could hold her own but had a heart as soft as a puppy's fur.

The drake's triangular, wedge-shaped head leaned toward Recoana. Jenny caught the strange rumble, clatter, and click of the drake, speaking aloud. Karaktilla could also speak mind-to-mind in speech that humans and other beasts could understand.

Anandita was there already, wheeled chair several paces back, golden cloak wrapped around her, dark-haired Hypatia, standing at her side. Jenny's heart swelled with the love of Anandita and her son, an addition to her family she had not quite expected, though she had longed for it for many years. A large portion of the township had gathered already, standing about or sitting in wheelchairs, hoods and cloaks wrapped around them to keep off the spring drizzle.

Even Hakim L'Ouverture had shown up, and the head of the Green Clan did not usually venture far from the fields.

Tegan's mothers were there as well. Inaya and Winney stood hand-in-hand, watching over the children from the township's school. Winney had clearly put some of the older ones in charge of the younger, but she always had one eye on the littlest. That was how things worked in Go No More: Every person had responsibilities that suited them, and everyone cared for each other. It was the way of things. Children here learned young that you pulled together, or died apart.

"What do you suppose the drake wants?" Jenny asked as they grew closer.

Bocan shook his head.

"It can't be anything good," he rumbled.

Unfortunately, Jenny had to agree. As they grew closer, the drake's mind speech became clearer.

::I have visions of the princess,:: Karaktilla said. *::And need you to attend to what I say!::*

Some of the council members appeared to be arguing with the purple drake.

"Fools," Bocan said. "Arguing with Karaktilla is a useless and foolhardy thing."

Jenny had to agree. The council needed to listen. It would not do to put their petty human squabbles in front of the drake.

Rafiq's voice rose and fell in argument, and John the Dairyman seemed to be backing him up.

Anandita shook her head in disgust. Jenny did not blame her. She searched the crowd to see who else was there, and how they were taking it all.

There was her mother, Danika, taking notes as usual.

Damson stood nearby, green hair in tight braids wound around her head, sharp ear points practically quivering with tension. Arms crossed and feet braced, the elf looked as if she wanted to strike somebody.

Jenny grinned. It was nice she wasn't the only one who became weary of the seemingly constant bickering of the council members. Danika looked annoyed as well. The set of her shoulders as she wrote was one of her tells. Mostly though, her mother looked worried.

Jenny veered toward her mother, Bocan in tow. They threaded through the clumps of gathered townspeople.

"What's happening?" she asked.

Danika's eyes flicked up, but she kept scribbling. "The drake said she's been getting visions."

"And?"

She finished whatever she was writing and looked at Jenny properly, mouth set in a straight line. "And she wants Anandita to come with her. To Wy'East. To look into the crystal orb again."

Jenny nodded. Anandita's report from the orb ended up helping a lot with the Battle of New Salem. Jenny would likely hear all about it at dinner, unless her lover would be en route by then. Jenny's mind ran through all the things Anandita would need readied to travel drake-back. She would need to check with Anandita and Hypatia when this gathering was done.

Danika wasn't finished. "Anandita says she trusts the drake, but the esteemed council members don't seem to agree."

Jenny groaned, wishing for a moment she was still with with Tegan and the others. But Aphrodite had needed to check in with Charles Wong and the council. Speaking of which, where were the mages?

"I can't believe I came back for this squabbling," she groused.

Danika quirked her mouth at Jenny. "Not looking forward to your turn on the council, are you?"

Jenny threw up her hands in horror. "That's the last thing I want."

Her mother laughed. "I think you inherited that from your great-grandmother Molly. Stories say she was all action and no talk."

"Ass-kicker Molly," Jenny replied, raising a fist in salute. It was because of Molly that the Steel Clan wore the winged wheel emblem.

Great-grandmother had been the leader of a motorcycle clan way back in the Pre-Reckoning times. Outlaws, they called themselves, trading in marijuana and fighting an entity they simply called The Man. Jenny was not certain what exactly it was about trading in cannabis that made Great-gran an outlaw. Pre-Reckoning times sounded really weird.

Bocan poked her shoulder. "Pay attention."

He pointed a big blue hand toward the drake.

Jenny and her mother both startled and stood at attention, facing Karaktilla.

::We need to work together!:: the drake broadcast. *::The threat is greater than we imagined.::*

"What is the threat?" Jenny said out loud, lifting her voice to rise above the clamor of the crowd.

A film fell and rose on Karaktilla's nictating eye, and the drake looked directly at her. Jenny fought to not shiver beneath the steady gaze of the giant reptile.

::The exact threat is as of yet unknown.:: Karaktilla spoke directly into Jenny's mind. Jenny was never certain if others could hear when the drake did that, though she had heard that Karaktilla could pinpoint one mind in the midst of a throng.

::The only thing I know for certain,:: the drake continued, this time sweeping the council members with her gaze, *::is that if you do not figure out a way to help the princess, we all may perish. We are beginning to think that Elzabetta has the power to straddle both the realms. Perhaps that is why her souls wander. Perhaps her souls are attempting to connect with this realm, and all of her mother's work has been to keep her away from the gates between our realms. But whatever the case, we know that the princess's health is key to the well-being of the realms.::*

"That is ridiculous!" Rafiq said, sputtering.

Anandita raised a hand to stop him.

"We must listen to Karaktilla's counsel. She speaks true words. I can sense it.... And much as we hoped difficult times were over and the battle had been won?" She pulled her cloak more tightly around her shoulders. "I think we all knew that the battle was not the end of the war. Silverhair will not be satisfied until she gets what she wants."

Jenny stood stock still, listening to her lover.

"And what is that? That you think she wants?" someone said. Jenny didn't see who.

::*Power. Power over all beings is what she wants. And if Elzabetta perishes, I fear that will be exactly what the Queen shall get. But if Elzabetta finds her liberation, Daraktal and I believe that all the realms have a chance not only to survive, but thrive.*::

Damson spat on the ground in anger at the drake's words but did not speak.

It was Bocan who raised his voice next. "The gold-arsed royalty Underhill want everything that is anathema to us here. And we know that the healer and drake are correct."

"You can't know..." John the Dairyman began, but was hushed by those around him.

Bocan continued. "It is why my parents left Under-hill. Why so many of us have left Underhill." He gestured to Damson, and to the trolls that had arrived at some point, Jenny did not know when, but their large, deep blue bodies now towered above the rest of the crowd.

"Queen Silverhair is far worse than the warlord Wulf, and a far greater threat to us," said Aphrodite, striding forward, pushing her way toward the gathered council members with Charles Wong at her side.

"Don't you think we know she's a threat?" Rafiq

blustered. The council head did not look pleased to have been called out. "How many souls has she stolen? Do you think we have forgotten?"

Bocan growled deep in his chest. Rafiq closed his mouth, and John the Dairyman blanched even paler than he usually was.

"How dare you speak so blithely of stolen souls when my mother sits, half wraith, half human under my father's care?"

"I beg your pardon, Bocan," John the Dairyman replied. Rafiq said nothing.

Bocan grunted.

Jenny clapped a hand on her comrade's arm, then raised her voice again to speak. "Those of us in Go No More follow the founders' wishes that we all live free and share what we have with one another. That none shall lord it over another. Is anyone here telling me they wish to change that?"

She scanned the crowd. There was some grumbling and mumbling, but mostly people looked from her to Bocan and shook their heads no.

From the back of the crowd, Hakim L'Ouverture shouted, "We shall be subject to no one! We shall live free!" The head grower raked the crowd with his gaze and lifted a fist. "We shall be free!"

The township answered in kind.

"We shall be free!" they roared.

Jenny nodded, feeling the power of it in her bones.

These were a people of healing and weaving, of growing and teaching. They were also, all of them, a clan of warriors, no matter what path their talents and apprenticeships had led them on.

Tears prickled at the back of her eyes, and she felt proud. Proud to be a member of the Steel Clan and prouder still to call herself a friend and champion of Go No More.

SILVERHAIR

The Holly King's throne room was stifling.

While Queen Silverhair's domain was all pale wood, flowing curtains, and sunlight, the Unseelie King's lair was made of towering gray stone walls that enclosed the space like a tomb. The walls were hung with bright tapestries, which softened the cavernous space slightly, and a fire blazed on the massive hearth large enough to roast an ox. At least the King had provided her with a high-backed chair, cunningly designed with a small curved roof to keep the heat from the fire contained.

Usually, Silverhair would have sent an envoy to the King, or demanded he come to her. But this was a delicate conversation that needed his good will and good temper.

A conversation she did not want overheard. Not by her people. Though she did not doubt there were spies crawling the walls of this place. She had plenty of those herself. But a spy or two was different than an entire court. With a spy? At least the news would be in singular, albeit dangerous, hands rather than fodder for gossip amongst the courtiers, used as currency for advancement, bribery, and power mongering.

"Elderberry wine?" the Holly King asked, shifting on his massive chair. They both sat near the fire and while Queen Silverhair had welcomed its warmth at first, she now could not stand the stinking burn and heat of it.

But it would not do for a queen to look uncomfortable, so she bore it silently. All negotiations were a form of battle. And it would not do to show her weakness to this king.

"Yes. Thank you."

The King snapped his bejeweled fingers, and a courtier glided forward, carrying a silver flagon and matching goblet.

She sipped at the fragrant wine, enjoying the slight hint of tart among the sweet.

"And your daughter? She is well? Looking forward to the nuptials?"

"She is well enough and will be ready when I tell her to be ready."

The King raised an eyebrow.

Queen Silverhair cursed inwardly. She needed to guard her tongue. That was a slip, and showed the very weaknesses she sought to mask.

"Oh? I had thought she was amenable. My son is handsome, is he not? What is the problem?"

The Queen lowered her goblet, ready to reply, but he continued.

"Is it that he is Unseelie and she is Seelie? I should think that would be a boon for both our realms and that that *boon* would be understood."

His voice was sharp, almost menacing. Queen Silverhair did not rise to the bait. She calmly swirled the red wine in her metal cup, as if thinking. As if his words did not alarm her in the least.

"You know how young people are," she said. "They always think they know what is best for themselves. She is not yet wise in the ways of diplomacy and politics. But she will become so."

The king grunted. "That makes a certain amount of sense."

Silverhair smiled and sipped at the wine. Her daughter did not want to marry the son of the Holly King. Silverhair knew it. Her daughter did not want many things that must be done. Her precious jewel had become a selfish brat. She saw now that she had coddled Elzabetta out of her own weakness. Out of her own desire to keep one remaining part of her dead husband near her.

But that had gone on too long. Elzabetta must learn, or Elzabetta must pay. Her daughter's wandering souls would ever remain lost. Regaining them had been an abject failure, so she must use her daughter's life in some other way.

To shore up the power of Underhill by allying her court with the Unseelie King.

"I have to admit to some misgivings myself," the King said, crossing and recrossing his legs. He wore heavy, hideous brocade unlike Queen Silverhair's light, watered green silk. She supposed that when you lived in eternal winter rather than eternal spring, your tastes ran to the heavy and gaudy instead of light and refined.

"Your realm is not quite stable, is it? Still crumbling. If your daughter is resistant to the match, this makes me wonder if I should not withdraw my offer."

His steel-gray eyes were fixed on her in challenge.

Silverhair gripped her cup and then forced herself to relax her face and smile.

"My realm is still changing, it is true. However, that does not mean we are not stable. Nor does that mean we are not a good ally to your court. Together—" she leaned forward "—we shall be stronger. With our children wed, our rule shall be unshakable."

"And the upstart humans will get their due." The King leaned back against his cushions and snapped his fingers. That same, silent courtier moved smoothly forward to refill his cup. He inclined his head at the Queen's. She shook her head. She had had quite enough of the Holly King's wine. She had had quite enough of him.

She hated needing him. But he was correct. The Seelie realms were unstable still and Underhill was cracking. An alliance between the two courts was the only thing she could think of to save it, now that her original plan had been lost.

Oh, she had lied and assured him that Elzabetta was fertile and could bear a healthy child, when there was no way to tell. Not really. And Elzabetta's souls still wandered who knows where, though the child had seemed better lately. Strangely better.

Silverhair had not been regent for as many hundreds of years as she had been without learning what to say and what to keep behind the closed curve of her lips.

"Our children should be quite happy together," she said, smiling.

The King slowly returned her smile. "Whether they should be happy or not is immaterial to me." He took a hefty swallow of wine and set the metal goblet down on a wooden side table with a smack. "All I care is that if this is to be done, it be done swiftly, and the power of our realms secured. If Seelie queendom crumbles into dust, things will become so much less...convenient for us here."

Silverhair fought back a snarl. The Seelie realm had always been the stronger of the two, and if it fell? It would take his reign down as surely as it would take her own. But a marriage was far better than a battle. There were battles enough to be fought with the humans without dividing her resources to war with the Holly King, too.

No. If marriage it must be, then Elzabetta would simply live with the choice, the way Silverhair herself had lived with the choices of others, for good or for ill.

"For future generations," Queen Silverhair said, raising her glass.

"For future generations," the King nodded, picking up his goblet to return her toast. He wiped his mouth with the back of his hand and leaned toward her.

"Now. There are options other than marriage if you are willing to get your fine hands dirty."

The Queen frowned. What was he talking about? "Why not marriage? I thought we were agreed."

The king shrugged. "You have said your daughter is able to bear a child, but I still have seen no proof from any alchemists or physicians. My intelligence reports that the princess still is not well, and your pet alchemist has fled."

"How dare you..."

The Holly King smiled and raised a placating hand. "I mean no insult, Queen Silverhair, against you or the princess. I simply wish to ensure that, whether a child is born or not, your realm and mine are safeguarded for the future. Now. Would you care to hear what sorts of loyal subjects I have at my disposal? What monsters I have yet to unleash?"

Queen Silverhair exhaled, took a sip of wine, then smiled.

"Do tell."

An alliance which would unleash Unseelie creatures upon the human realm might do quite nicely.

This arrangement might be better than a marriage after all.

CARONDEL

Carondel paced the room, from window to the single bed just wide enough to fit him, and back again.

It wasn't a bad place they had put him. Comfortable enough. Cozy, with warm wood walls that gleamed in the early spring sunlight filtering through the sheer white curtains.

The curtains were hemp, like everything else in this place, including the tunic and pants they had given him. He wore comfortable, well-made brown wool socks on his feet. *Wouldn't do to leave a man his boots.* The guard had said that, grinning, when he took the mud-encrusted leather pair. Carondel missed those boots and wondered where they were.

He might need them, should plans go in his direction. And if not? Well, in that case, he would likely never need boots again. The room was simple. Along with the bed, there was a single chair, and a few precious books the schoolteacher had lent him. Old, battered things from Pre-Reckoning, as the humans called it, plus one that looked new, encased in a sturdy hemp-covered binding.

But much as the alchemist loved study, he could not focus on the books today. He was restless, and his fingers itched for his alembics and retorts. For his herbs, and a mortar and pestle, and for his own library, filled with arcane lore and more magic than he had the time or chance to try.

But here he was now, throwing his lot in with humankind. He hoped it was the correct choice, though there was never truly a way to tell. Every action changed the shape of the future, and besides, Carondel was an alchemist, not a prognosticator like some.

His magic was in the doing, not the knowing.

A knock came at his door. He stopped his pacing and waited. Soon enough, he heard a key in the lock and the guard's rumbling voice talking with someone whose voice was pitched much higher.

A woman, perhaps?

She soon stepped through, someone he had not seen before. The woman wore the apron of a kitchen worker over an undyed hemp shirt, heavy dark trousers, and boots. Her light red hair was pulled back into a neat bun. Her feet looked to be about the size of his own. For a moment, he wondered if he could steal them from her....

She was a pretty woman with some pockmarks on her face, and hazel eyes set over a beaky nose. The woman shouldered the door shut behind her. He heard the snick of the lock. The guard had shut them both in together. With a few long strides, she crossed the room and set the tray down on the small table next to the single chair.

The scent of some sort of meat soup reached out to grab his nose, along with the fragrance of freshly baked bread and butter. Carondel's mouth immediately filled with saliva.

One thing he would say for the people of Go No More: they ate well.

Once the woman had finished with her task she turned, making an urgent motion with her hands.

"I haven't much time," she said. "My name is Skaadi, and my brother wants me to tell you we are on your side."

"I don't understand," Carondel said. This was quite unexpected.

The woman shook her head impatiently. "We can help you. We can help you escape and get you back to the Queen."

"How? And who are you? Why would you do this?"

She tilted up her chin. "My brother is one of Wulf's men. He disguised himself and we escaped together. Joined the caravan. We've been hiding out here ever since. He joined a construction crew, building housing, and I'm working here in the kitchens."

"Why would you help the Queen?"

"Why wouldn't we? You think we truck with these upstarts who don't even know their place? Besides, Wulf was always good to us. Gave us things. Made us promises...though I guess those promises are moot now."

"Is Wulf dead?" Carondel asked.

The woman shrugged her thin shoulders. "That's what we heard, but you never know. He may have disappeared somewhere. Or gone Underhill."

Carondel had heard talk that the warlord was dead, but it didn't hurt to get information from a different source. He tapped his lips and placed a hand on his growling stomach. He would eat after the woman had gone.

"How many of you are there?"

The woman grinned. "Not many, but enough. These soft-hearted fools took us all in, no questions asked."

Carondel found this hard to believe. From what he could tell the Steel Clan were no fools. Nor were the mages or healers here.

"Oh, they ask plenty of questions," Skaadi said. "Gave us all a right good grilling. But we still have these…"

She pulled a leather thong from beneath her tunic. On it was a small round of copper stamped with the crest of the Queen.

Carondel had seen their like before. These amulets were cheap enough to make and barely had any magic to them. They were not a true seal—like the one he had stolen—but they could offer some protection to those who wore them.

"Can you get me one of those?" Carondel asked.

The woman's eyes narrowed. "Not sure. But you tell us what you need, we'll do our best to get it for you. Work on a way to get you out of here."

A sharp rap came on the door.

"I've got to go. But you think on what I said. You need anything? You just ask for Skaadi."

Carondel nodded. The key rasped in the door.

"Thank you for the soup," he said.

"No problem. Jamie and Porrac are good men. Good cooks and brewers too." She paused at the door and dropped her voice. "Almost seems a shame to bring them down."

And then she slipped out of the door. He heard it shut and lock again.

He strode to the window and stared out at the township, at the people bustling about. He could barely hear the echo of hammers and the pounding from the forge. It was a good place, this Go No More, far better than New Salem ever was. Better than Underhill. He wondered if they would allow him to stay here. Make amends.

As he stood musing, the red-haired knight walked by, accompanied by the large, pale blue halbtroll who glanced up as though he'd heard the alchemist's thoughts.

Carondel stepped back from the window. He was not sure why. He just had a feeling that the red-haired Knight and the blue halbtroll would read something on his face even through the warped and wavering glass.

"Superstitious nonsense," he muttered, then sat and took a bite of the fragrant brown bread, groaning at its deliciousness.

Would he be better off here in Go No More, asking

for help from these Knights? Or was his lot better off throwing himself on the Queen's mercy?

All his instincts protested, kicking out at that last, but he had to ponder it all the same. When the weave of fate unwound itself to show you different possible turnings, only a fool would not pay attention. He had to decide what it meant that this woman Skaadi had walked through his door and made him such an offer. He also had no way to tell whether he could trust her. Case in point, why had an outsider been allowed to serve him food? He sniffed at the soup suspiciously, his nose not detecting anything unwholesome. His stomach rumbled, loudly this time. He was hungry.

Perhaps he could use this woman Skaadi for his own aims. To help Go No More safely get more people into Underhill without needing to bust through the gate after all.

With more than one charm on hand, who knew what was possible?

He looked down at the bowl of soup once again. Poisoned or not, a person had to eat. He picked up his spoon and tucked in.

TEGAN

Tegan let Case and the others move on ahead. Per needed a moment alone, and though Starlight's input would have been welcomed, the lynx was clearly annoyed and had sulked off into the oak grove somewhere, likely following Abyad's dog. Fine. She would return when needed, Tegan was sure.

Tegan closed per eyes and slowed per breath, reaching into per mind for the flow of water held in the clouds above and from a stream per sensed nearby. Tegan called upon the spirit of place. Tegan called upon the spirit of all places.

Mboli.

"Lend me your wisdom," per whispered. "Let me see the patterns of the flow of water. Let me see the pattern of the stones in the stream. Let me see the patterns of the riverbanks that guide the water. Let me taste the patterns that guide the breeze. Let me not be confused by the rush around me. I am water. I am stream. I am rock. I am wind. I am fire. I am flow. I am magic. I am all that is, all that was, and all that shall be…"

Tegan rocked with the words, energy mounting. For one moment, per felt it. Per felt it all.

"Tegan." Case's low voice jarred per from the prayers. Blinking, Tegan opened per eyes and looked into his own. So clear, so beautiful.

The magic flowed through per, towards him. He gasped. Tegan leaned, ever so slightly forward. They both leaned, drawn like bowstrings, vibrating, humming…

And then stopped. Right before their lips met in a kiss.

Case cleared his throat. "Abyad sent me back. He felt some concern that you were missing."

Tegan shrugged and looked up into the oaks. "I needed a minute."

"The magic?"

Per nodded. Case stood at per side in silence, though Tegan could feel his heartbeat, hearing the soft huff of his even breathing.

"It isn't just you, you know."

"What do you mean?" Tegan asked.

Case cleared his throat and shifted, weapons clinking softly. "I asked the djinni one night when you were off somewhere."

Tegan turned to look at per comrade, and the object of per lust. His face flushed with discomfort, but he held per gaze steadily, as a true warrior always faced a challenge.

"I wanted more information about what is happening to you. So I can help."

"You knew this? You saw this?" That was bad. It meant that Tegan had not been holding per shit together as a warrior should.

Case reached out and gripped per shoulder. "Tegan. I know you. I see you. You think I haven't noticed the increased magic? Or your troubled eyes come morning?"

Per stared at him in silence.

Case shrugged. "The djinni says that this is happening to many humans now. Even as Underhill weakens, magic rises in this realm. It must be why the Queen is so desperate to steal our souls. You are part of the shifting power between the realms."

Tegan wrenched per eyes away from his, taking refuge in the green of the trees, the scent of woodsmoke, and the feel of water trickling through per veins and misting from the sky.

Breathe, Tegan. In. Pause. Out.

All three of Tegan's parents had thought per would become a mage. Tegan had the strange, uncanny skills for it. The extra senses. The ability to manipulate the elements. And the ancestors spoke loudly in Tegan's head all the time, too. Per usually ignored them. But lately, they'd grown so loud it was not possible.

It also was nothing per had ever wanted. Though Tegan respected per comrades from the Mage Clan, Tegan had never wanted to be one of them, preferring the rough and tumble camaraderie of the Steel Clan Knights. Tegan had found a place there. A home.

But now, as the magic rose inside per, and as the ancestors' voices were joined by the voices of Goddesses and Gods, Tegan questioned everything per had always thought about per life.

And now, to find that per was not alone? Tegan shook per head.

Now was not the time to stand in an oak grove and brood. Now was the time for action. So, Tegan steadied perself and looked at Case, who gave one slow blink, almost as if he was waking from some strange spell himself.

They quickly headed toward the smell of smoke and the small cabin tucked into the edges of the grove. The warriors and scouts ringed the cottage, and the white-skinned djinni waited on the path.

"So much for a stealth welcoming committee," Chase muttered.

Tegan smiled, grateful for anything that lightened up the situation.

"Not like the Raven Priestess wouldn't know every damn thing that happens in her oak grove."

"You have a point."

All Tegan's senses were on high alert. Despite the lighthearted banter, there was no telling what they were walking into. Not with the Raven Priestess, her seriously uncanny animals, and possibly a traitor elf who used to be a friend. The djinni's magical tracker had led them here, and so, they would enter.

The wood plank cabin was tiny. It had to only contain one large room. There was some sort of outhouse a few paces behind, and the smoke curled invitingly from the stone chimney. The place looked solid and well built, well chinked between the plank walls, with a roof from salvaged PR metal. The wavy, corrugated kind. Tegan wondered how long it had been here. And how the Raven Priestess had found it.

There was no no telling with her. She was a strange one, which only added to her attractiveness. The priestess was a dark-skinned, comely woman Tegan would not mind bedding.

"If only I could trust her not to stab me in bed."

Case smiled, like one of the priestess's wolves.

"Nothing like a little danger to spice up bed play."

Per grinned back. He was right. Which was probably why Tegan was also drawn to the silent djinn, who watched their approach with black eyes. Though Tegan had to admit that it was Case who had captured a corner of per heart. Something Tegan had never thought would happen, but here they were, heading towards the unknown as usual. Ready to do what must be done.

Tegan crossed the narrow porch and rapped on the front door before stepping back, one hand on the pommel of per machete. As per fingers touched the leather-wrapped metal, per felt an answering spark of magic.

Well. That was new.

The door opened, and there she stood, raven feathers fluttering, set in silver pins that anchored the dark coils of her hair. Black eyes staring out from above beautiful high cheekbones and smooth dark skin.

"I was wondering when you lot would arrive."

"Do you have the elf?" Tegan asked.

The Raven Priestess smirked. "I do indeed." Her eyes scanned the porch and the edges of the cabin, though Tegan knew the woman was scanning far beyond where her eyes could see.

"The wolves are standing guard inside. There is not much space for all of you indoors. Certainly not for those that are surrounding the cabin right now. But you three? You should fit just fine. If you don't mind being cozy."

Tegan felt Case tense at per side. He was right to be concerned. It would not do to crowd into such a small space. Harder to fight and control the situation.

"Bring him out," Tegan said.

The djinni stood, arms crossed, saying nothing. Waiting.

The Raven Priestess considered the three of them for a moment, then gave a sharp nod before shutting the door.

The three moved backward.

"Case, go tell the others what is happening. But then I need you back here."

He nodded and strode off the porch to alert the others. He could decide whether they still needed guards around back or not.

That was one good thing about working with the clan. Tegan trusted every one of them to make decisions on the fly.

The door opened yet again, groaning slightly on old hinges. Two enormous wolves nudged the elf out.

Tegan's lips curled down at the sight of the too-skinny elf, pale green hair in tangled braids.

Peridot, the traitor. The one who smoked and drank with them. The one who had shared food and laughter in the public house. The one who had broken Damson's heart and put everyone in danger. He looked gaunt and weary. And well he should.

"Hello, pig fucker," Tegan said. Peridot stepped onto the porch but did not speak. The Raven Priestess followed, a bird on each shoulder.

She was creepy as fuck.

And then something shifted in the wind. Abyad's black cloaks fluttered around him. And when Tegan looked at his face, his white skin was almost waxy, and those black eyes blazed with an inner fire.

Sweat broke out on Peridot's brow, despite the chill in the air and the light patter of rain on the porch rooftop. He looked as if he were straining against something. Tegan felt the slight pressure of djinni magic in per own head. Heard Case's boot fall on the porch boards.

"Holy Mother," he said, "what the fracked earth is going on?"

"Abyad?" Tegan asked, "what are you doing?"

The Raven Priestess held up one hand as if to stop per questioning.

"I asked you," Tegan repeated, "what the fracked earth is going on?"

"He is probing the elf's mind," the Raven Priestess interjected, voice as rough as a crow's. "You'd best not interrupt."

Tegan threw more shields up around perself, not about to let anyone in, and not wanting the backsplash of any magic that might arise.

Case clutched at his head.

"Shields, dammit!" Tegan snapped.

Case nodded shakily and swallowed hard.

Peridot let out a high, keening sound from deep in his throat that raised all the hairs on Tegan's head.

Per braced in per boots, ready for him to bolt. But he did nothing, just stood still, face twisting, fingers clenching. Tegan's guts twisted from the pressure and the strangeness of the magic. The Raven Priestess seemed as implacable and unruffled as the ravens who sat, stolid, on each shoulder. The smaller of the two wolves whined, and the second set a paw upon its companion's neck. Whether to stop it or to comfort it, Tegan did not know.

"How long?" Tegan grunted out, and then with a snap, the pressure lifted. Peridot took in a gasping breath and fell to his knees on the porch.

"I think I have the information we need," Abyad said, training those frightening black eyes per way.

"Then shall you come inside for a cup of tea?" the priestess asked, voice mildly amused.

Tegan nodded. "We'll come in." Per looked at Case.

"I'll stay outside," he said.

"So, that leaves the warrior mage and the djinn," said the Raven Priestess. "Perfect." She was already retreating indoors, dragging the staggering elf behind her, crowding with the wolves into the opening until they disappeared.

"Abyad," Tegan said, "next time you're going to pull a stunt like that, give me a warning."

"As you wish," the djinni replied.

Tegan glowered at the djinn, gave Case a quick raised fist salute, and stepped across the threshold into who knew what?

CHAPTER 33
ANANDITA

The wind blew fresh in her face, and an errant bit of cloak flapped annoyingly near her ear. No matter how well she secured the thing, and no matter how well secured she was to the drake's back, the wind at elevation always tugged and pulled and broke something free.

Anandita clucked in annoyance, even as her heart soared with the drake's wings. She didn't have time for this. She didn't have time to be whisked away on drake-back to go consult a crystal ball.

There were herbs to grind and poultices to make and apprentice healers to instruct and new towns-people to take care of. All of Go No More was in an upheaval instead of preparing for spring after a long, quiet winter. Winter had been anything but quiet, and consequently, Anandita, Tokki, and Recoana were behind. The only one who seemed prepared for the new season was her father and thank God and the

Asvini for that! Anandita was grateful for her family, that was for certain.

Her parents and aunties would make certain Hypatia was well cared for in her absence, but still, she worried, and hoped that Doc Warren and the other healers had enough resources to deal with any crises that might emerge. Thank God that the mind healer, Jimena, had proven to be a sound ally and skilled, no-nonsense worker. She had been a boon in dealing with the refugees, not only because of her specialty, but because she had seen firsthand the devastation the so-called warlord Wulf had caused.

Anandita had to trust that things were well in hand back in Go No More. The Vedas taught that every person had a responsibility toward themselves, the ancestors, the Gods, and other human beings. She had come to learn that responsibility did not always look the way she thought it would.

Sometimes, the responsible thing was to accomplish all the tedious, daily chores that kept hearth and home together. Other times?

It meant doing the thing she secretly loved and longed for. Like flying high above the fields of Go No More, strapped to the back of a large purple drake.

Flying drake-back was the most exhilarating thing she'd ever felt in her life. Breathing deeply behind the protective folds of her cloak, Anandita released the worries she carried, and allowed herself to simply feel.

She felt free. Powerful. The views were astonishing, and she drank in the sight of Wy'East towering up ahead, its snowy peak shimmering and sparkling, reflecting the early spring sun. She blinked against the dazzle as Karaktilla and her consort, Daraktal, both banked, heading to the landing place in front of Karaktilla's cave.

Too soon, the mighty purple drake was kneeling by the stone face next to outcroppings that formed a set of steps that Anandita could thump down on her clever prosthetics. She called them stubbies, though the engineers who designed them had some fancier name for the cunning metal caps with rubber-lined rocker plates on the bottoms and a well-padded cup that fit over the ends of her knees. It was as strange being this low to the ground as it was to be high up on drake-back. Though Anandita used her stubbies off and on, she far preferred her wheelchair.

Finally, clutching at the stone face, navigating the roughhewn steps without tripping on her cloak, Anandita reached the ground.

The red drake, Daraktal, had already entered the cavern. Anandita followed, with Karaktilla taking up the rear. The vast cave was cold and silent. It was strange entering the great cavern with no fire roaring, and no tea steaming on the hob.

But as soon as Anandita had that thought, there was Daraktal, taking care of both those things. He breathed out a small burst of fire that set the laid logs quickly blazing and busied himself collecting jars of herbs from the shelves nearby.

That was interesting. It showed that the two drakes had grown even closer since last time Anandita had seen them. As a matter of fact, they reminded her a lot of the way Jenny had fitted into her and Hypatia's little household. The thought gave her comfort.

Meanwhile, Karaktilla moved towards the vast round table with the massive crystal orb set in the center. A step stool led up to a wooden chair that was just the right height for Anandita to stand upon in her low prosthetics, giving her a platform from which she could gaze into the ball.

The purple drake, of course, dwarfed both table and the orb. Everything in this cavern was designed for her magnificent bulk.

The drake poured some sort of unguent over the surface of the ball and spread it about with one mighty taloned hand. That was new, as well. Anandita did not remember this preparation from the last time.

The unguent smelled of tree resin and flowers that would not be in bloom for another month. It smelled of the time between winter and spring. Anandita inhaled deeply, filling her lungs and her nostrils, until her head swam. She coughed and then blinked to find Karaktilla staring at her with one of those strange, reptilian eyes.

::Tell me what you see.:: The voice rang in Anandita's head. She sent up a prayer to Saraswati and one to the Asvins, the healers. She had learned the hard way that when one asked for wisdom—particularly wisdom that might be difficult to bear—that one should also pray for healing.

The two needed to go hand in hand or the world might face another Reckoning. Anandita vowed to stave that off with all her might. Her job was to heal, and apparently her job was also to seek out wisdom. So...

::Stop stalling. It is good to pray to your Goddesses, but now that you have done so, it is time to center yourself, and See.::

Anandita jerked with surprise, hands smacking the smooth wood surface of the table. She hadn't realized she was avoiding looking in the orb, and yet she was.

She slowed her breathing down, called upon all her senses, softened her gaze, and looked.

And there inside the orb was Tegan, shouting to the sky, kpinga in one hand, machete in the other, stance wide, boots braced. The Knight stood in front of a gate, three drakes at per back. Magic swirled through the air around Tegan, in a myriad of colors.

Karaktilla passed one talon across the orb, and the vision changed to that of a princess with pale green-gold hair, sleeping in a bower, surrounded by green.

The sleeping princess's face looked troubled, but the image shifted quickly yet again to a straight-backed elf with hooded eyes. And then Queen Silver-hair, in a different scene still, sitting in a cavern in front of a large, warm fire, talking with a rotund and sleek elf wearing finery the likes of which Anandita had never seen. Above his head was a crest of holly, reminding Anandita of the queen's oak leaf crest.

"Elves and their trees. One would think they were dryads," she muttered. And then she saw the princess once again, surrounded by warriors. Human warriors in russet-colored leather. There was magic. More magic. And a battle.

Anandita peered into the crystal, seeking more, but the visions grew cloudy and slowly disappeared, leaving behind a crystal orb, with clouds and striations, and clear places in which she caught her own reflection. A woman with dusky skin and hair as dark as night. Was that what Jenny saw when she looked upon her with eager eyes?

::What did you see?:: The drake's voice in her head drew her back all the way.

"I saw many things," she replied, blinking as she looked around the cavern, trying to acclimate to this place once again. "Battles to come. And magic. More magic than I have ever seen before."

::Yes. We too, have seen such things, but wanted confirmation that our sight was true. Magic increases, and the balance of the realms is in flux.::

Anandita inhaled the fragrance of steeping mountain herbs and realized her mouth was dry. Daraktal sat on a pile of bright cushions on the large, woven rug near the hearth, reading. The tome was propped on a pillow, and he carefully turned pages with a long metal stick. The sight was a strange one and made her smile.

::Tea is ready,:: Daraktal clicked and rumbled. *::Very well done, healer. Now sit.::*

Anandita climbed her way down and moved across the cavernous floor, prosthetics thumping beneath her thighs. Finally, she eased herself onto a cushion and removed the chafing metal stubbies, then drew a small pot wrapped in waxed hemp from her leather belt pouch. Sighing, she slid up her trews and removed the soft stockings that protected her knees and began to rub warm oil into her flesh, soothing the abused muscles, flesh, and tendons. Anandita was strong, but clearly needed more practice with the prosthetics.

Soon enough, after she stoppered and rewrapped the pot of healing ointment, a steaming bowl of tea was set by her side. She inhaled the steam gratefully but left it to cool for a moment.

Then she settled down to tell the drakes what she had seen in as much detail as the knowledge seekers desired.

She also wanted to find out as much as they knew, in return.

CHAPTER 34
PERIDOT

Peridot never thought of himself as weak. No, he was always the cunning one. The one hedging his bets. The one pulling the wool over so many people's eyes they never saw him coming. Or going.

But look at him now. Sweating in an overheated one-room cabin guarded by two fucking wolves, a pair of ravens staring at him with their black, beady eyes.

But worse was the Steel Clan warrior staring at him with per own dark gaze. A scarred right eyebrow lifted when the Knight caught him looking. Something had changed about per recently, though the elf could not pinpoint exactly what it was. The tightly muscled warrior reeked of magic in a way per had not before. It was ancient magic from a faraway place and smelled a bit like the black-shrouded djinni currently staring him down with black eyes and unnaturally pale skin, paler even than the long fall of Silverhair's main. Pale as a lizard, startled from its underground cave.

A lizard with very sharp teeth.

"Who do you work for?" Tegan's voice cracked through the cloying air, hitting him like a slap.

"I work only for myself," he replied.

"You lie," the djinni growled. Both wolves growled in concert, hackles raising. Peridot fought to sit up straight, hands cradling a tea mug, unconcerned look on his face. He fought to not show the fear that coursed through his veins, setting the silver blood thrumming inside of him.

The wolves sniffed the air, scenting him. He just hoped the djinni could not smell his fear as well.

"What he means," the Raven Priestess said, voice dry, "is that he works for everyone in order to best suit himself."

He hid a wince. She was not far off the mark. The only way Peridot knew to keep himself safe was to pretend he held at heart the best interests of whomever wielded the most power in the moment. He gulped at the cooling tea from the mug still clutched between his narrow fingers. Buying time.

"You might as well tell us," Tegan said. "Things will not go any better for you if you don't."

"As a matter of fact—" the djinni leaned in "—we may have to string you up in the forest. Hang you upside down in one of those mighty oaks outside, dangling from one leg."

The djinni looked at the Raven Priestess. "Would that not be a fitting offering to your God?"

The priestess said nothing. Peridot could not tell if she was offended or intrigued. Either way, he did not like it. His thoughts scrabbled inside, like rats seeking a way out from a collapsing tunnel. He needed to find a way through this impromptu tribunal.

He should have been cleverer. Instead, it seemed he had walked directly into a trap.

Perhaps it is for the best, his own thoughts whispered. *Give up. Give over. Give in.*

Never, he growled to himself. *Never.*

"I don't know what you are speaking about," he said out loud. "I served the Queen. Yes. You knew that. I served until she decided I was not worthwhile anymore."

"So, then what?" Tegan scoffed. "You decided to come back to Go No More? Throw yourself on our mercy?"

He glared at the warrior, who stared back, unperturbed.

"I would like to treat with you," he said, licking his lips. "Cut a deal, as you humans say."

Tegan barked out a laugh, harsh as one of the ravens who shifted on the back of the priestess's chair.

"You do, do you? What would you have that we would want?"

"I could get you safely through the gate to Underhill," he said.

The djinni sniffed the air as if seeking out the truth or falsity of Peridot's words.

"And why would you do that?" Tegan asked.

Peridot's gaze flicked between the warrior and the djinn. The priestess seemed to be keeping out of this discussion. He wondered where her loyalties lay.

"Because I am sick unto death of all of this," he said, tasting the words as they left his lips. He found that they were true. He *was* sick of it. Tired of the politicking and the machinations and the subterfuge. Tired of running and hiding and scheming. Tired of being on the wrong side, though he wished he had figured that part out before. He realized now he had it good in Go No More. Life was far better there. Even the struggles were better than what he had to put up with Underhill, beneath the iron fist of Queen Silverhair and her magicians.

And there was also Damson, though he had ruined that, hadn't he?

"I want a fresh start," he said. "Safe passage. I want to return to Go No More."

Tegan laughed again, shaking per head. "Of all the...you think that we will trust you there? You think you did not break Damson's heart? You think you can just return, unmolested?"

He pondered for a moment. The warrior was correct.

He set down the mug with a soft click, then looked from the warrior to the priestess to the djinn.

Should an elf ever choose to gamble, now would be the time.

"Set me to whatever ordeal you must. I will face it. But know this: I have something both Go No More and Queen Silverhair can use."

"And what might that be?" Tegan raised that scarred eyebrow once again.

"Information. Information about who holds what

magic, and who wants what form of power. I have information that the Queen is treating with the Unseelie court, even now. And I also know where the Go No More waterworks are most vulnerable, and where the seed stores are hidden."

Tegan's lips narrowed, and per fingers clenched as if the Knight wanted nothing more than to rip Peridot's head from his shoulders.

He sat completely still. Waiting.

Tegan never took per eyes from his face, but it was clear per next words were directed at the djinn.

"Can you bind him? Put a geas or something on his sorry elf ass?"

"I have already done so," the Raven Priestess replied. "As soon as he crossed my threshold."

Peridot's breath caught in his chest. "When?"

"The first sip of tea you took was an agreement. Whosoever claims hearth right in my home takes on an unbreakable obligation to me and mine."

Both wolves stood now, flanking either side of her chair.

"Unbreakable?" Peridot repeated.

The priestess shrugged. "There is always a way out."

"And what is that?" Peridot whispered the words, so softly he was not certain she heard him.

"There is always death."

Peridot sat frozen in his chair, feeling the chains of magic tighten. He knew this day was coming, and here it had finally arrived.

"Tell me what you require," he said. "And I will do it."

"That you will," Tegan said. "We're sending you back Underhill, magicked up to your teeth."

"And then?"

Tegan and the djinni shared a glance. The djinni nodded. Peridot was not certain what had passed between the two, but Tegan looked satisfied.

Peridot was not sure if it was good that he would live to see another day, or whether the promised death upon betrayal would feel like a sweet release.

Then the djinn's magic hit him, and Peridot began to sweat.

CHAPTER 35

TEGAN

As the djinni continued to work his magic, a buzzing started up inside Tegan's head. The amulet at per breastbone burned and bit. Magic, Tegan thought, but not the djinn's magic. This was per own magic rising like solstice-tide inside per skin. Drumbeats sounded. Voices chanted in a language Tegan did not know. Per feet twitched in their boots, longing to follow the rhythm, marking out the dance of power. The dance of life.

Per stood still trembling, the power building, building, building inside the raven witch's hut, building inside the djinni as a breeze whipped his cloaks around, dark cloths fluttering like wings. And yet, they were indoors. There was no wind. There were no drums. No singing, no dancing...and yet it all was here. Now. Inside this humble home, inside Tegan's breast. The power beat with per heart, rising from the djinn, rising from Tegan.

Per magic rose to greet his, spilling out. Tegan heard a choking sound. Per eyes snapped open.

The elf's eyes bulged. His body bowed back and forth, writhing, as if trying to escape. His hands scrabbled at his chest, clutching his throat....

Building, building, building, building, the pressure grew until Tegan felt per veins might burst from per skin.

"Stop!" The Raven Priestess's voice was a crack of lightning.

The winds stilled. The drums ceased. Tegan stood, panting. The elf collapsed onto the floor, tumbling from his chair.

Abyad simply smoothed down his robes, looking calm, though there was a strange light behind those black eyes. The slight madness of magic. Tegan had seen it before and she saw her own fearsome magic reflected back in his eyes.

He gave her a quick nod of acknowledgement as the Raven Priestess stood over the elf.

"Rise," she said, "Peridot, sit in your chair. All of you. Sit."

She helped the groaning elf back into his chair. Peridot was as pale as Abyad and looked about to puke.

"Sit. I will make more tea and we will talk."

The Raven Priestess looked at the djinn. "And you will tell us what you found."

Her eyes raked over Tegan, but she said no more, for which Tegan was grateful.

Tegan had enough trouble to contend with, without raising the priestess's ire.

The magic Tegan had avoided per whole life had decided to arrive full force and all per wanted to do was race home to Go No More, immerse in a blistering-hot tub, eat a good meal...and get counsel from per mothers.

But there was work still to be done. And a Knight did not shirk per duty. A Knight did what they must to protect the people and to honor the ancestors and founders of Go No More. Tegan could not help to wonder, though....

How was per to honor per own ancestors? The ones now knocking at per breastbone and the base of her skull?

No time for those questions. Not now. Tegan sat, accepted a mug of tea, then turned to Abyad.

"Will he do what we need him to?"

Abyad took a sip of tea, as unconcerned as if this were a genial visit to an ordinary person's home. And as if he had not just magically manipulated Peridot to make sure the elf would work for the benefit of Go No More, all the while making it seem as if he still worked for the Queen.

"Let's keep this conversation short, then," Tegan said. "We need to get this pig fucker back to Go No More."

And Tegan needed to get a handle on this wild magic before the battle they were courting came to call.

CHAPTER 36
JENNY

Though her trip to the gate with her comrades was short, it was good to be back in Go No More. Charles Wong was safely delivered, and conferring with Aphrodite. As she hammered a board into place, Jenny's thoughts returned to Tegan and the others, still out in the field following the djinni's lead. She hoped that gilded arsehole Peridot wasn't giving them too much trouble.

If they'd even found the treacherous rat.

Jenny wiped a bandana across her broad brow and paused to squeeze some water down her throat. She and Bocan were taking a turn with the construction crews.

Though it wasn't Jenny's first choice, part of living in Go No More was that everyone went where they were needed. Sure, Jenny and Bocan worked on security, keeping the town safe. And the Knights were still training the new people, but Haryath and Amarpal were in charge of security patrols today, leaving Jenny and a grumpy Bocan free to lend a hand.

Bocan couldn't do much with his one good arm, but he was still stronger than most humans and had been put to work carrying supplies. Jenny, hammer in hand, was nailing together some of the new dwellings rapidly going up between the fortified gates and the growing fields beyond. The Go No More council had gotten permission from the Confederated Tribes to build on the otherwise wild land, making room for the refugees in need.

Jenny didn't mind the labor. The air was warming up, and she was dressed simply in her sumac leather trousers and an undyed hemp shirt, now mottled with sweat.

They'd been working all morning when the shouting began, and the alarm bell newly installed at the main gate began to ring frantically.

Jenny dropped her water and tools, leapt off the ladder she'd been working on, and ran toward Bocan who stood like a blue ox, good arm holding a wooden bucket filled with newly forged nails. His large bald head whipped about, flat nose sniffing the air.

"What is it?" Jenny asked.

His brow wrinkled in confusion. "Smells like trolls, but not any trolls I know."

Just then one of the Sikhs came running toward them.

Amarpal. Her face looked grim beneath her turban. She carried a weapon in each arm.

"There's been an attack in the forest near the waterworks! Come quickly!" Amarpal didn't wait for a reply but sprinted back toward the other end of town.

Bocan gave his bucket to a strapping girl of about seventeen winters.

"Take this to the head carpenter and tell him we might need backup. Anyone able to fight."

The girl nodded. Jenny and Bocan picked up their own weapons and raced after Amarpal, running through the township, joined by other Steel Clan Knights boiling out of the garage, plus Swan the bowyer and two workers from the forge.

Winney and some children were on the school porch.

"Stay put!" Jenny called out. "And keep the children inside!"

Winney nodded and herded her charges back into the building just as John the Dairyman raced out to join them.

Jenny put on speed, leaving a tiring Amarpal and the wounded Bocan behind, racing towards the edge of town, past the great waterworks that kept Go No More in potable water and kept their fields supplied during the dry summers.

The waterworks had been sabotaged before. She hoped that wasn't the case again. Pain in the ass for the engineers and mechanics and for the growers in the township, too. With planting season coming up, that was the last thing they needed.

Jenny's broadsword was in her right hand, buckler

gripped in her left. She raced on, not sure if the threat was still present.

And then she heard roaring and screaming. The bellowing avalanche roar were trolls' voices giving call to comrades, but the shrieking? That was human and that signaled something bad.

"What in the fracked earth are strange trolls doing here?" she muttered, pounding toward the woods just outside of town.

Racing among the towering firs and hemlock spruce, she smelled troll, then she saw them. There, in a clearing too small for their bodies. Huge, hulking brutes with dark blue skin, they looked like Bocan's da, for sure. But meaner, with an oily glint in their half-feral eyes. Jenny swallowed down bile and took in a calming breath.

Then, with a bellow of her own, she entered the fray, swinging her broadsword low, dodging a nearby tree, aiming at the hamstrings of the closest troll.

Two other trolls had a human woman between them. That was the source of the shrieking.

The trolls were pulling the woman apart, one grasped her arms, the other her legs, both trying to move at once.

Jenny cursed, wishing for Tegan, Case, and Jerrod. As it was, too few Knights battled far too many trolls. Amarpal and Haryath were swinging mightily, beaten back by a host of mountainous trolls. There were at least a dozen. She had never seen so many in one place before. Where in the nine worlds had they come from?

One troll bled out on the ground in the center of the melee that eddied around it. Feldspar, Recoana, and Bocan's da all raced in, brandishing cudgels and wicked axes, bellowing like oxen.

And then the ground began to roll.

CHAPTER 37
BOCAN

Standing on the edges of the forest, Bocan roared, fighting to clear his head. His arm was on fire and the fight was a maelstrom around him. There was Da, axe in hand, slicing through the Unseelie trolls, for Unseelie was what they had to be.

They looked like the trolls Bocan knew and yet their energy was different. There was something wrong about them, something off. A thing he did not recognize. Whereas the Seelie Court was evil in its own way, the Unseelie had gone even further down the road of power for power's sake, rather than power connected to the life-giving source that fed all things.

"Gods of Earth and Stone be with me! I fight for Go No More!" he shouted, and felt the earth beneath his feet answer. The power of his Gods rushed through his body, rumbling upward to fill him, skull to heel. Here was the support he needed. His pain faded for a moment. Though his injured arm was still not strong, his left hand carried a long knife and his right hand carried magic. But where to aim?

Haryath, Jenny, and Amarpal, along with half a dozen more Steel Clan Knights, were a whirling blur in shades of red attacking the trolls, who had must have come through a temporary gate.

Better that than another permanent gate. Temporary gates only allowed in small numbers and closed quickly. If Unseelie creatures had access to a main gate?

Go No More was in deep trouble.

Damn them all. Damn them all to whatever level of Unseelie hell they were bound for.

With a mighty slash, Amarpal sliced through one large troll's neck, sending an arc of dark, silvery blood into the air. How she had the power for it, Bocan did not know, but he heard the clunk and tang as her blade finally hit bone, and saw the troll fall to its knees.

"Bocan! Your back!" Jenny shouted.

He whirled just in time to block a bellowing troll, taking the brunt of the blow on his injured arm before moving beneath the troll's arm when he raised it to strike another blow. Bocan jammed his blade into the fetid armpit and was covered in spurting dark, silvery-blue blood. It spattered hot onto his skin, and stank of sulfur, which was strange. His arm was on fire again, screaming at him for entering the fray.

The soil beneath his boots grew slick with blood.

Blood that would feed the trees ringing this small clearing for the coming year.

"Gods of Earth and Stone! Gods of power and

might! Fill me with your strength! Help me make this right!" Bocan rhymed like a witch, standing tall. His eyes rolled back in his head and his flesh trembled. The power rumbled through him. Despite the pain, he felt as strong as a mountain. As terrifying as an earthquake. As bold as a stone flung from a sling, arcing towards its target. The ground around him bucked, throwing the fighters off kilter, both troll and Steel Clan alike.

"Aim for the strange trolls, jackass!" Jenny yelled as she careened past, sword gleaming.

"I am aiming for the trolls," Bocan muttered, focusing his magic, trying to channel it only towards the beings doing harm, and not towards his comrades. He imagined the magic coursing inside him could channel through his right hand and move like his axe.

Sweat popped up on his forehead. This was much more difficult than simply letting loose and allowing an earthquake to topple everything in its wake. This near to the waterworks, that could spell disaster.

The roaring inside him increased, as did the bellowing and shouting around him.

The power built and built. The firs and spruce around him creaked and groaned. Bocan loosened his muscles, forced his breath to deepen, and sent a blast of power up through the troll's large flat hairy feet.

The Gods of Earth and Stone began to shake the trolls apart, muscle by muscle, bone by bone.

The Unseelie creatures shrieked and screamed, making sounds no troll should ever make.

"Step away!" he bellowed.

"Step away!" He heard his da answer. "Disengage! Step away!"

He had to get the Steel Clan and the other Go No More people clear of the Unseelie trolls before...

Sure enough, the earth that moved through him sliced through each troll. Their deep blue, mountainous bodies began to crack and crumble, fighting the power as they were crushed beneath their own weight, crumbling into rubble.

One final troll, blue skin cracking, stared at Bocan, lips moving as if trying to curse him. It fell, crumbling to its knees, arms out as if they could reach Bocan, crumbling into blue rubble, rocks, sinking slowing into the earth.

The earth opened, swallowing the troll.

He saw the silver seam of the temporary gate flash and then it was gone. There was nothing left to show a battle had been waged besides damp, churned-up earth and panting, gasping comrades, all around.

They were so beautiful, tears leapt to his eyes.

Still standing, Bocan breathed in the spring air, and looked about himself, amazed. His eyes came to rest on the square, blood-spattered face of his da. Da dropped his axe and held out his big blacksmith's arms. Bocan staggered into his father's embrace, smelled the oil, and sweat, and woodsmoke scent of him. Comfort. Home.

"You did good, my son."

Bocan burst into tears just as another shout went up.

"The Eastern Gate! Attack!"

"Hypatia?" Jenny asked.

Anandita's son bounced on his feet at the edge, next to a fir. "Come quickly! Now!"

His da released him and picked up his axe.

Bocan's tears dried and his blood chilled. What had brought misfortune to Go No More? What had made certain that half their warriors were gone, leaving the township vulnerable?

"Bocan." Jenny was at his side. "We have to go now."

"Go on ahead," his da replied. "We shall follow."

Jenny looked from his da to Bocan, and gave a sharp nod before running off, following the other warriors except two that were injured too badly to run.

"What is happening, Da?"

"The bitch Queen is taking her due. You fit to move?"

Now it was Bocan's turn to nod. He gathered up the shattered pieces of his heart, cradled his injured arm, and began to walk as fast as his legs would take him.

He did not yet have the strength to run, but hoped he got there in time to help his friends.

CHAPTER 38

ELZABETTA

Her maidservant was a pretty hob named Dara. She was short of stature like all house elves, with dark hair and eyes to match. Elzabetta's favorite, Dara was one one of three hobs that served the princess in turn. Mother trusted no one anymore, so all servants that dealt with royalty had to trade in and out to keep them on their toes. And to hold the Queen's favor.

It seemed to Elzabetta that things had not always been thus. There was a nursemaid she remembered loving as a wee elf. That hob had cooed and clucked over her like a mother hen.

Until the day she had been sent away.

Dara finished folding and smoothing Elzabetta's garments, shutting them away in the cunning cupboards built to look as if they were carved plants and trees emerging from the polished wood walls.

"Will that be all, Princess?"

"Yes. You may go and eat your lunch now."

The hob turned toward the door.

"Although..."

The hob paused, a question in her eyes. "Yes, my lady?"

Elzabetta thought a moment. "Send Tarioc to me, please."

The hob waited, as if for further explanation. Elzabetta just stared. Dara colored, embarrassed, then dropped a curtsy and left. That was one thing Elisabetta had learned from her mother: explain as little as possible, particularly to those who were in your service. Elzabetta might not like it, but she had learned the technique, nonetheless. One thing her mother knew was politics and control. And while Elzabetta appreciated neither, sometimes it was good to have tactics in one's pockets.

Soon enough, there was a soft rapping on the door.

"Enter," she said.

Tarioc strode in, straight-backed as always, face a mask, green hair plaited neatly, pale eyes sharp with interest.

"You sent for me, Princess?"

"I did. Shut the door."

He did as she said and then headed toward two comfortable chairs set near one of the large windows.

"Not there," Elzabetta said, voice sharp. "Move the chairs farther from the window."

He nodded and did so unquestioningly.

"You can establish a sphere of silence, you know," he said, once they were both seated.

"Of course," Elzabetta said, inclining her head. She

did not know that. There was so much she did not know....

She could see in his eyes that Tarioc knew that she was lying. She had never been taught some of the things that she assumed would only come to her when she was Queen. Though when would that day come? And did she even want it?

Tarioc was a good enough subject and politic enough to not mention any of this. He simply waited while she closed her eyes, drew in a breath, and reached inside herself, seeking the power to do what he suggested.

There was nothing there. Her scattered and shattered souls still wandered, wherever it was they had gone to. Oh, inside herself were still three souls, and her pulse beat strongly. But she doubted very much that it was enough to work the magic required. Though she was stronger now that the alchemist's experiments had ceased, there was no avoiding the fact that her souls were not complete.

"Elzabetta." Tarioc's voice was quiet, gentle, as if speaking with a spooked animal. "You can do this. There is no reason you cannot."

Her eyes fluttered. "But my souls..."

"Some of your souls may be wandering but that does not mean you do not have contact with them."

Her eyes flew open. "What? Then why?"

"Because your mother is cruel bitch."

Elzabetta's breath caught in her chest. Her eyes widened.

"Yes, it is treason for me to say so, but it is true, nonetheless. And you know it."

She sat stock still, her pulse thrilling in her neck at the danger of it, the transgression.

"Can I trust you?" she whispered.

"I would tell you that you can, but really, Princess, you should trust no one. Not even me." He leaned forward, steepling his fingers beneath his narrow chin. "Though I pledge to you, I have only your best interests at heart. Your best interests, and the interests of this realm."

She said nothing, weighing his words.

"But I entreat you," he continued. "Try again. Seek the place of silence."

She closed her eyes and steadied her breathing once more, focusing on the flow of air moving in and out of her nose and through her lungs.

"Feel it," he said. "Reach for it."

And she did. She sought out the stillness at the heart of the deep pool that rested in the center of her souls. And Tarioc was right. Dancing far away, along the edges of her consciousness, she could feel the other parts of herself yearning to return home.

But that was an experiment for later. For this moment, she breathed into the stillness, feeling the pool expand within her, then around her, with a thought and a breath. She pushed on it, sending the stillness it farther outward, until both she and Tarioc were surrounded by the power of silence.

Stillness wrapped them like a muffling blanket.

The very air she breathed felt hushed. She opened her eyes and blinked.

"Well done," he said.

"How did you know?"

"I have watched you. And I have been studying. My mother is a faery healer and knows many things. She had made quite a project out of studying the gifts of elven royalty, going back thousands upon thousands of years."

Elzabetta tilted her head. "You are a shrewd one, are you not, Tarioc? And filled with surprises."

He shrugged and bowed his head. "Now that we are enclosed in your sphere of silence, Princess, why did you call me here?"

"You have a plan," she said. "A plan to get me out of here."

"I told you so. We discussed this." His brow furrowed.

"Yes. We discussed this, but we did not discuss what our next steps must be, and what effect it will have on the realms Underhill should I depart."

"I do not know the answer to that, Princess. No one does, even though your mother thinks she does." Tarioc leaned forward again, face solemn, voice urgent. "All I know is that things cannot continue this way. Your mother is killing you, and her increasing instability is rocking the realm. I planted a spy mirror in the throne room, and I fear her actions. Right now..."

His voice trailed off.

Elzabetta sat up. Alert. "Right now?"

"She meets with the Holly King."

Elzabetta sat back again, flapping one hand as if batting away an insect. "I know all about that. She wishes me to marry his son and bear a child."

Those final words choked her throat. None knew if Elzabetta could bear. It was difficult enough for any elf to quicken and carry a babe to term. And for her? It seemed unlikely.

"But that is no longer the case." Tarioc's words cut through her self pity.

"What?"

"Oh, she still wants you to marry and consolidate the power of Seelie and Unseelie courts, that is true. But now she is working directly with the Holly King."

"What do you mean?" Her head swam with confusion.

"Right now, they are working together to attack the human realms."

The silver blood inside Elzabetta's veins grew cold. Her mind sharpened with anger.

"How dare she?"

Tarioc shook his head. "That is what she does, Princess. She destroys."

Elzabetta saw it all, in a flash of clarity. The years of destruction her mother's anger had wrought. Including on Elzabetta herself.

"I feel that you speak the truth," she said. "And if the Unseelie and Seelie are courting one another? We most certainly need to act. As quickly as we can."

CASE

Riding his motorcycle, armed to the teeth, surrounded by comrades, was usually one of Case's favorite things. Not this time.

This time, Starlight was back with Tegan, and Case had Peridot riding pillion. Peridot was a nervous passenger, which made things a pain. He jerked and pulled instead of relaxed and leaned the way a good passenger did. The elf's fear was likely compounded by the speed. Case made sure to keep the bike burning klicks fast enough that the elf would not leap off the bike and disappear into the fields and woodland flanking the cracked PR highway.

He didn't trust the pig fucker. Not one ounce. Case barely saw the landscape around them. Barely noticed the *drip drip drip* of early spring. He was too busy keeping track of the elf at his back and pondering what the fuck was going on with Tegan.

His comrade had him worried. Per magic was rising.

He could feel that. But he could also feel Tegan fighting it and he wasn't certain whether that was bad or good. There were always murmurs that Tegan should have been initiated as a mage but had chosen the Steel Clan instead.

He never quite understood all that, because Tegan was one of the best warriors he knew, and didn't seem to have any more magic than anyone else that he could see. But clearly that was not the case. Clearly Tegan had hobbled perself somehow.

And the magic had chosen this time to bust free. That worried him most of all. Magic seemed to be increasing as of late, and Case wondered what portents rode the wind.

He also hoped his turn was not next. He liked his life with its limited amount of ordinary magic. Being an ass kicker and a parent suited him just fine. Becoming a mage? Not so much.

The dragoons hit the stretch of road that was Case's favorite. It was a long, winding ribbon of road that headed through the green fields outside Go No More where the Green Clan did their work. They kept the township fed and with plenty of hemp and cannabis for the needs of the weavers, rope makers, and those who made cannabis-infused products, plus had good surplus for trade. Go No More was not wealthy, but always had enough to share.

And that was all that mattered in life, wasn't it? To have friends and family taken care of and have enough to offer others.

Tegan's bike swerved and shuddered ahead of him.

Starlight jerked hard, but the lynx's claws held, gripping the leather pillion.

"What the fuck?" Case said, the words muffled beneath his scarf. He put on more speed, Peridot clutching at his shoulders almost painfully, but Jerrod's bike was already at Tegan's side, carrying Abyad. The djinni was doing something with his left hand and the bike straightened again.

Case pulled up alongside Jerrod, who slowed and pulled down his kerchief.

"What's happening?"

"Trouble," the Knight shouted back.

Case clamped down a burst of irritation.

"I can see that. What kind of trouble?"

"Magic. Tegan's magic. Abyad is trying to keep per under control until we get back home."

Shit. This was the last thing they needed, but he had to trust the djinn. Peridot stiffened behind him. Case shouted back, "Don't try anything!"

The elf did not reply. Case, Tegan, and Jerrod all opened throttle and the bikes sped on, arrowing toward home. They were so close. The fields sped by, the bikes aimed toward the new structures outside the gates.

There should have been construction work happening, and yet there were no carpenters up on the buildings, and the townspeople that were around?

The township was armed for battle. What in the fracked earth was going on?

"Hang on tight," he called back, and gunned his engine. With a swirling scent of burning oil, they headed toward the fortified gates where townspeople stood holding spears, rakes, and hoes, faces grim or pinched with fright.

Now that they were close enough, he could hear a strange, uncanny roaring that made him want to piss his leathers.

Skidding to a stop, he cut the engine, kicking hard at the stand that held the bike upright. He swung his leg off and simultaneously collared the elf, dragging Peridot down with him.

"What are you doing?" the elf said.

"You stay with me."

He dragged him towards the nearest person he saw, which was thankfully Hypatia. Anandita's kid had a good head on his shoulders.

"What's happening?"

The boy's usually golden-brown skin looked pale.

"Two attacks," he said. "First trolls, and now some creature...I don't even know what it is."

"Wyvern," spat a townsperson.

"Wyverns are *here*?" Peridot's voice was choked. "That's very bad."

"No shit," Case replied, mouth dry. His head whipped around at the sound of running boots. It was Arrow. The dark-skinned elf barreled toward them and punched Peridot right in the face, jerking Case's arm. He released Peridot, who fell to the dirt.

"Traitor! Oathbreaker! How dare you return to this place?" Arrow shouted as the two of them wrestled on the ground.

"Halt!" Case shouted, just as Damson came

running up. Great. Now Case was surrounded by angry elves.

"We've no time for this!" Damson yelled. Case looked at Damson. Her pale skin looked pinched, and peaked, as if the elf had been under an undue amount of stress.

"Case, you are needed. I can take care of these two."

Case looked from Damson to the other two elves still struggling on the ground, then scanned the township.

Bocan limped towards them, supported by his da. That was not good either but might work to Case's advantage. He did not one hundred percent trust the elves to guard each other, but a wounded halbtroll just might do.

"Bocan!" Case shouted. "Help Damson guard these two!"

Bocan's big head came up and he looked half confused, then his face cleared. He conferred with his da and they both nodded, Bocan waving one arm as if to shoo Case on his way.

As Case ran off with the other Knights towards the eerie roaring sounds, he spared a thought for Tegan, but had no time to check on his comrade.

As he rounded a half-finished building, what he saw made his blood run cold.

It was a rusty red and mottled green creature that looked like a small drake. But where the large drakes that were friends to Go No More had four, strong stout legs, this had only two. Its muscular belly tapered into a long, sinuous tail and ended with a sharp, wicked-looking barb. Each leathery wing was also tipped with a barb.

Case just hoped the barbs only sliced and did not also drip poison.

Jenny whirled and jabbed, slicing at the creature, red braids flying around her determined face as Flex the faery fox nipped at the creature's heels. The wyvern roared, belching acrid brown smoke tinged with fire.

Case heard his comrades running and saw why the townspeople had formed a sharp cordon. They had to keep this creature from entering the town itself and threatening the children. He spared a thought for his own son before examining the creature's movements, looking for a way in that would help Jenny and damage the beast.

It was most definitely a thing out of the legends of the ancients, reminding him of some of the illustrations he had so loved in the schoolroom as a child.

Creatures of legend come to life once again... though why he still found it strange, he did not know. But knowing such things existed did not take away the fear drenching him in cold sweat. His heart pounded in his chest, and he prayed to whatever God was listening that his son was safe, his comrades were safe, and that Go No More had not been breached.

Then, bellowing "We ride for Go No More!" Case ran into the melee, broadsword in hand, a larger match to Jenny's sword. The heavy sword fit neatly in his hand as he raced towards the beast to help his comrade, still seeking a clear pathway through the slashing tail, the biting fox, and Jenny herself.

And then a second creature appeared.

"Fuuuuuucckkk!" he shouted. This one was the rich green of beetle's wings, and slightly larger than the first. He pivoted, dirt flying, veering towards it, reaching the creature the same time as Tegan's thrown kpinga arced through the air and smacked the beast's long throat.

The wyvern shook its head and undulated its long, snake-like neck, trying to dislodge the many-bladed weapons as Tegan's lynx growled and harried one of its stubby legs.

"Case! Clear!" Tegan shouted and he stopped, knowing his comrade had more blades to throw. They whistled past his head, thunking into the creature's flesh as it screamed and shrieked. The sounds rent the air, splitting Case's head.

He snapped his head around. Tegan stood proudly, fierce grin slashing per dark face, eyes alight with battle lust.

He had never seen a more beautiful or stirring site in his whole life.

CHAPTER 40
TEGAN

The creatures roared in challenge and screamed in pain. Per comrades dodged and parried around per, and Starlight snapped and leapt, face stained with wyvern blood.

This was what Tegan was born for, not the magic coursing through per veins. Tegan was built for battle. Tegan was built to protect those that Tegan loved.

Tegan had sworn to fight for Go No More, and so Tegan would.

Every blade Tegan threw hit true, slamming into its target, doing its part to take the creature down. Starlight growled and dodged, and bit with snapping jaws.

Per comrades raced to back up Jenny, who valiantly fought with the first creature. The orange-red blur was her faery fox trying to trip the beast, while dodging the wicked tail.

Then, through the shimmering seam of a temporary gait, a third wyvern appeared.

Holy earth and ancient ancestors.

Tegan began to pray, sending the words out above the melee like mighty blades in flight.

"Mboli. Great River. Flow through me. Increase my power. Increase my magic. Increase my chance at life."

The words flowed unbidden from Tegan's mouth. It was a prayer per never would have said before this moment, when something deep inside—some primal urge—stepped forth. The power grabbed Tegan by the scruff of per neck, taking over.

Kpingas gone, machete in hand, she felt the magic flow freely, coursing through per muscles.

Tegan lifted the sharp machete to the sky and howled like a wyvern. Howled with the fire of life. Per howled and was filled with life-giving water. Per howled with all per might.

"Yes!" per voice echoed above the sounds of the skirmish. "I am Tegan! I am warrior mage!"

Per shouted to the sky as the pulse of people and beasts yelled and shrieked and clamored. Tegan felt them all. Every Green Clan member with rake and hoe. Every bowyer. Every weaver and cook with whatever weapons they could grab to hand. Starlight and Flex. And overhead, the shrieks of Serena the owl.

"I am warrior mage! The power of Mboli flows through my veins! I am here! I am here! I am!"

And then, four more beasts busted through the open gate, thrashing and roaring, tails whipping warriors into the air and slamming their bodies to the earth.

Tegan ran shrieking, swinging per machete,

surrounded by comrades and suddenly, Aphrodite and Charles Wong were there, hurling fire bolts and glowing orbs of magic toward the beasts.

Per comrades' aims were true. The beasts shrieked and raged with all their might, but Go No More was stronger still.

In a circle around them, the townspeople bellowed, holding the line, including the refugees who realized they had a stake in protecting this place.

So precious, every last one. Tegan felt their rage and fear and channeled it into the twining flow of magic.

Tegan swung per machete and every bit of magic inside flew down per arm and through the blade. Machete struck flesh and muscle and bone, crunching and cracking, impact jarring up per arm. Tegan pulled the well-oiled blade free, then leapt and whirled, and smacked again, slicing out to slit one snakelike throat.

Tegan shut per mouth against the spray of hot, strangely colored blood that stank of bonfires and sulfur.

Tegan was not thinking anymore. Move. Respond. React. Attack. The battle clicked through per mind and Tegan saw five paces ahead, acting before the wyverns could shift and move. The magic steadied Tegan, and filled per whole being, setting per limbs alight with the buzz and joy of battle, and the lust for life.

Tegan danced amidst the maelstrom. Tegan leapt, and bared per teeth at the strange beasts, even as a tail lashed out and the barb sliced open per cheek.

Tegan laughed.

This was power. This was life.

Warrior mage. The words echoed inside Tegan's head. *Warrior mage. Warrior mage.* But what did the words mean?

And suddenly, Tegan knew, and the magic flowing through per limbs and coursing down her blade? She could manipulate it.

Tegan narrowed focus on three of the strange, drake-like wyverns, and calling upon the power of Mboli himself, Tegan thrust per magic out the tip of the machete's blade, but did not strike with the metal itself. Instead, Tegan sent the flow of magic, aiming it down the serviceable metal of the machete, and from there it branched out, ramming straight into the great beast's throats, hitting them all at once.

The roaring choked off into whimpers. The creatures' eyes grew large. They thrashed, smacking warriors with tails and wings, bodies flying outward.

"Clear!" Tegan shouted. Per comrades could not hear per. They continue to slash and strike and yell.

"For Go No More!" Jenny shouted, slashing out with her deadly broadsword, raising her buckler against a striking wing.

Tegan planted boots on churned-up ground, slick with blood.

"Clear!" Tegan shouted once again. Heads snapped up, and warriors scrabbled outward toward the protective circle of the townspeople and their weapons. But still, some comrades battled with the beasts.

Tegan filled per lungs a third time.

"Clear!" Per voice was stronger than ever before, as if per breath itself was tinged with magic.

And suddenly, the human bodies were gone from the circle, the animals stood panting near per feet, and all that was left were two wyverns—for that was what per mind called them—jaws open, black tongues lolling, staring back with strange, uncanny eyes.

Tegan sent an extra jolt of magic. It flew toward them like mighty arrows. Like the thundering of a river down a mountain. Like a sudden storm.

The creatures grew larger and larger and larger, as if being magnified by a spyglass held in the fist of the Gods. Their mouths opened and shut, shut and opened, as if trying to cry out.

And then the wyverns exploded outward into ten thousand shards of blood and flesh.

And Tegan stood tall in the heart of it, battered and smiling in the spray of life and death.

CHAPTER 41

PERIDOT

Peridot sat at the long, gleaming wood bar, surrounded by excited chatter and banter he was too exhausted to pay attention to. He nursed a mug of brandy wine as Porrac and Jamie bustled about, serving sweaty, filthy, exhausted Knights and all the townspeople who had crowded the place.

The two men were so similar, and yet so different from each other. One with dark skin, and tight curly hair, the other pale as milk, with rosy cheeks and fair, fine hair that stuck in wisps around his forehead, a result of sweat from the kitchens, no doubt. But they moved in similar ways and told similar jokes.

Peridot wondered if that was the way of people when they had lived and loved together for many years. Not that he was likely to ever find out such a thing. He was more likely to get a knife in the back than find someone to love long term, the way Jamie and Porrac had found one another.

He took another sip of the rich, sweet wine, rolling it across his tongue as he mused. Though the mingled scents of the public house were getting to him. He could ignore the clamor, but his sensitive nose wrinkled at the smell of unwashed bodies, the meat and tuber stew, plus beer, cider, and cannabis smoke.

At least the brandy wine kept his stomach settled.

It was a sign of how traumatized and exhausted people were that they had come to the town's gathering spot without sparing time for the bathhouse. The folks of Go No More tended to be clean, overall, and not overly fond of the drama that he sometimes encountered from humans in other places.

But tonight? Getting drunk and sharing tales of the Unseelie beasts seemed to be the order of business. The bards who usually played on the small stage across the hall moved from table to table now, collecting snatches of stories that they would later weave into skillful songs.

They wouldn't even need to embellish much. Not this time.

Peridot himself wished to drink as many cups of brandy wine as the bartenders could spare, but he also knew that getting drunk was unwise. But he needed something to blunt the edges of what he had seen. He still shook from it. Though Bocan, Arrow, and Damson had kept him to the outer edges of the fight, the terror of seeing those wyverns still hit home. And then receiving word about the Unseelie trolls? That had shaken him to his core.

If ever he had thought he could still play double

agent, and if ever he had thought that working for Queen Silverhair might still be in his best interests?

Those strategies were gone. The Queen was evil, through and through. Not just a grief-stricken mother who had lost her only love, and then born a child with damaged souls.

Peridot had been lying to himself. He saw it clearly now, as he stared into the murky depths of his cup. He had chalked up the Queen's soul stealing—horrible as that was—to her grief and desperation. But this turn? Working in concert with the Unseelie against the humans?

For some reason, for Peridot that was a step too far. To treat with their historic enemies meant Queen Silverhair was irredeemable. She played a game he could no longer guess the rules of.

It also meant there was no way to save his own skin.

And that is the brunt of it, isn't it? he thought to himself. Peridot was fucked. He was welcomed nowhere. An exile of his own making.

Porrac pulled a foaming beer from a tap and Jamie smacked his ass as he skirted by, heading for the kitchens.

Peridot had thrown away a chance at what Jamie and Porrac had. He had betrayed his best friend, Damson, twisting things so far that she had resorted to torture. He still felt the pain and shock of it, and if the new mind healer would consent to help him, he should seek her out.

But more than that pain was the regret of what he

had lost. He had lost Damson's love and good opinion. He had forfeited a chance at something more.

He also found, sitting on a stool in this crowded, noisy place, that he missed Go No More and the humans here. He missed the easy camaraderie. He had missed this public house and sitting with the sense of people working to one purpose around him.

He had ruined that. He no longer belonged.

Even now he was flanked by guards. The djinni sat to his right side and Damson, once his love and best friend, was now an angry, bristling stranger on his left. Behind him, standing near the long bar swilling beer, were three Steel Clan Knights, and more on the broad porch outside, and sprinkled through the hall.

There was no chance he could walk free, nor did he belong as one of their party.

He was good as a prisoner now, and he deserved it. There was nothing left for him Underhill, even had he wanted to return. The Queen would as easily throw him to a wyvern as any of the people here would slit his throat.

"See what you have wrought?" Damson said, practically spitting into her cider. His old friend bristled with anger. It only made her more beautiful.

"I do. I do see it." His words were soft, and he could not meet her sharp and wounded eyes.

"You have to go back in," the djinni said, startling them both.

"Are you out of your fool djinni mind?" Damson said, leaning across Peridot to spear the djinni with blazing emerald eyes.

Black eyes blinked back at her, unperturbed.

Peridot waited, enjoying the feel of Damson's closeness, and knowing he did not deserve even the kind warmth of her next to him.

"It is the only way for him to help fix any of this. He has to go back in, and he has to help us."

"And you trust him." Arrow's voice came from behind. When had the dark-skinned elf arrived?

"You cannot trust him," Damson said. "He forfeited all trust when he betrayed Go No More and sold us to the Queen for who knows what? This pig fucker does not deserve to even sit among us. Why is he not locked up with the alchemist?"

"So they can plot together?" Arrow spat.

Peridot's head reared back as if he had been smacked. His mind was whirling with pain, regret, and one slender spark of interest in what it was the white djinni had to say.

The djinni raised one eyebrow, looking from Damson to Arrow, then back at him. Peridot gulped down his remaining wine and waited.

Once it was clear that he held their attention, Abyad spoke.

"Of course this elf cannot be trusted, but I have a feeling he has had a change of heart. Shall we condemn him without giving him a chance to act upon this change?"

Damson slammed a fist on the bar top but said nothing.

"What do you propose?" said Jenny, the red-haired

Knight, who leaned on the bar past Damson, with the massive, pale blue hulk of Bocan standing at her back.

"I propose that I put a lock and key into our spy here and send him back Underhill."

"The alchemist insists we rescue the princess," the halbtroll's voice voice rumbled out.

Peridot was shocked. First, that the alchemist would say such a thing. And second, that a member of the Steel Clan would share that information with the likes of him, and in such a public place.

Perhaps battling Unseelie trolls and wyverns had rattled the halbtroll's thinking.

"Oh, you are going nowhere," Bocan said, as if reading his mind. "The djinni here will make certain of that. You shall be tethered to the djinni by your agreement, and in the end, you shall be forever barred from Underhill. You know this, so you might as well choose to help."

Damson glared at the halbtroll, but avoided Peridot's gaze, so he turned again toward the djinn. Those uncanny eyes blinked at him, holding secrets of the ages. Peridot wondered how old the djinni was. He felt older than Underhill itself. Old as the wind. Old as time. Peridot felt a hot breath of wind move across him, driving out the icy chill from heart. The djinn's voice whispered inside his mind: *You could have your life back, if only you comply.*

Peridot did not think it would be such an easy bargain, this.

The djinni finally spoke out loud again, but softly,

pitching his voice to reach only Peridot's ears in the midst of the clamor and crush.

"You can have this. It will take hard work and the rebuilding of trust. But if you do this thing, it is possible. Many things are possible."

Peridot reached a hand up to swipe his face and realized that tears were coursing down his cheeks. A novel experience for one such as he.

"I am so tired," he said. "Tired of running, tired of scheming."

And as he spoke the words to the djinn, he found that they were true. Enough of his self-pity. It was time he took responsibility again. Peridot straightened his spine and spoke.

"Tell me what to do."

"I need to speak with the alchemist again," Bocan rumbled, "and we all need some food."

"And a bath," Jenny quipped.

"Very well," the djinni replied. "Let us go our separate ways and gather more information."

"Where shall we meet again?" Arrow asked.

"Who said you were invited?" Tegan said, stomping through the crowd. Per must have come in from the porch, considering the scent of cannabis clinging to per clothing and hair.

"If you do not trust me by now," Arrow said, "you will never trust me. And I believe for whatever venture the djinni has in mind, you will need my help."

Abyad nodded sharply.

Damson spoke, voice reluctant. "It pains me to say it, but Arrow is correct. We need her. We need everyone. We will certainly need all the mages available. And perhaps the mind healers too."

"All right," the djinni said. "We shall reconvene in two hours' time."

"And meanwhile," Jenny chimed, "you get locked into a room upstairs."

Locked in a comfortable room was more than he deserved, Peridot was sure. Whatever it took, he would not throw this chance away.

He just had to figure out how to stay alive, and find his purpose once again.

TEGAN

The shower and subsequent soak had done as much to ease Tegan's tortured muscles as the cannabis, but per still vibrated with tension and the aftermath of battle and magic combined. Per prodded the cut on per cheek. It was tender, but not deep, and should heal just fine. And if not, well, scars were sexy.

Per did not want to sit through another Gods-damned meeting, necessary as they were. Per wanted sex. And a lot of it.

And with one person in particular.

Per had somehow made it through, soaking in the tub and listening to the fears of per comrades, while returning the heated glances Case sent per way. There was something about battle—both the buildup and the aftermath—that brought things into sharp focus. Anger. Fear. Hope. Lust. Whether there was love there, Tegan was not yet willing to say, though per loved all per comrades in one way or another.

But Case? That did not bear thinking about. Not yet. Maybe once they got through the next fight, per would see about that. See whether building a life with Case and his son was the right thing to do.

Perhaps Tegan was deluded, thinking that a notorious cat-about-town like perself could settle down, whether with one person or two....

Not that Case was any blushing neophyte himself. Per had seen the way he looked at her. And at the djinn, too. And would not that be a wonder to experience? The thought of the three of them together made per skin heat.

Yeah. Before a meeting, Tegan might be better off giving perself some relief. Release some tension so per didn't bite some fool council member's head off.

The meeting could wait. Or per comrades could fill Tegan in later. Irresponsible? Right now, per did not give a fuck.

Tegan was headed back to per small home when Case's rough voice called out from behind.

"Tegan."

Per slowed down, letting him catch up. They fell into step and rounded the corner leading to a tidy row of small homes. Some were a single room, others had sleeping nooks, or, in rarer cases, a proper bedroom or two. Case and his son, Jason, lived further down in a place with both bedroom and sleeping nook. Tegan had been to their comfortable home many times, having quiet conversations with a comrade or three, or playing games with Jason. Tegan really enjoyed the boy. He was clever and humorous, without being cruel.

Why was per thinking about Jason? And Case's home?

In a dark corner beneath a cherry tree barely beginning to bud, Case put a hand on Tegan's shoulder, stopping both per feet and wandering thoughts.

"Tegan," he repeated, voice rough, "are we doing this?"

"I don't know. Are we?" Tegan replied.

"I notice we are not walking toward the public house. So, what I want to know is, what are we doing?"

Tegan arched an eyebrow. "I was heading to my home for a few moments alone before facing pushy council members. What are you doing?"

"I want you," he said.

Tegan's heart slammed into per throat. Case's fingers on per arms felt like brands of fire. Heat and wet pooled in per pelvis. With a growl, Tegan grabbed Case's blond hair and pulled his face toward per own.

Their lips met. Press of flesh, tangle of tongues. He whimpered, back in his throat. Tegan growled again in response. The kiss deepened.

"My place," Tegan snapped out. Releasing perself from him, per stalked off. Case cursed then followed, steps quickening.

It took everything to not run toward per front door. Tegan clicked up the latch and shoved inside, not even bothering to remove per boots.

As soon as they were inside, Case did not even wait for per to light a lamp before Tegan's body was pressed against the door, lips on per neck, hands on per ass.

"Boots. Off." Tegan said, shoving him away. "Boots. Leathers. Shirt. Off."

Case laughed. "Who put you in charge?"

Tegan scowled but did not stop shucking boots and dropping leathers to the smooth wood floor. Per noticed Case did the same, until he stood before per, pale flesh naked in the faint electric light beaming in from the street outside. His heavy cock bobbed at his thigh, beginning its rise. It was as red as his cheeks and lips.

"You aren't naked," he said, striding toward her on bare feet, eyes intent.

"Got distracted."

He reached out and yanked the shirt over Tegan's head. Per gasped as the cool air hit, nipples tightening. But per own sex was still hot with need.

Per leapt toward him like a wildcat leapt on prey. He caught per. Met per power with his own.

Muscle to muscle. Bone to bone. They kissed, and grabbed, and stumbled backwards, Tegan steering their bodies toward the curtains that marked per sleeping nook, and a well-appointed bed, throwing back curtains, throwing back the wool comforter, revealing clean hemp sheets, as soft as spring.

As soft as the inside creases of Case's knees. As soft as the head of his tumescent cock. And then per mouth was on him. He groaned beneath per.

"Tegan. Gods. You."

Tegan was a storm, rolling over him. A wild animal. A person possessed. A warrior. A lover. A mage.

He flipped per, rolling them both deeper into the

bed, and then his mouth was on per sex, teasing per own erection.

Tegan groaned and growled and scratched, shuddering as wave after wave of pleasure rolled through per body. Case held per hips steady with calloused hands. Tegan bucked, and shoved, and reached, and drew his cock back in per hands. He shouted and shoved a finger inside per. Tegan returned the favor with a finger of per own.

Case was panting, pleading, calling out per name, and then joined with Tegan, until they were falling, flying, tumbling, screaming each other's names.

The magic lighted Tegan's souls. Per pushed and licked and kissed and cried out, until all was heat and shuddering movement. Magic. Lust. Love. All crashing through per like a storm.

And with a bellow, Case's body tensed. He shuddered, moaning, and collapsed on top of per. Tegan grabbed his head and pulled it toward the juncture of per shoulder, where muscle made a pillow next to bone.

He fit there perfectly, as if the spot was his, and his alone.

Though Tegan had a feeling he might share, if and when the time was right. And per might, too.

But first, Tegan wanted more.

"We have to go to this pig-fucking meeting," she groaned into the easy silence. "But after? We're doing this again."

"For an anarchist, you have some strong, authoritarian tendencies."

Tegan smacked his ass.

He grabbed per hand and kissed Tegan.

It was as soft as mist in the morning, and just as sweet.

I am so fucked, per thought.

But Tegan did not mind.

CHAPTER 43

SILVERHAIR

Queen Silverhair swept down the long, dark corridor, sage-green skirts sending up gusts that caused the torches in their troll-wrought sconces to judder and shake, casting strange, Unseelie shadows on the walls. Like an arrow sprung from a twanging bow, her aim was unerring. With firm and graceful steps, she headed once again for the Holly King's lair.

Two guards stood outside the large holly doors. She paused, eyes flicking toward the carvings of boar hunts and feasting, the Holly King himself at the center. Disgusting creatures, the Unseelie. Nobility should never hunt and kill. That activity was for the lesser elves and beings better suited to the task.

She felt a pang at having yoked herself to such an elf but swept the thought away.

"I must speak with your liege," she snapped out, voice filled with command.

The lefthand guard flicked her eyes toward the one on the right, who nodded and bowed.

"If Your Majesty would wait but just one moment, I will alert the Holly King that you are here."

Silverhair balked at the insult, but simply nodded. Arguing with a guard would do no good. He slipped inside a crack between the carved doors, closing it too quickly for her to see inside, but not so quick that she could not hear the King asking what the fool thought he was doing.

She smiled. Good. The King was in a foul mood? Well, so was she.

Within moments, the double doors opened wide and she was ushered in, blinking slightly at the increase in light. Every candle in the kingdom was lit, it seemed, and the fire crackled merrily on the hearth, the scent of mulling wine filled the air of the chambers.

The King and his son sat cozily before the fire. The prince had the good grace to leap to his feet, while the sovereign looked at her with lazy, hooded eyes, full lips turned downward in a slight frown.

"Queen Silverhair!" Prince Galen said. "Please, sit. Take my chair. I shall get myself another."

A courtier already hurried forth, a well-padded chair thrust in front of their body, moving like an ungainly animal.

The Holly King's son was a tall, handsome elf with hair black as night falling across his broad shoulders. He wore a rich blue tunic that complemented his skin, which was the creamy underside of a dove's wing. The eyes that regarded her were the color of the purple crocus.

If he did not wed her daughter, Queen Silverhair might bed the prince herself. Eyes on the Holly King, she sat in the offered chair.

"Well met, Your Majesty," Prince Galen said, once they were all seated. "What brings you to our realm?"

The Holly King said nothing. So much for their earlier cozy chat. Tables turned quickly in the Unseelie realms, it seemed.

"Prince Galen," the Queen replied, tilting her head his way. She did not answer his question.

"Your daughter," he continued, smoothly, as if nothing in her behavior was amiss, "she did not accompany you?"

"No. She did not wish to," Silverhair replied. "Her health, you know."

It was as good an excuse as any, though they both knew it was a lie. Galen had the good grace to look uncomfortable.

"Might I come to your court to pay my respects to Princess Elzabetta?"

The King barked out a laugh, and Silverhair's eyes sharpened.

Did the young fool actually *wish* to marry her daughter? Or was he simply playing his father's game?

"Your father and I are undecided on that course of action. Other things are now in play."

Confusion marred the prince's brow. So. That was intriguing. The prince was not privy to his father's recent machinations. And why should he be? Did Elzabetta even know that she was here?

"Father?"

The Holly King shifted on his large, sumptuously upholstered chair. Not quite a throne, it was still clearly the seat of power here. "Marriage is not off the table, but with the princess's health still uncertain, Queen Silverhair and I are trying other methods to achieve our aims."

"Which have failed," Silverhair spat, turning on the Holly King. "You told me you were sending your most dangerous creatures, and yet, they were either killed or turned tail, running to Underhill in defeat."

She bristled with anger, holding herself in check only with the reminder that, should he wish it, the Holly King could have her imprisoned here.

Or killed.

Either action on his part would spell out certain war, but he might not care.

The King shrugged as if her words were of no consequence. As if several of his best warriors had not been killed, and by humans, no less.

"It was but a test incursion. To assess exactly how well trained and fortified these humans are." He picked up a golden goblet—the source of the mulled wine scent—and drank. The lack of wine cup near to hand for her was a direct insult then, and not an oversight. "Does it bother you, their deaths?"

His voice was unctuous. Disgusting.

Her fingers curled on the arms of her chair; she wanted to slash at his smug face.

"Wine, my Queen?" Galen asked, nervously waving a courtier near.

"Leave it!" the Holly King bellowed. The courtier scurried back to her place near the wall as Galen subsided back into his chair.

"You are in my realm, Queen Silverhair. Do not forget it. You are here at my invitation and shall not question how I use my own people to our ends."

She looked down at her lap, breathing slowly in and out through her nose. When she looked up again, a smile was pasted to her lips, tugging them upward by force of will.

"Of course. I meant no insult. I was simply concerned that things had not gone according to plan."

The King drank again, then motioned for another cup to be filled and placed on a small table brought to Queen Silverhair's side.

"My plans are long and far reaching, my Queen. As, I am certain, are your own."

He lifted his cup toward her. Queen Silverhair lifted her own. A salute. A false declaration of truce.

She forced herself to swallow the spiced wine. Forced herself to continue smiling as the liquid traced its way into her belly.

"To success," she said, voice brittle and bright.

Galen looked from her to his father, and back again.

"To success," the prince said, though it was clear he was bewildered.

The King said nothing but drained his cup and motioned for some more.

Silverhair and the dove-cream prince shared one, long look. Taking each other's measure.

It was time, once again, for the Queen to take her own. She needed to regain control. Perhaps Prince Galen was the answer, after all.

Whether as secret ally, husband to Elzabetta...

Or consort to the Seelie Queen.

CHAPTER 44

TEGAN

Tegan walked toward the large greenhouses near the fields outside the township gates, exhaustion dogging every step, though the signs of spring soothed per souls.

The meeting had gone on long into the night and included several argumentative council members.

Though Tegan had planned to meet with Case again after, they were both too weary, and he needed to get back to his son. And then the meetings started all over again come morning, and lasted through the day.

Finally, midafternoon, Tegan had wrenched perself away, unsettled. Per needed the counsel of per mothers, especially Inaya.

Tegan followed the stepstone path that approached the largest greenhouse, a metal-framed monstrosity filled with wavy new glass. One solid tug on the wood door, and per was surrounded by warm, steamy air. It felt good on Tegan's muscles, which still ached from riding, battle, and the tension of magic running through per flesh. Per was going to have to get used to that.

While the soak and sex had loosened per up some, Tegan's muscles still protested the abuse.

"Child." Per mother Inaya was a handsome, dark-skinned woman with a craggy face and long, luxuriant locks that, as far as Tegan knew, had not been cut since Inaya was a girl. They were tied back today with a purple wrap that matched a purple tunic worn over heavy, hemp canvas trousers.

Inaya patted a seed into a soil-filled tray, then turned, brushing off her hands. She opened her arms, and Tegan walked right in. Per mother smelled of green, growing things. Of the musk of cannabis. The sweet almond of her hair oil. The rosemary growing outside the greenhouse doors. Inaya smelled of comfort and of home.

Though Tegan equaled per mother in height, per mother still kissed Tegan's brow as if per were a toddling youngster.

"Walk with me and tell me what has painted that face of yours with trouble."

Tegan trailed after per mother, who walked through the shelves and benches filled with seed starts and already burgeoning plants. Inaya was one of the head growers of the Green Clan, under the tutelage of master grower Hakim L'Ouverture. Inaya would be named master grower herself one day soon, Tegan was certain.

The carefully tended rows of seedlings would soon

grow into their main crop of hemp and cannabis that kept the townsfolk in clothing and rope, soaps, conditioners, tinctures, infused honey, and of course Tegan's favorite, smoke.

The Green Clan cultivated all sorts of food plants as well, plus the yellow brassica that made biofuel for what machinery they had, including the Steel Clan motorcycles.

Tegan admired per mother more than per could say. Both per mothers actually, and Tegan's father too.

It made Tegan wonder about family. Case and Jason...

"So, what did you need to talk about child? Your magic. It's growing, nah?"

Inaya's eyes were on the plants, not looking at per, but Tegan felt per mother's dark eyes all the same. Her fingers were busy, nimbly plucking shriveled leaves, patting at shoots and poking at soil. She added a bit of water or compost tea here, adjusted a heat lamp there...naturally doing all the things that were part of ordinary life of a Green Clan grower, all things that Tegan had been raised around but were as foreign to per as another language.

Tegan understood blades and bikes, and unfortunately was going to have to come to understand magic as well.

"How did you know?" Tegan asked.

"I can smell it on you, child. You're different. I can feel it too. Magic is rising everywhere. It was only a matter of time that your own destiny came to collect its due."

The words unsettled Tegan, but per said nothing, simply enjoyed the simplicity of being among the plants with per mother once again.

Finally, Inaya paused and examined Tegan. Tegan was a grown adult, with responsibilities and leadership of per own, but in Inaya and Winney's eyes? Tegan was a beloved child, all the same.

"What am I to do, Mother?"

"I cannot tell you that until you tell me more. What happened out there?"

Tegan reached for the words. How to convey the feeling of standing at the water's edge? Of words, flowing unbidden from her lips? Of, yes, per magic building? And that magic striking out in battle with a wild power Tegan was uncertain per could harness.

"Mboli," Tegan said, pronouncing the name that was at once familiar and strange. "Mboli happened."

Inaya frowned. Thinking. "He came to you?"

Tegan nodded. Inaya looked back at the plants and then at Tegan once again.

"I pondered this a long time. Discussed it with Winney and Angel, even. I wondered when this would happen."

"How did you know?" Tegan kept asking that, but could not ask anything else.

"You are my child. And Mboli is of my ancestors." Inaya grasped Tegan's hands. "Mboli is of our people, and it is time you knew more."

Tegan sagged with relief. Finally, information...

"Mboli is the spirit of everything. He is especially active in rivers and tall trees, but he is also in the smallest whisper of air, in the kisses of lovers, on the tip of the warrior's arrow....."

"Is he a God?"

Inaya shrugged, prodding the soil in a small pot, testing the moisture levels. "Our ancestors did not call him a God, though that is as good a name as any, I suppose."

Per mother fell silent, the way she did when thinking. Tegan had learned to let her be. Per ran her own hands lightly above the small green fronds unfurling from black soil. The plants moved, as if reaching for per skin. Tegan drew per hand back and looked down. The sprouts looked taller than before.

And then per felt Inaya's eyes, watching, keen with interest.

"You could have joined the Green Clan, you know."

Tegan laughed. "What? And give up my kpinga? No thank you."

Inaya gave per a knowing look but did not push. Tegan felt tight with discomfort all the same. Per mother had seen the plants, just as Tegan had. And what did that mean? That the plants had reached up like that? Tegan had never paid enough attention to plants to know if that was something they did in response to everyone.

Or just people who belonged to the Green Clan. And Tegan.

Her mother patted her palms together, brushing off the soil.

"Mboli is in birthing and dying. Water and fire.

Earth and air. He is in the smallest and the largest things, animating them all."

"Is Mboli the spirit of good, then?"

Anaya shook her head. "Neither good nor bad. Mboli simply is."

"What good is that?" Tegan asked. A spark of anger coiled inside per tight belly. "I have no use for a being who cannot decide which side they are on."

"Ah, child, did not your mother and I teach you? And your father too?"

Tegan crossed per arms like a petulant child. "Teach me what?"

"That life is more complicated than good or bad. That evil and compassion have some small hold in each of us. Why else do you think the Reckoning occurred?"

"Because a bunch of selfish pig fuckers decided they were more important than everybody else." Tegan practically spat the words. The seedlings recoiled.

Inaya clucked her tongue and waved a gentle hand over the plants, who—Tegan swore it—relaxed and unfurled another centimeter or so.

"But how did they become that way?" Inaya said. "Are we not all born the same? If bad and good were not seeded in each heart, there would be no need for weapons, would there, light of my life?"

Tegan's mouth scrunched up. Per hated philosophical talks. Abstraction. Give per a blade in hand or a naked body writhing between per thighs. Give per a good smoke, a lazy soak, or days spent riding.

Tegan needed action.

But which action was the right one?

"You tricked me," Tegan said, glaring at per mother.

Inaya threw her head back and laughed, teeth flashing with mirth. "I simply told you the truth as I know it. Your mind and heart did the rest."

When per mother laughed, Tegan could not stay annoyed for long. Per cracked a grin.

"You saying I tricked myself, woman?"

Inaya shrugged. "If the boot fits…"

Tegan exhaled noisily. "All right. Enough. I'm ready to smoke a bowl after all this talk. And didn't you promise me dinner?"

Inaya patted Tegan's shoulder, then drew per into another embrace.

Much as Tegan said per preferred the open road to the settled life per mothers had, it was nice to know that home was waiting when per returned.

Just as quickly as Inaya hugged Tegan, she released per.

"Let me clean up, and then we'll go find your mother. Shall we invite Angel, too?"

"Might as well make it a party," Tegan replied.

Dinner with all per parents. Not something Tegan got very often, but one per needed right now. Badly.

The world had turned on its head, spinning like a child's toy. Tegan wished per knew where it would stop.

CHAPTER 45

CARONDEL

A rap came on the door, and Carondel heard the lock open. The smell of stew preceded the woman carrying the tray of food. Skaadi.

She looked up at him, but said nothing until the door was closed again, the guards safely on the other side of the heavy door.

Skaadi made a show of crossing the room and setting the tray on the small table near the window where his one chair was. He spent many hours a day here, staring out at the township. Go No More was a bustling place. A good place, it seemed. He wondered if it was a place that would accept him, should he live through this ordeal that was to come.

"What do you have for me?" he asked, keeping his voice quiet.

She slid a palm into her pocket and brought out a copper disc carved with the Queen's seal. It gleamed in the early spring sunlight. Carondel gasped to see it, but quickly covered the sound with a cough. She had done it. She had come through, and perhaps his plan would work.

Skaadi's eyes narrowed. She knew that he was hiding something.

Carondel found he did not care. All he cared was that she had brought the thing. He moved to take it from her palm, but she closed her fingers around the copper disc.

"How do we know that we can trust you?"

Carondel slowly withdrew his hand and looked at the woman.

"You can't," he said. "You should not trust me. Just as I should not trust you. But sometimes we have to move and act regardless."

She stared at him for a moment, weighing his words, then nodded and held out the disk again. But her fingers were still curled toward her palm.

"You must help us. You must help us get a message to the Queen." Her face was urgent. "Tell her there are humans who would help her out here. Help renew the reign of Underhill. Bring true power back to the land as opposed to these sniveling whiners here...."

Skaadi glanced out the window, looking as if she was about to spit.

Carondel was puzzled, and did not bother to hide it

"Why would you not wish the power for your-selves? Why do you want to give Queen Silverhair more power?"

Skaadi's eyes darted about the room as if looking for lurkers, and Carondel realized they were both still standing. He crossed the small space and grabbed a ladder-back chair that sat against the wall near the washbasin.

"Please sit," he said, motioning to the more comfortable chair by the window, next to the tray of steaming stew, brown bread, and mug of water.

Skaadi dipped her head and did so. He sat across from her after making certain that the window was shut.

"You should eat," she said, "before the stew gets cold."

Carondel waved a hand. "Food can wait. I need to know your answer. You asked if you could trust me, and I said you could not but that means I also cannot trust you. So I need more information."

She smoothed her apron in her lap.

"We do want our own power," she said, looking up. "But that will take years to build. To gather resources. To gather enough people on our side. To get the tools and weapons we need. But the Queen..."

Skaadi's eyes took on an avaricious gleam.

"The Queen has all of that and more. She can come in and make the Knights docile and crush their power. And she will reward us with our own power for helping her, so we can live free in our own way. The way men and women ought to live. Not this."

She swept a hand toward the window, indicating the town square. "This is not the way of things. We want to return to the way things were."

Carondel schooled his features into placidity. It wouldn't do to annoy the woman, but he did need to understand, and this plan of theirs? They clearly did not know Silverhair if they thought she would relinquish one ounce of power to their cause.

"You liked things under Wulf."

"We did. A person knows where they stand when there's a powerful leader. There's proper structure. You can put your shoulder behind something like that."

"And after you get what you want from the Queen, who would be that leader for you? Your husband? Yourself?"

Skaadi pursed her lips and gave her shoulders a small shrug but said nothing.

"Fair enough," Carondel replied. "I shall use this amulet to return to Underhill and give the Queen your message. Or I shall try. While this amulet should mask my entry, I may be struck down the moment they clap eyes on me. So don't expect too much."

The whole thing was a gamble. Gambling on this ordinary seal to mask who he was well enough to get him through the gate, and gambling that the Queen's seal would lend enough authority to get himself and the princess out. If he showed it to the right people.

Or both he and the princess could end up dead.

Skaadi nodded again, and stood, twitching her apron into place over her canvas trews.

"That is all we can ask. And if you need any more help from me, please let me know. I can get you bread and cheese, maybe some fruit or jerky, and a bag to carry them in. And we can get you escort into the woods after we break you out of here."

She held her chin proudly, as if it were she going into the silver bitch's lair.

Carondel stood and gazed down at the human woman, so fierce, yet so bitter. He wondered what had turned her so.

"I may need escort," he replied. "But I may not."

"What do you mean?" Her head snapped around, eyes suspicious.

"There may be a way I can convince the Knights of Go No More to escort me themselves."

He smiled.

Skaadi grinned back, like an arctic fox.

"You can do that without betraying us? Well, then you have my blessing."

There was a knock on the door.

"Guard's getting antsy. I'd best get back to work."

"You'd best," he replied. "Thank you, Skaadi."

"I just do what's right."

She stepped forward, knocked on the door three times, it opened, and then she was gone. The door bolted and barred behind her, and Carondel was left staring down at the copper disc inside his palm.

"Now, the experiment."

He walked back to the table by the window and shoved the tray aside. Setting a clean hemp handkerchief upon the rough wood, he lay the gleaming amulet upon the bleached cloth and then carefully withdrew a pouch that hung on a thong around his neck beneath his tunic.

In that pouch was the Queen's own signet that he had stolen at the Battle of New Salem. He had hidden it from his captors through a bit of cloaking magic. Too bad such a spell only worked on objects, not living, breathing beings. Such a thing would make sneaking about much easier.

He held the signet up to the light. It gleamed as if possessed of magic. The sundered triangle and cracked oak leaves were as terrifying and beautiful as Queen Silverhair herself.

He set the signet down next to the copper disc and began to hum, tracing his hands in triangular arcs, forming knots and symbols above the two. The metals began to vibrate, tuning to each other, until finally they snapped together, melding their energies.

The Queen's seal lent its power to the copper disk. Energy built. His humming grew louder, his motions, steadier and more precise, until power poured from his palms. Carondel put all the remains of his magic into the signet and the disk, working until sweat popped onto his brow.

Then he pulled his hands away, and with a sigh, the disk and signet pulled apart and fell, right and left, on to the white cloth.

They both gleamed as if brand new and the figures were etched more deeply than before.

He placed upon his palms over one, then the other, and smiled.

"The magic is the same," he said, and that was good. It meant that he had options. Options for himself, but options also to sneak someone else into Underhill.

Or to carry someone out.

There were many things he could do with this power.

He could do as Skaadi asked and get a message to the Queen. He could alert her guards. He could carve himself a new place within Underhill. He could be killed....

Or he could help the Steel Clan.

He could rescue a princess and bring her to a new home.

It was only the last, he found, that kindled a glimmer of hope inside his breast.

And Carondel had not felt hope in far too long a time.

CHAPTER 46

TEGAN

The rains had stopped. It was a beautiful early spring day. Tegan wished it was a day to simply enjoy. Sparring with friends. Going on a ride. Wandering through the forest with Starlight. Heck, even helping with the construction crews.

Instead, Tegan stood in the center of the practice ring, Starlight at per heels, a kpinga in per right hand, machete in the left. Boots braced against the earth. Ready? Not really. But wasn't that the way with all tasks? You didn't know what you could do until you did it. Failure or success all came in the attempt and how you faced it.

The mages had told Tegan there was no need for all the steel, but Tegan simply did not feel right without them. What is a warrior without per weapons?

Your weapon is your mind, Inaya had said. Though Tegan knew per mother was correct, that did not mean it felt right inside per bones. So, weapons in hand, per looked at the comrades and friends surrounding the fences that separated the practice field from the horse paddock and bike garage.

The sounds of construction continued from the distance, while the acrid scent of the glassworks and forge filled per nostrils along with the dust of the ring and the lingering scent of biofuel from the bikes that always seem to cling to Tegan's leathers.

Good sounds. Good smells. All mingled with the scent of Douglas fir, hemlock spruce, and pine, and of the herbs in Anandita's garden, and the taste of Case's lips.

Their kisses from the night before still lingered, causing per to wonder what might yet come. But Case was not here to watch per, to support per. He had work of his own, escorting Peridot and Carondel to the permanent gate. Tegan would rather be there than here, but every person had their duty.

Turns out, getting tested for magic was Tegan's current lot.

Head grower Hakim L'Ouverture stepped forward, walking staff thumping on the hard-packed dirt. An old man with a nut-brown skin and cheeks as high and round as new apples, he had dark eyes that were shrewd, yet kind. The locks that Tegan knew flowed down almost to his knees were wound into a massive beehive on top of his head. He gripped a corn pipe in his teeth, though no smoke rose from it. The staff was both a tool for walking—he had sustained a grave injury to his leg in childhood and it had mended badly —and a weapon as deadly as Tegan's own.

"You must be tested, Warrior Mage."

Tegan's head snapped back as if he had struck per.

"Do not call me that. That is not my name." Despite having shouted that very title in the thick of battle, Tegan was not comfortable with it. At least not yet.

"Very well," the head grower replied. "Tegan. Tegan is your name, and a strong name at that. But whether you accept or reject the title Warrior Mage is up to the ancestors and the elements themselves."

He paced the ground in front of per. "We humans have little say in the matter. Once Mboli has taken charge, the best you can do is comply. Bend where he bends. Flow where he flows. Stand firm where he is firm."

Tegan shook off the trembling and the tension in per limbs, inhaled deeply, then went into the long, fourfold cycle of breaths would tap not only into per center, but into the earth and sky itself.

"Good!" Hakim L'Ouverture called out. "Tap into your soul, sibling! Call upon all that is and ask it to be with you. Call upon Mboli himself. Call upon The Way."

And Tegan did. Tegan closed per eyes and called upon Mboli, upon that essence per encountered at the waters deep in the forest. The magic began to float in and around per skin like water. Tegan tasted it, a sweetness lapping at per tongue, filling per sex, and flowing through per blood, until it seeped into every part of Tegan's body, then flowed out into per souls.

In this moment, for the first time, Tegan felt a glimpse of what Inaya told her that Mboli was. Not simply water...that Mboli was all things: good or bad, high or low, dark or light, earth or air, fire or water.

All was connected by The Way.

All was drawn to and from that source that flowed through life itself.

Tegan loosened per limbs and took in a breath from the soles of per boots to the Bantu knots of hair on per head.

Eyes opening, Tegan looked at Hakim and then at her mothers—Inaya and Winney—and her father, Angel, who stood near the horses that were his closest companions, sharing the paddock with Karaktilla the drake. Tegan turned, looking toward per comrades near the bike garage. Jerrod, standing tall, his daughter, Tokki, at his side. And Jenny, red hair shining, looking worried. Bocan, cradling his injured arm. He should have been abed, but if Jimena could not make him? No one could.

Bocan's father stood farther back with Recoana and Feldspar, forming a blue wall of trolls. Next to them, the slender elves—Arrow and Damson—looked on as well.

And there was the Raven Priestess, dark feathers fluttering in her coils of hair. She had been called from the woods to witness this ordeal, and to help with the coming battle.

The council members stood behind the wooden gate, watching, as did Jimena, Anandita, and some of the township's children.

Not one of them was wishing per would fail. That thought alone warmed Tegan. Lent per strength.

Inhale. Exhale. *Mboli be with me.*

"I am ready," Tegan said.

The testers stepped forth.

In stepped Charles Wong in his long, embroidered robes, and Aphrodite, resplendent in a blue tunic and boots made of black-dyed leather. They were there in case the magic grew out of control.

Then Bocan moved into place. Earth.

Abyad the djinni moved into the circle like a black clad wind. His face was veiled today, so only his ghostly hands and black eyes showed. Air.

Angel's people opened the large, double paddock gates, and Karaktilla rumbled closer. Fire.

Mboli had already tested Tegan with water, so per carried that perself.

Hakim L'Ouverture pounded his staff on the ground three times, each blow ringing through per bones.

"Begin!" he shouted.

Tegan bent per knees. Per had faced many battles but had never faced off against friends in this way.

Tegan wondered if per was ready, but then remembered the thing Jenny's mother, Danika, had taught them long ago.

A warrior is never ready. But a warrior is always prepared.

And Tegan was.

"I fight for Go No More!" per shouted. Karaktilla roared in answer, and a burst of fire leaped from between the drake's jaws.

Starlight hissed, and Tegan braced perself, raising the kpinga to strike against the fire.

CHAPTER 47

BOCAN

Bocan didn't know if he could do this. He had tried to convince Recoana or Feldspar that they should be the one to test Tegan.

Feldspar had insisted that it be Bocan.

Tegan is your comrade and you are the one among us with the strongest earth magic. It is your task. You must do this.

Fracked-earth pig fucker. And so here Bocan stood, in a loose circle with the other testers, on the packed-dirt sparring ground. Serena circled overhead. That should have calmed Bocan, but only tugged at his nerves. With drake fire sure to happen, he just hoped the owl would remain safe, feathers unsinged.

::Don't worry about me. I'm just here to make sure you don't do anything foolish, halbtroll. Like do yourself further injury.::

Bocan snorted and flipped off the snowy owl, who gave a hoot of laughter.

The moment of levity helped, which he was sure

was Serena's intention. His arm still ached like ten trolls were pounding it into steel, but the tension in his belly felt looser now.

Inhale. Exhale. Center. Focus.

Focus on his comrade, who needed his help right now, even if that help meant his best attempt at knocking per to the ground.

Tegan looked so small and fierce in the center of the circle. Ready, waiting, with Starlight at per side.

He felt the drake's first burst of flame almost before he heard it. It sounded as if a giant was working the blacksmith's bellows. The flame raced toward Tegan with a whoosh.

Tegan threw up a kpinga and channeled the fire down the blade and back toward the drake. The return volley didn't go very far, but the knots of hair on per head remained unsinged, so he guessed that was good. Maybe Tegan would get through this testing after all.

Before Tegan could fully recover, Abyad sent a gust of wind to batter per. Dirt eddied and twisted. The backdraft caught Bocan, and he braced himself against the onslaught.

Tegan dodged and wove, dancing like a dervish in the wind, face grim and determined. The wind whipped up shards of dirt and pebbles that stung Bocan's skin and battered Tegan's face.

At Tegan's feet, the lynx growled and braced herself, as if one animal could face down the wind, forcing it to cease. Then Starlight leapt forth, racing toward the djinn, whether to bite Abyad or cause him to...there. He dodged out of Starlight's way, and a blast of wind went wide, shaking the apple trees at the edge of the horse paddock.

The djinni quickly recovered and flung another blast toward Tegan.

Per held up both weapons, bouncing wind and stones off hard metal, but Bocan could tell Tegan was struggling already. Tiring. Fighting with magic took as much muscle as fighting with steel, but until one was used to it, fighting with magic drew on resources that could tap a person out as quickly as a blow to the head.

Hakim L'Ouverture motioned with his staff. It was Bocan's turn.

"Gods of Earth and Stone, be with me," he prayed. "Help me test my comrade Tegan without harming per."

Bocan reached deep into the earth beneath his feet. And then deeper still. Past the bedrock upon which the town of Go No More was built. Deeper and deeper his energy traveled, seeking out the magic held in soil and stone.

He felt the collective breath of the people gathered around him. They inhaled, and then paused, just as he inhaled himself, pausing before exhaling. The rumbling began.

The watchers jerked and swayed, yelping as the earth bucked and rolled beneath them.

Bocan held firm even though his arm throbbed and using his magic in this way made his head feel as if it would be crushed. The pulse of magic was still too much for his body and mind to bear; he had to learn to channel this earth power without it killing him the way it had almost killed him at New Salem.

He shoved more magic outward, feeling the ripples echo through the earth. His eyes rolled with the effort, his resolve weakening. The rumbling decreased. Tegan yelled, teeth bared, standing firm, barely touched by Earth, which was not right.

Tegan's task was to take each element, incorporate it, and use it. Make it part of her own magic.

Bocan saw now per was failing. Tegan had deflected both fire and air and stood barely touched by earth.

Hakim L'Ouverture shook his head.

Oh, the trick per had done sending the fire back to Karaktilla was a start, but not good enough. Not to get through whatever battle was coming. Not if they were to break the princess out from Underhill.

They all needed to be at full strength. And Bocan certainly was not. And since Bocan could not do this thing? Tegan had to. Which meant his comrade must be tested.

Tegan must. Not. Fail.

He drew in breath. Reached past the pain. Past the roaring in his ears. Past the wind and the fire and the water gathering in clouds overhead. Bocan had to do this thing. He centered again, raised his one good arm, and called upon the powers.

"Gods of earth and stone! Move through me. Be with me. Every troll and every rock. Every mountain. Every glacier that ever passed through this land. Ancient ones. Underground dwellers. All of you, please, heed my call. Be with me. Test my comrade, Tegan. Pour through me... Stone of stone. Rock of rock. Earth of earth. Flesh of flesh. I am here. I am Bocan. Half human, half troll, one with the earth!"

And the rumbling began again, this time in earnest. Bocan gritted through the pain, Starlight nipping at his boots, Serena circling overhead.

And Tegan, body shaking as the earth rolled, weapons raised...

CHAPTER 48

CASE

The dragoons were on horseback.

His big brown mare, Pie Face, was a beautiful, good-natured animal, and his saddle was comfortable enough, but this still was not Case's favorite way to travel. He far preferred the rumble of steel between his thighs and the speed of the road. While Pie Face could gallop just fine when needed, there was no galloping to be done on these narrow, wooded trails, green with spring growth and alive with the soft trills and calls of birds.

But horseback through the woods it was because the scouts wanted to do reconnaissance of the surrounding area, and that meant diving into places where the hogs wouldn't go.

So here he was, with an elf he didn't trust riding pillion at his back. At least it wasn't the alchemist. Jerrod was stuck with that pig fucker. They had drawn straws and Jerrod had lost.

Haryath and Amarpal were in the lead, their

sumac-colored turbans, dyed to match their leathers, bobbing up ahead.

Who knew where Jessie and Litha were? Scouts were always scouting. He just hoped they were within whistling distance because Case didn't trust the forest around the gate. They still didn't know who had made the thing, and after the wyverns and trolls attacking so close to home? If those Unseelie fucks could come through temporary gates, who knew what might already be moving through this more permanent one.

"So much for Magic's Bane shutting down the gate at Wimal falls." He shook his head. They'd all been so naive. Thinking their troubles with Underhill were over. That the soul stealing would cease. That there would be no more permanent gates erected within a day's ride of Go No More.

And look how all of that had turned out.

Case sighed. At least it wasn't raining. His waxed hemp canvas cape and hood remained stuffed into one of Pie Face's saddlebags, with a spare for the elf, though frankly, Peridot could fuck himself and die of a cold, for all Case cared.

Pie Face gave him a look over her shoulder as though telling Case to settle down.

"Sorry girl," he murmured, and forced himself to relax and breathe more easily. Sure enough, his thighs had started pressing into her sides. Making her antsy. Case couldn't help it. He would rather be back in Go No More, supporting Tegan. Per was undergoing some sort of test the djinni and the mages had decided per needed, which was bison shit as far as Case was concerned.

Tegan was the best of them. Per didn't need this headache on top of everything else that was going on. But that purple drake and Anandita had concurred, saying they'd seen something or other in the drake's damned crystal ball.

And Tegan had been shouting something about being a warrior mage during the battle with the wyverns. Which was troubling as shit. So, Case couldn't wave it away, much as he wanted to.

A blond head emerged from a narrow pathway up ahead, bouncing at a trot. Litha, the head scout. She was followed by Wasco apprentice Jessie, who had a much smoother seat. But then, the Wasco were horse experts, and she had likely been in saddle since before she could walk.

"What do you see?" Amarpal asked, slowing her horse. Case reined back Pie Face, making room for the two scouts on the trail. The small group of dragoons all paused.

"Tracks," Litha said. "Large." She sluiced some water down her throat, squeezing it from the leather skin they all wore strapped to themselves somewhere.

"What kind of tracks?" Amarpal asked, voice purposefully patient. Case stifled a grin. He knew the Sikhs both had spiritual training as rigorous as their physical training, but even they had to fight petty things like impatience sometimes.

"Sasquatch," Jessie said.

"Sasquatch?" Jerrod chimed in. "Are you fucking kidding me now?"

Case thought he'd heard tell of those creatures but had never seen one. But after the wyverns, anything was possible, he supposed.

Litha snorted and shook her head in disagreement.

"This was a group of tracks. Everyone knows Sasquatch travel singly," she said, turning to Jessie.

Jessie shrugged. "I saw what I saw. Those footprints were big. And humanoid."

"What else could it be?" Case asked.

Peridot's voice came from behind his shoulder. "Trolls."

Litha looked past Case, at the elf, gaze intent. "What would you know about that, elf?"

"I know that Unseelie trolls attacked Go No More a few days ago and now you see big prints. So, what else am I supposed to think?"

The elf's words made sense, but made Case feel uneasy, nonetheless. He turned in the saddle, one hand shooting out to grasp the clothing beneath Peridot's chin, dragging their faces too close for comfort.

"If you know something about this and aren't telling us..."

The elf met his gaze, barely flinching.

"I know. I'm dead. But I'm dead already. So, what does it matter?"

That was certainly not reassuring. Case gripped tighter. The elf's snowy skin flushed, and his breath rasped.

"Case," Haryath said, voice sharp with warning.

He released the elf and turned around as Jerrod sidled his horse up next to him, Carondel riding pillion and looking slightly ill.

"What do you think, alchemist?" Litha asked.

Carondel looked around, eyes skimming the firs and spruces, pausing for a moment on a downy woodpecker before returning to Litha, who simply waited. That scout was more patient than Case would ever be.

"I think this is all very bad," Carondel replied. "Queen Silverhair has never before treated with the Unseelie. To do so now..."

Case scoffed. "As if you gilded-arse fuckers are any better than the Unseelie. As if the Queen hasn't done enough damage on her own. As if I haven't myself seen whole villages dead, marked with her seal. And you..."

Case cut off his words, blood boiling. He needed to calm down or the mission to get these two pig fuckers to the gate unharmed was going to fail. Because he was going to kill the alchemist in his stained green robes.

Carondel pursed his lips. "You are not wrong. But don't you see? The Queen always had a line before. To not work with the Unseelie Court. Oh, they had an uneasy truce, to be sure. Because otherwise how would anyone live? But to form an active alliance, and now Unseelie creatures walk for the first time in human realms? This is bad. Very bad."

"I don't get it," Jerrod said, keeping his voice dry. "Explain it to me like I was a child."

The alchemist looked from face to face, brow furrowed, looking as if he was weighing his words.

"Spit it out, elf, or we will get it out of you at the

point of a blade." Case's words were bitter. Angry. And he did not care. These gold-arsed pig fuckers were stealing away every chance the people of Go No More had to live in peace. Just when they thought things were getting better, things went to shit again.

Case was sick unto death of it all.

"The Seelie..." the alchemist began. "So far, the Seelie are the only ones who have had the magical technology to open permanent gates between the human realms and theirs. And that is only because of millennia of human, fey, and elf alliances. In the times when the realms were sequestered, there were still humans who decided to work with the Seelie and their ilk, and vice versa. This allowed for the gates to open. But now, Post-Reckoning, as you call it..."

"We know the history." Case's face and neck were hot, and his right hand itched to punch something. "What I care about right now is that these Unseelie fuckers now have free access to our homes. Because of your fracked-earth queen."

Carondel looked ill. "It appears that might be true, though I still hope not. I hope that the Seelie are opening the gates and allowing the Unseelie through."

"And how is that any better?" Jessie spat. The young apprentice's face was dark with anger and fear.

"I know you do not want to believe this," Carondel said, "but trust me. It's far better than the Unseelie having access themselves. Because once they do..."

He traded a look with Peridot.

"Once they do, what?" Case snapped.

"We're all dead." Peridot's answer hung in the air

like a dust mote in a watery sunbeam. The only sounds came from birds, and the horses' harnesses as the beasts shifted slightly, anxious to be on their way.

Haryath broke the silence. "All right," the Sikh said. "Did you see any other signs of them? These possible trolls?"

"Sasquatch," mumbled Jessie. Haryath gave the apprentice a sharp look. Both Jessie and Litha shook their heads.

"Just one grouping of tracks, headed toward the stream," Litha said.

Haryath nodded, exchanging a look with his sister, Amarpal.

"One of us has to go back," Amarpal said. "And warn Go No More they might be at risk of a second attack."

"While the rest of us," Case finished the sentence, "get these two pig fuckers Underhill, and figure out if we can get the princess out."

At this moment, it didn't seem like much of a plan. But it was the only plan they had.

Haryath consulted with one of the other Knights, who nodded, then whirled her horse around, heading back to the township.

"Do we need a different pathway?" Jerrod asked.

Litha nodded. "There's a branching just up ahead. That should take us out of the path of the trolls if they're still around and get us to the gate in good time."

"Lead on," Case said to Litha, and the scouts

turned their mounts around and began trotting through the forest.

Case made a clicking noise, urging Pie Face forward as well.

They were heading into danger, that much was sure. But exactly what kind of danger? He did not know. All he knew was if any more of his comrades died, these elf fuckers would pay.

He touched the amulet at his breastbone and sent a thought to Tegan, wishing per strength, then set his focus on the path ahead.

CHAPTER 49

PERIDOT

The djinni and that bitch of a Raven Priestess had done something to curtail Peridot's magic. He had submitted to the djinn's arcane mumbling and hand gestures, figuring that a djinn's magic would not hold much sway over magic born Underhill. Damson? Damson could lock him up and throw away the key. But a simple air djinn?

Sure, he had felt the pressure in his skull, but thought that was just the probing of strange magic. He was wrong.

Peridot tried to reach out several times, en route into the forest, and been quickly thwarted. It was as if his energy bounced back to him, or he was swaddled in cloth.

He could still feel his magic and he knew he had access to the basics, but enough magic to form a gate on his own? No. Even establishing the smallest, temporary seam in the fabric of things was beyond his current abilities.

So, he sat impatient on the back of this stinking brown horse behind this Steel Clan Knight who clearly hated his guts.

Well, that was fine. Peridot and Case had never been close, even before Peridot had betrayed those who called him friend. That made this easier.

Damson wasn't here. Neither were Jenny or Tegan. And the trolls that he had called friend were also back at Go No More. Testing Tegan in some strange ordeal that he did not quite understand.

"Warrior mage," he muttered to the wind. He had never heard of such a thing, except in ancient legends passed down by some of the Seelie historians. Those legends said that once upon a time there were humans who were equal to the elves in magic and cunning.

Peridot had never believed it. Humans had always seemed so weak to him. So fragile. With their short lifespans, and their illnesses, and all the rest. But he had also seen enough just recently to prove that humans had more power than that.

Who knew? He still had to decide on a plan, and where his loyalties lay. His heart and souls told him to throw his lot in with his longing. And his longing was for the camaraderie of Go No More. Perhaps he could acquit himself well enough on this mission to gain a place back among them. Even a tentative place would be a start.

He weighed his options and once again found that attempting to curry Silverhair's good graces no longer held any appeal. The court was boring at best, and a nest of vipers at worst. And the Queen? She might just as well see him dead as continue to use him as a spy.

Upon entry to Underhill, hopefully Silverhair would believe that he still worked for her. He had information aplenty to impart in case he was brought before her. But would he be? Or would he be immediately imprisoned, even killed?

His gut roiled with the tension of it all. Peridot found that for the first time since his best friend and lover, Damson, had been forced to torture him, that he was afraid. Afraid of what might come. Afraid he would not be up to the task.

But he had to try. Had to try to save the humans and the princess, whom he frankly did not care much about. Elzabetta had always struck him simply as a spoiled, pampered brat that everyone fawned over, though she was sickly and held no real power.

But saving her? The humans said she was the key to saving the realms. Peridot still wasn't certain exactly what that entailed because he was not privy to most of their plans.

He only knew his part, and even that was vague, other than the aim. His job was to get in and do reconnaissance, and perhaps to question Queen Silverhair under the guise of proffering information. False information, of course. Though hopefully she would not scent that on his skin.

Peridot was to do all of this while the alchemist snuck in behind him to do some research on his own.

It was Carondel's job to approach the princess and

see if she was in agreement and readiness to depart Underhill.

He only hoped they both were up to the task. But there was no telling what would happen once they were through the gate. The gate that someone Underhill had built. The gate that was letting Unseelie creatures roam free.

Grimmer times he had never seen, and never hoped to see again.

He felt a pang of conscience that he had been a part of bringing these times to bear, of loosing a greater evil upon all the realms.

As if he could feel Peridot's tension, Case turned his head and spoke over his shoulder.

"You okay back there, elf?"

"Fine," Peridot replied, "just tired of being on horseback."

Case nodded. "We're almost there. Then we'll be rid of each other, have no fear."

Peridot wished his discomfort had to do only with riding pillion behind an enemy, a man who hated and mistrusted him.

But it was the unknown he was walking into that caused his discomfort. And the fear that perhaps he was the enemy himself.

CHAPTER 50

SILVERHAIR

Silverhair paced the vast throne room, with its large, curved windows framed in blond wood. Her sage-green skirts swirled past the flowing sculptures made to look like trees, with sprites and birds alighting in the branches.

She paused only to look up at the portrait of her husband. Her one love besides her daughter.

But her daughter had lived to disappoint Silverhair. Her husband's only disappointment to her was his untimely death. That wound still gnawed at her heart. But she could afford no weakness now.

With a breath, she steadied her mind and paced on.

The Holly King's plan had made Silverhair feel slightly ill at first, but the more she pondered and the more they plotted, the more excited she became.

A frisson of pleasure filled her limbs. She had not felt such energy since she was Elzabetta's age, and certainly not in the years since her beloved husband had been slaughtered long before his time.

Yes. This alliance between herself and the Holly King was far better than any marriage between daughter and son. Silverhair would maintain her full power, working with the Unseelie king as equals. And she would have use of Unseelie creatures of great and terrifying power.

But first, she needed to shore up the plan with a trusted confidant.

She could not trust Elzabetta's guard. Not anymore. She had trusted him once, but recently noticed a change in the way Tarioc looked upon her daughter. It was not the look of a lover, but almost worse. It was the look of a mentor or a friend. She could not trust that he did not fill Elzabetta's head with dreams, making her child want more than what was her lot.

Whom would she speak with? Whom could she trust?

Betrayal was everywhere Underhill. The Queen herself had cultivated that in recent years. She had found it best to not let any courtier feel too comfortable with their morsels of power. But after she herself had been so badly betrayed, any alliance she formed among her own people would be uneasy.

The Holly King himself, she knew she could not trust. They both knew it and would act accordingly. That alone promised a measure of security. Seelie and Unseelie would keep each other in check. That was the only way to consolidate their power.

Her own people, though? Who had the skills

needed to negotiate and help her plan? And who could be properly bribed to have her back?

She looked out one of the large, arched windows, gazing for a moment at the orchard just outside. Blossom. Leaf. Fruit. The way of the elven trees. All cycles Underhill came all at once, in a dance of fertility and temporary death.

Until recently, as rot slowly crept in from the edges, seeking out the center where she stood. The rot she had hoped to arrest by forcing her daughter to heal.

She saw how wrong that was now. She could not force Elzabetta to be whole. It was Elzabetta's fragmentation that she would use now, slowly draining her daughter's life force to accomplish what must be done.

She needed more magic for the battles sure to come.

And Elzabetta was just the one to provide it.

Now, who would help her fashion the future of the realm?

Silverhair resumed her pacing, walking past the empty thrones, barely noticing the spark of light hidden against the cushion of her own chair.

CHAPTER 51
TEGAN

Starlight stumbled, big furry paws scrabbling for purchase as the dirt ring tilted once again.

Tegan pushed off the dirt, regaining per feet, and braced against the rolling of the earth just as another blast from Karaktilla's mighty wedge-shaped head hit again. Abyad's wind caught the edge of per kpinga, almost wrenching it from Tegan's hand.

Starlight raced from challenger to challenger, doing her best to distract them as Tegan whirled and danced, fighting and deflecting, parrying and dodging.

::That is not what you are meant to do, child of mine.:: Tegan felt Mboli's voice within. The spirit of water, the flow of all things.

A lick of flame singed one of the knots on per head as a gust of wind slammed into Tegan's back, rocking per just as a mighty shake of earth came from below.

Tegan was failing and knew it. What did Mboli mean? What was the way?

Tegan fought to regain center. Fought to tap the magic seated in her souls. But the warrior instinct was too strong.

To attack and deflect, and to integrate the lessons, learn your enemy. Danika had said that to Tegan when Tegan was but an apprentice. To learn the enemy, you must practice the techniques of the enemy, eventually integrating them into your own.

A blast of earth power slammed upward, jarring Tegan's bones. Per hit hard, falling to the right knee, teeth snapping down, Tegan tasted blood. A gust of wind rocked per back on per heel as Karaktilla bellowed out another blast of fire.

Braced on one foot and one knee, riding the bucking earth, Tegan raised machete and kpinga to block the flame.

Per inhaled, fighting not to cough, breathing in the fire. The air. Kneeling there on the rolling ground, buffeted by wild winds, Tegan fought. Fought down per instincts. Fought down per own nature. Tegan tried. Tried to open. Open to the fire. To breathe it in. To drink it in. To let it flow through. Per felt fire meet water, and it was good.

Tegan swore. Per hurt. Badly. Mboli laughed inside per skull, as heat and cool wet twined within per, their magics feeding each other.

"Ha!" Tegan cried out through the pain. Maybe per could do this after all. With a wild grin on per face, Tegan leapt to per boots once again. Per could do this.

"Warrior mage!" Tegan shouted. "Warrior mage!"

And then the earth exploded beneath per feet. Tegan heard Bocan bellow and then scream. Per head whipped around to see per comrade fall as a burst of air ripped both blades from Tegan's hands.

The earth shook one more time. Per weapons flew in the wind. The machete pommel cracked against Tegan's skull.

Tegan fell, hitting hard, and lay panting, feeling the fire and water rolling together inside of per. And outside, felt air and earth crashing and clashing, until finally, the rumbling stopped, and the air stilled.

Per head throbbed. Per mouth was filled with blood. Fire and water ran through Tegan's veins. Per could taste their magic. Taste the possibility of more.

And yet, Tegan had failed the test. Tegan was not a Warrior Mage. Tegan was simply what Tegan had been before: a Knight of the Steel Clan, and a human with some magic. Just like the rest of per comrades.

Per groaned and rolled over, trying to sit up. Jenny ran toward Tegan and knelt, "Comrade. Are you okay? What happened?"

"I failed," Tegan replied. "That's what happened. Help me up."

Jenny held out one hand, clasping Tegan's forearm and pulling per upright onto unsteady feet.

"You're going to have a knot," Jenny said.

"No kidding," Tegan replied.

Charles Wong and Aphrodite walked toward per, looking resigned. Was that a flash of disappointment in their eyes? No matter. Tegan looked at Aphrodite.

"Well, that only half worked. What is next?"

Abyad was at per side. "You did not integrate." His voice was flat.

"No shit? Pig fucker," Tegan replied.

::*Knight. Come to me.*:: Great. Now the drake wanted to rub it in, too.

"Guess I have to talk to the big lizard now." Tegan sighed and turned toward the purple-scaled beast.

"I suppose we all should do that," Abyad remarked.

Tegan rolled per eyes at the djinn, then winced at the pain. Per sheathed the machete and tucked the kpinga into the straps on per back, then squinted toward the drake, who had a wisp of smoke curling from one nostril. Weird.

"Okay. Let's get this part over with."

Tegan limped toward Karaktilla, Jenny at per side, but en route, per realized Bocan was still on the ground. His partner, the mind healer Jimena, crouched over him. Anandita was in her chair to one side. Both healers seem to be engaged in something or other. Jimena's hands rested on the halbtroll's temples as Anandita dug a small pot of something from a bag carried on her lap.

Tegan looked at Jenny. "Will Bocan be okay?"

Jenny shook her head. "I don't know. I hope so. The big oaf keeps overdoing it, no matter what we tell him."

"Well, Tegan said, voice dry, "the mages here thought it was a good idea for him to practice his magic again."

"We thought it would be safe," Charles Wong

remarked. "How were we to know he would injure himself with magic?"

Tegan threw up per hands. They were at the drake by this point. Taken looked up at the giant purple triangle wedge of a head with its slow blinking eyes and shimmering scales.

A light rain began to fall. Tegan tilted per head back, welcoming the cool wet. Per would prefer a shower and then to soak the aches from per bones in the bathhouse, but for now? The rain would do.

"Drake," Tegan said, "I failed."

::You did not fail, Knight.:: The drake clicked and clacked her jaws, but the words sounded English inside Tegan's head. *::You have both fire and water within you now, and are stronger than before.::*

Tegan frowned. "Yes, but I thought that wasn't good enough. Not to face Silverhair's people and whatever Unseelie shit she decides to unleash...and then get the princess out."

It wasn't that the Steel Clan and the mages couldn't fight the queen and her guard. They had done it before. It was that this time the Queen was well prepared. And this time they intended to steal something far more precious than a halbtroll's human mother. Stealing elven royalty was a different trick and required all the magic, strength, and cunning they could muster.

"What's next?" Jenny asked.

::I have a plan,:: Karaktilla replied.

"I hope it's a good one," Tegan said. "But can I bathe and eat first?"

Karaktilla made a strange clacking and rumbling noise that Tegan took for laughter.

::Very well. You and your comrades do what you must. I shall remain here and speak with these two mages.::

"You do that," Tegan replied, weary to the bone. Per turned to Jenny. "Let's go see how Bocan is. And then I really need a fucking bath."

CHAPTER 52

ELZABETTA

There was a scratching outside the window.

Tarioc motioned Elzabetta to be quiet. She sat still in her padded chair and watched. The tall elf crept soft as a cat on his green leather boots toward the large wooden-framed arches where white curtains billowed in the soft, apple-scented breeze.

Blade in hand, he peered through a gap between the curtain and the window frame, then reached through the open casement to grab what was beyond.

Elzabetta stifled a gasp and heard a strangled whisper.

"Do not hurt me. I have come with a message for the princess."

"Carondel?" she asked, recognizing the voice, even distorted as it was by Tarioc's grip on the alchemist's collar. The warrior snapped his head towards her.

"You know this fiend?"

Elzabetta sighed.

"Of course, I do. And you do as well. It's Mother's

pet alchemist. Or he was," she said, crossing the floor toward the window. Tarioc held up one pale hand to stop her, then sheathed his blade and dragged the alchemist over the windowsill, dropping him on the floor with an unceremonious thump.

The alchemist looked aggrieved, and a flash of anger crossed his eyes but was soon extinguished. He looked gaunt. Much thinner than when she had seen him last, and more ragged. Also, there were no stains upon his fingertips from his vile experiments. He looked almost browbeaten, sorrowful, if such emotions were possible for one who had done the things he had done.

She hardened herself against him. The alchemist's experiments on her and the scores of humans whose souls he had helped her mother steal would not be easily forgotten or forgiven.

Tarioc reached through the curtains and shut the window, latching it firmly.

He pulled his blade again, pointing it at Carondel's throat.

"Rise," he said.

The alchemist complied, smoothing down his tunic and setting himself to rights.

"Turn. Hands upon the wall," Tarioc commanded.

Carondel complied, which was astonishing. Elzabetta had never seen the alchemist so cowed by anyone besides her mother. His fire was gone. His arrogance too. He was a broken elf. Elisabetta wondered what he had seen in his time outside of Underhill. What had happened to make him so?

Once Tarioc was satisfied that Carondel was unarmed, he raised an eyebrow toward Elzabetta.

"It is fine, Tarioc. He is fine. Thank you. Let him sit."

Tarioc looked to stand guard behind the alchemist's chair.

"Let us all sit," Elzabetta insisted.

"I do not think that is wise, Princess. I would prefer to keep to my feet."

She inclined her head. Tarioc gazed back steadily.

It seemed that Elzabetta would not win this battle, and it was likely he knew best.

"Very well," she said. "Come, Carondel. Tell us why you are here."

The alchemist shifted nervously in his chair, glancing at Tarioc.

"You can trust Tarioc as well as you can trust anyone," Elzabetta replied. "If he cannot be trusted, I am already lost."

"Besides, elf," Tarioc spat, "it is I who do not trust you. Speak if you are going to, or be gone."

Elzabetta shut her lips, impatient with the drama, but she also could not blame the warrior. She did not trust Carondel at all, yet they did need to know why he was here and looking chastised. But the fact remained that both of their positions were precarious. And if the Queen found out Tarioc had disobeyed her orders? He would be dead or exiled in a trice.

"Carondel," Elzabetta said again, voice firm with command. "Tell me why you are here."

Carondel cleared his throat. "Might I trouble you for a cup of water?"

"Out with it," Tarioc spat.

"Tarioc," Elzabetta's voice was lined with metal, "please get Carondel a goblet of water."

Tarioc scowled at the alchemist—he knew better than to scowl at her—but crossed the room and poured water from a pitcher into a goblet nonetheless, setting it down with a click on the small table near the alchemist.

Being princess had its power, when she remembered to use it.

Carondel drank thirstily, cleared his throat again, and finally looked at her. Truly looked at her, as if seeing her for the first time, which was strange since he had known her since she was a swaddled babe. She wondered if he had ceased to look at her because he was ashamed.

"I have come with a message from the Steel Clan."

Elzabetta furrowed her brow.

"I do not understand. Who are they?"

"Human knights?" Tarioc interjected. "They wear blood red and are the ones who stole..."

"Yes," Carondel interjected. "The large halbtroll stole his his human mother from my laboratory before I was even done."

Elzabetta was filled with sudden fury.

"How. Dare. You?" She wished her eyes were weapons, to slice the alchemist to ribbons.

He looked down at his lap, having the grace to look ashamed at least.

"I apologize, princess," he said. "What I did to you…it was a terrible thing. I never should have complied. I should have chosen death over that. I know that now, though…sometimes I still forget. The magic calls me, and your mother? Still holds sway. She imprinted something in my souls to make me wish to do her bidding. I have tried to break this but have not had full success."

"I'll be happy to break whatever is necessary," Tarioc muttered.

Carondel and Elzabetta both ignored her guardian. Carondel held his eyes on hers, as if forcing himself. She held his gaze right back.

"I cannot say it is all right, Carondel, because it is not. Nothing shall ever replace the lives of those who were stolen. And nothing can make the torture I endured at your hand a thing that shall ever be right. But you did not come here to speak to me of such things. Did you? No. You would not have risked it. You have another mission."

She leaned forward in her chair, anger displaced by a quickening excitement. "Tell us what this mission is."

"We wish to help you escape, Princess, if that is what you desire."

A frisson of heat raced up her spine and set her cheeks to bloom. Her heart raced. Her palms grew wet. But her throat was dry.

"Water, please, Tarioc."

He looked at her with concern and raced to fill a goblet, placing it directly into her hands. She drank deeply and gave a delicate cough. Would freedom finally become possible? She barely dared to hope it. Barely dared to pray. But in her heart, she found, she longed for it with all her might.

She and Tarioc had spoken of such things, but she had never believed it was truly possible. And now help had come from outside.

"Tell us more," she said.

Tarioc stalked forward and, hooking his long fingers on a chair, he placed it near the other two, forming a small triangle. Finally, he sat.

"Yes. Tell us, alchemist. How do you propose to do such a thing?"

The alchemist took another sip of his own water and looked from Tarioc to herself.

"There is a plan. It is risky."

Elzabetta waved her hand. "Everything is risky, is it not?"

"True, Princess." The alchemist gave her a considering look. "You have grown wise in my absence."

"I have grown wise," she said, "because I am no longer exhausted from torture."

He winced as if she had slapped him.

"Yes. Yes. I can see that now," he said. "I am heartily sorry...."

Elzabetta held up a hand, finished with his apologetic stalling.

"Stop. Tell us what brought you here and tell us what must be done. Now."

CHAPTER 53

TEGAN

The water wasn't hot enough to soak away Tegan's exhaustion, but it felt good all the same, as did being clean. Nothing like a good scrub in the showers followed by a soak in one of the three large common tubs in the big bathhouse room.

Per sat in the steaming tub with Jenny and Bocan, tending to per bruised body and mind as well as a bruised sense of pride.

"I failed," Tegan said for the tenth time.

Jenny rolled her eyes. "Come on, Tegan. You didn't fail. Karaktilla said you were able to integrate fire with the water just fine."

"Yeah, but what about the other two?" Tegan muttered, still stung. "Didn't want to be a warrior mage in the first place."

"Good," Jenny said. "Now you're off the hook."

Tegan scowled at per comrade. "Off the hook doesn't save the princess. Off the hook doesn't get the job done."

Bocan groaned. "Can you talk more softly? Please? My head feels like Feldspar put me between the hammer and the anvil."

"Can you take up less space, you oaf?" Jenny quipped

The halbtroll splashed at Jenny, who just laughed.

"You're a strapping woman, and large yourself."

"I still don't displace as much water as you," Jenny shot back.

Tegan had to agree. Per also was in no mood for per comrades' verbal sparring. The new magic inside was disconcerting and making per irritable: fire and water, swimming around as if they owned some part of Tegan's body. Or per souls.

But Tegan didn't want to talk about that. Ever.

"I think you should show a little respect for those of us who were injured," per said.

"Yeah, show some respect," Bocan grumbled.

"What happened to you out there, anyway?" Jenny asked him. "I was watching, and you were pretty careful to not use your injured arm."

"Jimena thinks the magic at the Battle of New Salem did something to my brain. Injured it somehow."

"Well, that explains a lot," Tegan grumbled.

Jenny sat up, splashing water over the side of the tub, and shot Tegan a quelling look before turning her concern to Bocan. "What? How did we not know this?"

Bocan shrugged, clearly uncomfortable. "Jimena and Doc Warren both said such things can mask themselves. If a person is injured enough...they can seem fine, but the next strain can make things suddenly worse.”

Tegan felt a pang at per own self-absorption. Per knew Bocan was injured, but figured it was just like anything else. A Knight got through it. Or they retired.

“And you think that’s what happened?” Jenny asked. “When you were channeling out there today?”

“Yes,” Bocan said, running his good hand over his face, wiping away the sweat.

Tegan didn’t know why he bothered. The steam would only replace the moisture within a few seconds.

“I must have hit my head in New Salem when I was out of it, thrashing around on the ground.”

“You probably hit it repeatedly,” Jenny said. “The ground was really shaking, and you were lying directly on top of it.”

Per comrade nodded slowly, wincing from the pain.

“Yeah. When the earth moved through me again, I felt woozy, and then I blacked out and fell.”

“Did you hit your head again?” Tegan asked.

He shrugged. “I don’t know. All I know is my eyes aren’t focusing very well.”

And his speech was slightly slurred. Tegan had chalked that up to being tired, but now wondered if it wasn’t something else. He spoke as if his tongue was thick, and his words came more slowly than usual. Never a quick talker, Bocan, but he wasn’t usually thick-tongued like this, either.

“So, what’s the alternate plan?” Jenny asked. “You’re out of it, clearly, and likely shouldn’t come with us Underhill.

Bocan sank more deeply into the water. "I don't know. Jimena thinks she can work with me between now and then. Stabilize things. And Doc Warren has exercises she wants me to do."

"Well, fuck a pig," Tegan said. "You might be out of commission, and I'm not as useful as the drakes and mages hoped. At this rate, I don't even know how we're going to get through the gate and get Elzabetta out."

"Well, we have to hope that Peridot and Carondel are able to help with that," Jenny replied, looking sweaty and unconvinced.

"You trust them?" Tegan said.

"Gods of Earth and Stone, no," Bocan said. "Who could, after what they've done? But..."

"But they're all we've got," Jenny finished.

"But don't the mages think the gate will be fortified?" Tegan asked. Per exhaustion, coupled with the lazy heat finally penetrating per muscles, must have addled per thoughts. There was something per wasn't following.

Jenny grinned and rubbed her hands together, the twin moon orbs of her breasts bobbing as she moved.

"Well, there's a little something I haven't been telling you."

"What, you pig fucker?" Tegan said, though there was no heat to per words. Per was too tired and wrung out to make good on any threats anyway. Not unless the danger was real. And then per would kick ass, and after? Crash harder than a motorcycle tripped by a troll's foot.

"Karaktilla is calling in the drakes again." Jenny looked smug as a cat.

"The drakes?" Tegan quirked an eyebrow. "And what are they going to do? Storm Underhill?"

"Pretty much." Jenny was practically bouncing in the big tub. "They plan to blast it open and you're going to help. You know, directing the fire with your..."

She waved her big white arms, tattoos shifting and twining as she made what Tegan supposed were meant to be magical gestures.

Now it was Tegan's turn to roll per eyes, but inside, the fire and water moving through Tegan grew still as if listening. Attentive.

"And if that doesn't work," Jenny continued, "Karaktilla says they'll use their claws. Mess Underhill right up."

Tegan barely heard per comrade. The water inside per skin called to the water surrounding them all.

Mboli. The flow. Tegan knew the God—or whatever per ancestors had called him—was there. In the room. Watching. Listening. Being.

All right then, Tegan thought, as Jenny and Bocan discussed possible strategies. *If you are one with everything...then if you're in me, then I ought to be too. So why did I fail?*

The water did not answer. Tegan sighed, and decided Bocan had the right idea. His mouth and nose barely cleared the top of the water. Per sank more deeply, hoping the water would soothe per troubled thoughts the way it had eased per muscles and bruised flesh.

"I'm going to soak until I'm wrinkled," per announced. "And then I'm going to eat everything in Jaimie and Porrac's kitchen."

"Don't your mothers want to see you?" Jenny asked.

Tegan groaned and began re-twisting the knots on per head. Per had washed away the drake-singed bits and now needed to repair what was left. "I had dinner with them two days ago. Besides, I can't bear their worry. I'm going to tell them I have meetings."

"That will go over well," Jenny said.

"I'm a Knight of the fucking Steel Clan," Tegan replied, fingers tugging and twisting, neatening up the rows. "What are they going to do? Tie me up?"

"They are your mothers," Bocan said, eyes closed like a cat relaxing in the heat. "They can probably do whatever they please."

And now it was Tegan's turn to smile. Per had to admit it felt good.

Tegan didn't know it would be per last smile for quite some time.

CHAPTER 54

PERIDOT

The stone walls were lit by flickering flames set into niches in the walls. Surrounded by reflective copper, the warm light made pleasant pockets in the gloomy corridor. Peridot's boots were silent on the flagstone floors as he walked deeper into the place where elven courtiers never tread.

There was one advantage to being trained as a spy. Peridot knew many secrets. He knew things that elves would kill him for. He knew things that elves would pay good coin for.

He also knew things that would open doors that a prudent person would best keep shut fast and barred.

Queen Silverhair, it turned out, had met worryingly long with the Holly King in his Unseelie realm. This fact disturbed Peridot, and explained the appearance of the wyverns and Unseelie trolls. It also meant that Peridot needed to tread even more carefully to avoid her notice. If Silverhair were forming an alliance with the Unseelie court, any scruples she had left were long gone, and he did not wish to face her.

What those two were plotting could not be good. He was better quit of her court forever.

Peridot had learned much over each moonrise and sunset in the human realms. Mostly, he had learned to take what advantages were offered. His choice was now clear. If life Underhill were no longer tenable, he would throw in his lot with the humans of Go No More.

He stole deep into the bowels of Underhill. A place for servants and craftspeople, for trolls and sprites, hobs, and other humble folk.

It was also a place well used by those who had much to hide.

He continued down the passageway, past plain, dark wood doors, and further corridors branching left and right. Finally, the flickering flames showed him what he sought: a well-used door carved with a closed fist wreathed in laurel.

One would not notice the carving in passing. It was remarkable only if one knew the way, and what to look for.

Peridot rapped smartly on the wood thrice. Then paused. Then thrice again. Then paused. Then thrice again.

He stepped back to wait, hand on blade, ready to stab out should needs be.

The figure who opened the door was hooded, their face in shadow, but Peridot knew their form.

"Jacobus," he said.

"You should not be here." The other elf's voice was low, and wary.

"I must. I must speak to you and to the others."

"Do you agree to a Truth Teller?"

Peridot swore inside but had expected no less.

"I do."

"Enter." Jacobus stepped back and opened the door wide, showing Peridot a glimpse of a stone room hung with tapestries. He stepped into a space well-lit with candles backed by more of the clever metal frames. The room was filled with half a dozen elves of varied genders.

Not a one looked pleased to see him.

"What is he doing here?" Sapphire spat. There had always been acrimony between them. Sapphire had never looked kindly upon Peridot's face, even before she figured out he was a spy.

"Truth Teller Veridite," Jacobus said. He swept his hood from his round, pale face, ignoring the anger and suspicion that flashed through the room. An elf of many more centuries than Peridot stood slowly from a rocking chair, rising to face him. The Truth Teller.

Her face was gaunt, but her limbs looked strong and hail. Her hair was a deep rich green but her eyes, even in this dim space, were an uncanny, glowing gold so light it was almost white. Those eyes saw everything, and Peridot knew that the elf's ears, heart, and mind were equally keen.

"Why have you come?" the Truth Teller asked.

"I have come because this realm is once again in danger. I wish to help. And I also wish for your help."

"And why should we trust you?" another elf called out.

"You should not, but this one can tell you whether or not I speak the truth."

Those pale golden eyes bore into him. Peridot forced himself to stand still, though it felt as if a mole tunneled inside his head. He clenched his fists and fought to relax his jaw. He must bear this, and having a Truth Teller root about inside his head was far less torturous than what Damson had put him through. Veridite's magic sniffed here, sniffed there, then eased.

First test, passed.

"Speak," the Truth Teller said, voice crisp. "Tell us more."

Peridot inhaled, ready for the probing. The Truth Teller's touch felt lighter this time, at least.

"The humans outside are plotting to break in again."

"To what end?" the Truth Teller inquired.

"To free the princess and free the realm."

"For what reason?"

They were dancing now, with words, as Peridot opened to the other elf's magic. It was an intimate, discomfiting dance.

"Queen Silverhair has poisoned this realm and all others. Even now she treats with the Holly King."

"She does not!" Sapphire said. "She would never be so foolish."

"No?" Peridot asked. Half of him was surprised they did not know yet. That wasn't good. It boded ill for their required help. "Ask any of the courtiers when was the last time they saw the Queen. When was the last time anyone saw the Queen?"

The Truth Teller snapped her fingers for silence and turned to one of the other elves. "He seems to speak truth. But this requires confirmation. Swiftly."

The elf bowed his head and walked out, shutting the carved door behind him.

The Truth Teller broke her grip on Peridot's skull.

Peridot sagged with relief at her withdrawal.

"Water?" he asked. "Or wine?"

Jacobus filled a battered metal goblet and handed it to him. Wine then. It would do. He took a hasty gulp at the sour taste, and breathed deeply in the stuffy, shadowy air, trying to clear the memory of the Veridite's probing of his mind.

"Sit," Veridite said, returning to her rocking chair.

Peridot found a wooden chair with a thin pad and sat, careful to not spill the wine. He took another careful sip.

"Why have you returned, here, spy?" asked Jacobus.

"I returned here," Peridot said, looking at the elf who had once been his comrade, "because I am sick to death of what I have done. Sick to death of betrayal, suffering, and war. Sick to death of machinations and plans that never help but ever hurt. But mostly?"

Peridot looked around the circle. Not a one of them spoke. All waiting in the flickering candlelight.

"Mostly, I am sick to death of being in that bitch's thrall."

"And he speaks the truth again," Veridite said, rocking calmly, a pleased look on her gaunt face. "Welcome, brother. Now tell us, what is your plan?"

CHAPTER 55

CASE

By the time Case and the others got back to Go No More, the town was in full preparation for the mission.

Apprentices raced about, gathering supplies. Leather workers mended worn-out trousers and jackets and sewed plate metal into linings.

The forge clanked and smoked, working overtime. Doc Warren and Anandita supervised a crew rolling extra bandages and making tinctures and other medicines.

Construction had ceased, and the New Salem refugees looked confused and frightened as they trained with some of the Steel Clan Knights, preparing to protect the township, should it come to that.

With random gates erupting and Unseelie creatures roaming, every single person would be needed while the strongest Knights were gone, along with some of the best-trained town members, like Swan the bowyer and some others. A small troop of the Steel

Clan would remain behind to coordinate efforts on the ground and make sure the green New Salemites helped, rather than got in the way.

There had been discussions as to how large a crew would go to the main gate on this rescue mission, and much shouting over whether it would be an all-out assault and declaration of war on Silverhair and her court, or whether it would be a "blast the gates, get in and out again" operation.

There was no right answer, at least not that Case could tell. The only way to know which the right decision was would be was to try. And after that? They would either succeed or it would be too late.

Frankly, Case leaned toward war, but rescue—get in, get out—was what had been decided. Of course, things didn't always go according to plan, did they?

Especially when elves were involved.

He shook his head and walked his horse alongside Jerrod and the others. They were headed to the barn on the other side of the paddock from the Steel Clan garage, dodging running messengers and apprentices weighed down with weaponry.

Case dismounted, gave Pie Face a pat on the nose, then turned the lovely beast over to one of Angel's apprentices to curry, brush, and feed.

"Thanks, girl," he said, then turned to the young apprentice. "I'll be back for my saddlebags later."

The girl nodded and led Pie Face away, as Case trotted off to find the one person he wanted to see more than anything.

Tegan.

He found her barking orders at trainees, face tense with worry, whirling this way or that, offering instruction and correction with the confidence of an old-fashioned general from the schoolroom history books.

Wearing per sumac-red leathers, the knots of per hair wound more tightly than usual, Tegan turned. Per face cleared as per caught sight of him.

Case had to admit that warmed his heart.

They strode toward each other, clasping arms, holding each other apart so as not to grind against one another in the middle of the organized mayhem.

"You smell of horse," Tegan said by way of greeting.

"I do. And you smell singed."

Tegan gave a wry grin. "Damn Karaktilla shooting flames at unsuspecting Knights."

Case grinned right back. "How'd that go? Do I have to start calling you Warrior Mage now?"

Tegan shrugged, frowning.

"Tegan. Tell me. Did you pass?"

Tegan shook per head, looking down at the dirt beneath their feet. Clearly not wanting to talk about it.

"Later," he said. "Dinner?"

Tegan looked at him, dark eyes assessing, searching, wondering. He allowed some emotion to be visible on his face, his usual warrior's mask cracking for a moment.

Tegan gasped slightly, licked per lips, and nodded.

"Yes, dinner. I can get you..." Tegan cleared per throat. "I can get you caught up to speed on the alternate plan."

His heart thudded in his chest, thinking of all the

things he wanted to do with Tegan after dinner. Until per dashed his plans.

"We won't have much time, though. All of you who just went to the gate? You'll have to meet with the rest of the Steel Clan."

"Who's going into Underhill? Has that been decided?"

"You, if you want to. Jenny. Jerrod. Haryath and Amarpal. Swan the bowyer and some of the more skilled townsfolk."

Case exhaled. All their best, as he suspected, though having Jason's mother, Swan, there, in possible danger, while he was there as well? That made him a bit uneasy. Swan wasn't much of a mother—that was their arrangement—but still...

"All right. How can I be useful now? Unless you feel like telling me more."

Much as he wanted food and a bath, that would all need to wait. Besides, no use getting clean only to get filthy all over again.

"Follow me." Tegan spun on one bootheel and strode toward the garage where the bikes were kept.

Guess that was the end of that conversation. At least for now. Case followed to the large, open bays of the garage, with a glance toward the horse barn and his saddlebags, dreaming of unpacking, and yeah, a bath, a beer, and a pile of food.

"Hurry up, slowpoke," Tegan called over per shoulder. "Or I'll set you on greenhorn training duty."

Case groaned and picked up the pace, staring at Tegan's tight ass in those leather trousers. His cock rose, then quickly subsided. Yeah, when the township prepared for battle, everything else got put away.

Inside the garage was just as busy as out. Case greeted several of his comrades and a couple of apprentices. His son, Jason, ran toward him.

"Dad! You're back!"

Jason slammed into him, and Case's arms surrounded his son as he smiled down at him. The boy was the best part of Case's life, and he was away from him far too often.

They might have to look at changing that. Take more duties around Go No More. Fewer recon missions and battles far away.

But he had to get through this first. He patted Jason on the back, and the boy ran back toward Anandita's son, Hypatia. They were working with a couple of machinists on what looked like a tricky repair.

The place also boiled with mechanics and their apprentices. Everyone looked hard at work, fine-tuning motorcycles, fixing small parts, making sure everything was in running order.

"You'd think this was more than a rescue mission," he muttered.

Jenny heard him. Head snapping around, red braids flying.

"You think this isn't?" she said.

He lifted his hands. "I didn't mean..."

She shook her head. "I know. Sorry. We're all just tense. After, you know..."

After the trial, she meant, but didn't want to speak

of it in front of Tegan. Case got it. But he wished he knew what the fracked earth had happened.

"Where's Bocan?" he finally asked.

Both Tegan and Jenny shared a look and grumbled in a disgust that he knew masked worry.

"Pig fucker hurt himself again," Tegan finally said.

"Shit. All right."

"Are you here to work or gossip?" Jenny interjected.

Clearly there were a lot of sore spots he was dancing around here. That'd teach him to leave Go No More when his new lover was facing an ordeal that per didn't want to talk about and that had left another comrade injured.

Fuck.

"I'm here to work," he said. There was nothing for it. He'd find out later. "Give me something to do."

But he caught Tegan looking at him, eyes filled with naked desire. He stared back, leathers tightening, until per eyes bent toward per bike.

His own spark plugs needed cleaning. Badly.

Best get to it.

TEGAN

Tegan stood before the shimmering gate, kpingas at the ready, machete in hand.

It felt like it had taken them forever to get gear and plans together, and get the fuck on their bikes and out of Go No More. Too many council members argued for further reconnaissance and preparation. Karaktilla finally weighed in, backing Tegan and the Steel Clan.

Rafiq, John, and the others grumbled, but complied.

All the preparation in the world would not help them. The only thing left to do was fight.

Tegan studied the gate, tasting its resonance and comparing it with the magic coursing through per veins and whispering in per ears.

The gate was still a foreign thing. It felt alien to the forest. Not part of The Way, as per mother described it, and as Tegan was only now coming to feel inside perself.

Yes. Tegan could taste Mboli's magic. Smell it. It invaded every crevice of per being. Was this what mages felt like all the time?

How did they not go mad?

Tegan dropped into the practices that were as familiar as the feel of the machete in per palm. Slow heart rate. Slow breathing. Center. And then...something new.

Palms up, call to Mboli. Pray.

"You who flow through all things in this realm, flow through me now. Guide my thoughts, move through my hands, fill my magic with your power."

Done, Tegan ran per hands over per face. Per had no idea if the prayer was the right one, but murmuring the words out loud had calmed the last of per nerves.

"You good?" Case. Next to per. Tegan could feel him without even turning to look. The tingle of sex—one stolen hour the night before—still lingered between Tegan's thighs and on per lips.

Tegan reached out a hand and grasped Case's fingers briefly. He squeezed back, then let go.

"As well as I can be," Tegan said, "given the circumstances."

Per stared at the gate. Watched the mages tracing symbols. Saw the three drakes get into position.

"Case? What the fuck are we doing here? Remind me again why we are rescuing Silverhair's daughter, when she has been the cause of so much pain?"

"Because she is a victim, too, so it's the right thing to do. And because the mages and drakes tell us that her magic is the key to securing safety and power in our realm. Restabilizing things as Underhill slowly crumbles. And," he said, turning to Tegan with a grin, "to make the bitch Queen suffer."

That small upturn of lips lit up his beautiful, rugged face.

Tegan smiled back. "I guess that is a bonus. How about you? Ready?"

"Ready."

They stood in silence for a moment, listening to the sounds of preparation around them.

"What do you think is happening beyond the gate?" Tegan asked.

Case shrugged. "I don't know. All we can do is trust that Peridot and Carondel are doing what they said they would. If they aren't? Well, they're at risk now, aren't they? Like every other fucker inside."

"Death?" Tegan said.

Case just shrugged again but did not remark. Death was always a possibility, wasn't it? Every day, no matter how hard one tried to avoid it; and despite being trained for battle, every damned Steel Clan Knight would prefer to be growing old by the fire surrounded by fat, happy children.

"I wish I hadn't failed." Tegan finally spoke the words that were really bothering per.

Case grunted. "You didn't fail."

Tegan scowled, staring back at the shimmering gate. They really should have been conferring with Jenny and the others, but per wasn't ready. Not yet. Tegan had to get per shit together.

If Tegan's heart was not in the fight, the fight was

already lost. Self-doubt was a killer in more ways than one. But per couldn't seem to walk away from that sense of failure.

"I missed two out of the four elements."

"You mastered two more elements than most humans, Tegan. I don't know why you're so hard on yourself."

"Because if I had passed, I could have dealt with this problem alone. We could have avoided all this. Not put so many back into danger" Per swept an arm toward the gate. He grabbed that arm before it fell.

Tegan whirled. Stared at him, unblinking. Case trained his dark brown eyes right back, unblinking. Tegan gave the man that. He refused to look away.

"You don't know that," he finally said. "We don't know what's going to happen in there, just like you don't know what will happen when you tap into fire and water. Think, Tegan."

He softened his grip.

"Besides..." he said, not willing to let up. "Didn't our training tell us that it takes everyone to do their part? Isn't Go No More founded on those principles? A Steel Clan Knight faces no battle alone. So why the sudden need to go all lone wolf, Tegan? You feeling your ego?"

Tegan growled. He was baiting per, and Tegan knew it.

"Pig fucker," Tegan spat. "You know that isn't it."

"Then let us help. That's what we're all here for. That's what we've all trained for."

"If I say you're right, will you shut up?"

Case barked out a laugh.

"Maybe. If you're lucky. But don't count on it."

He bumped per shoulder. Tegan bumped back.

"All right," he said, "let's go talk to the drakes."

Unease still coiled in Tegan's belly, twining with the magic there. But some of the worry had lifted, just as Case had probably planned.

Was this what it was like to be seen? To be known? Tegan couldn't decide if per liked the feeling or loathed it. Maybe doing per own thing and fucking everything that moved was easier, but Tegan had to admit being seen by Case was also rather nice.

Per grabbed his face for a long, groin-tightening kiss, then smacked his ass.

"All right. Let's get this party started."

CHAPTER 57

ELZABETTA

Elzabetta was exhilarated. She had never been allowed much excitement, not in her whole life. She had been so sickly as a child, fretful even. And then her nursemaid was dismissed, and things grew worse. The hob was the only one who could comfort her.

And then the torture increased. And the countless human beings who had suffered and died... Elzabetta could do nothing about that now, except to make sure it did not happen again. Her mother's other plans? To marry her to the Unseelie prince?

That, she would thwart as well.

The best revenge was to live well, it was said. So, damn her mother and her plans. Elzabetta would live free.

Heart pounding, she had filled a small pack with two changes of undergarments, spare tunic and trews, her favorite hair comb, a couple of small mementos, some bread and cheese.

That was all she was allowed to bring with her from her old life. No gowns. No larger objects. No jewelry other than what she could wear, tucked beneath her practical riding clothes…. Looking out at the orchard, and the shimmer of bees alighting on the apple blossoms, Elzabetta did not think she would miss any of it.

Though Underhill was all she knew, Elzabetta was ready for a change. Besides, Underhill itself was changing around her. How many more years until it was a different place than the one she saw before her now?

After tracing her fingers over her father's ring, a heavy golden thing with an acorn carved in relief on the face, she tucked that into her pocket, then added her mother's sundered triangle and oak leaf amulet.

Someday, these might be currency, and until then? Reminders of her parents, who had loved her in their way. Even if Elzabetta shuddered at the madness of it.

Tarioc cleared his throat.

"We must leave, princess."

She nodded and walked across the golden wood floors in her sturdy riding boots. He silently ushered her down the long corridor. They walked swiftly and silently until her protector paused in front of a set of four carved knots and pressed the central one.

Elzabetta gasped as a door open into a dark passageway. A blue lamp filled with foxfire glowed, held by Carondel, who waited just inside with a small pack of his own.

Tarioc nodded at the alchemist and shouldered a

larger pack and two water skins that were propped just inside the door. He motioned Carondel ahead.

"You are next, princess. Please."

Tarioc fell in behind her. She was grateful for her boots on the uneven flagstone floors. Her soft slippers would have been torn to shreds before long, and who knew what conditions were like where they were headed?

That thought alone was enough to set her heart racing once again. A world outside her mother's thrall. A world of strange tastes, sights, and sounds. A world filled with humans and who knew what else?

A world she had never even been allowed to dream of. Not since her nursemaid had been taken away along with her stories of life in the other realm. Marian had family in the human world. Perhaps she was safe there, now. Elzabetta hoped so.

As they turned a corner into a long, stone corridor, the light increased, provided by torches mounted to stone walls by crude metal, and reflected by plates of what looked like copper. It was rather pleasing to the eye, though Elzabetta was so used to sunlight, she found she still needed to walk with care.

They passed heavy wood doorways set into the stone, some with muffled sounds inside.

The farther they walked, the more Elzabetta realized her stomach was not right. She swallowed, trying to ignore it, but the sense of illness and unease increased.

She adjusted her small pack more comfortably on her back and trudged forward.

"Are you well, princess?"

Tarioc's low voice bounced around her in the flickering light. Carondel slowed and peered over his shoulder, back at her.

"I am well enough," she responded. "Let us continue."

But the strangeness in her stomach increased. It almost felt as if some outside force tugged at her solar plexus. Was she an animal on a tether, being pulled by some unseen hand?

Sweat broke on her brow, and a sense of urgency pulled her forth. Elzabetta almost knocked into Carondel.

"Princess!" the alchemist cried.

"Hurry," she gasped.

Tarioc placed a hand on her shoulder.

"What is happening? Tell me. Why must we hurry?"

"Something feels very wrong!" She clutched at her belly.

"What is it?" Carondel asked, light and shadows dancing across his worried face.

"Something…" She bent over, gasping, as a mighty tug threatened to wrench her stomach from inside to out. "Something is pulling on me."

Tarioc's head snapped up and down the hall, then stopped at Carondel. "Do you feel anything, alchemist? Some magic?"

"It is very near!" Elzabetta cried out, almost bent in two.

"I sense only the faintest glimmer, coming from

just ahead. We should let the Princess guide us if she can."

"Can you, Elzabetta?" Tarioc was bent over her, wiping at her brow with a cool, damp kerchief. She must be in quite a state for him to take such liberties with her person.

"I think so. But hurry. It grows stronger."

Tarioc motioned Carondel ahead, then placed an arm around Elzabetta, supporting her weight.

"Let us keep moving," he said. "Tell us where to go."

She stumbled forward, following the alchemist's back, swallowing down bile, as the tugging sense increased.

Suddenly, she wondered if leaving her mother's home was the right thing to do. They had not even left Underhill, and already, things felt terribly wrong.

She felt frightened of what lay ahead, but found she was unwilling to return.

So, not knowing what else to do, she swallowed down her nausea and misgivings, then leaned on Tarioc. One step. Two. They followed Carondel down the dim, strangely lit stone corridor.

Without windows and sunlight to rely upon, it grew more and more difficult to get her bearings in the strange place. Trying to calm her lurching stomach and swelling head, she finally felt it.

Their destination. The place pulling at her.

She tugged on Tarioc's sleeve.

"To the left. Just here."

Carondel heeded her voice and stopped.

"Hold her," Tarioc said, and the alchemist rushed to do his bidding. She was transferred from one set of arms to the next. Carondel smelled faintly of caustic substances. A smell that brought back nightmares and brought her breakfast perilously close to the surface.

"Just. Lean me against the wall."

"Princess?"

"Leave me!"

Shocked, he gently complied, until she was resting, chest heaving, wiping at her mouth, leaning against rough stone. Tarioc traced the walls of stone, searching for something Elzabetta could not see.

Then, with a click, one dark stone groaned open. He manipulated something, and a panel slid open.

"By all the Ancient Gods, what is this?"

Tarioc turned to help her inside the space. An empty stone room, containing but two objects lit by a single lamp. A cradle, beautifully carved. Her cradle.

And next to it, a rough wood chair containing a skeleton dressed in simple clothing. Her nursemaid, the hob.

Elzabetta shoved a hand into her mouth, stifling a scream.

"What is this?" Tarioc asked. But he was not asking her. He spoke to the alchemist.

And, despite the horror of her nursemaid—missing no more—Elzabetta crept forward, pulled toward the cradle as if seeing what lay within was the most important thing in the world.

Except, she did not want to see it. Not at all.

A low chiming sounded faintly above her labored

breathing. A low chiming, and a soft voice, calling, "Come. Come."

And step by step, she did.

"Princess?" Carondel's voice was a whisper she ignored.

"Come. Come."

"I do not want to do this!"

"Elzabetta." Tarioc's voice, barely heard.

The pull was so strong it was almost all she could hear or feel.

"Come. Come. Closer. Yes."

How could she bear this? How could she approach this thing that caused the wrenching in her gut?

Elzabetta took another step, and still another, until finally, she stood at the cradle, Tarioc at her side, resisting the urge to reach out and clutch at his fingers and beg for him to not make her look upon whatever it was that rested here.

Instead, she took in a slow, shuddering breath, and forced herself to see. Forced her head and eyes to turn toward the cradle carved by her father's finest crafters. Made for her.

Inside the bed wrappings, once white but now pale gray, was a hollowed-out log the size of a small child.

And resting in that log was a glowing silver orb.

Elzabetta gasped, and all went black.

She felt Tarioc's arms reach for her before she hit the floor.

CHAPTER 58
CASE

The drakes were ready. This was really starting. Case's broadsword was in hand. Jerrod was at his side, Amarpal and Haryath nearby.

More than thirty Steel Clan Knights stood ready, waiting, as the the mages worked their magic, backed by Abyad the djinn, gesturing and calling to the air or whatever it was they did, trying to open a crack in the gate.

They didn't want Jenny's weird anti-magic to shatter the thing, because that would close it down, trapping the princess inside. Jenny stood well back for now, out of the flow. But not as far back as Bocan, who, last Case had checked, stood leaning against a fir tree near the healers, out of arrow range.

The halbtroll would stay on this side of the gate. He was too much of a liability to join his comrades, but he was too stubborn to stay home. So, they had compromised.

Case tried to keep Tegan in sight as much as possible as per stalked around the edges, unable to stand still.

He was worried about the new magic roiling through per. It was strange, uncanny, and unsettling. It didn't seem possible, but the magic made Tegan even more gorgeous than before.

Per skin practically glowed, vibrating with the power of the two twin forces—fire and water—pushing through per energy fields. Case knew this was part of Tegan's destiny, but he also wished he could spirit per away to a quiet cottage somewhere on the edge of town where they could make love for days.

They could raise his son together. Maybe take in a couple of the orphans from New Salem.

But that was a dream for a quieter time.

Instead, as usual, he stood, waiting for battle. Water skin tucked securely into the broad belt that held two extra knives that he'd honed the night before, tucked next to a small war hammer he'd had custom made by Feldspar. It was a blacksmith's hammer, a short, handled sledge that could do major damage.

It was dedicated to Thor, and used only during battle. Case wasn't the most religious man in Go No More, but called upon his Gods almost as easily as he called upon his friends.

Sometimes he even meant it.

Half gloves on, shield in one hand, broadsword in the other, bladder empty, feet braced, he was as ready he could be.

He watched Tegan check per kpingas once again

and adjust the grip on per machete. Per barked out orders at two apprentices until Jenny stepped forward and took over. That was good. The apprentices didn't need Tegan's overflow of nerves.

Case could have been helping with all of that, too, but he was too nervous himself. Too anxious.

He'd worked on calming Tegan down but needed to get his own shit together or risk becoming a liability in the middle of battle. Usually, he would be fine. He knew his role in battle: get in, smash as many heads as possible, stay out of the way of the halberds and pikes, dodge a few arrows. Make a few kills.

Today, though, he had been charged by both Bocan and Jenny to have Tegan's back, no matter what. And he would.

But that made him nervous all the same. Because suddenly, Tegan was more than just a comrade and best mate.

Tegan held his heart in per small, dark hands.

Finally, the mages stepped back, and the drakes prepared to move forward, purple, red, and black.

Case, Jerrod, and all the other Knights and apprentices moved even farther away from the gates as one after another, in quick succession, the massive reptiles took their places. First Karaktilla, purple scales glimmering, sunk her claws into the forest floor and blasted at the crack in the seam. She moved out of the way just enough for Daraktal, the slightly smaller red drake, to aim beneath her sinuous neck, shooting fire at a lower part of the seam. He was followed by the enormous black drake who blasted above Karaktilla's first volley.

::*All together now!*::

All three were in proper position and knew where to aim. It reminded Case of the way archers worked in concert, some aiming high, others low. But instead of arrows, the drakes sent out enough fire to decimate the forest if they were not careful.

He could smell burning fir and pine needles from the trees closest to the gates, and hoped that the few safety marshals they'd appointed were ready with buckets of water and dirt.

The heat was almost intolerable, even this far back. He could barely imagine what things would feel like nearer to the blast line, let alone in the pathway of the coordinated conflagration.

Case wet his kerchief and pulled it up over his mouth and nose, securing the damp cloth beneath the curve of his helmet.

Fire bounced off the magic, seeking out the crack the mages had wrought in the middle of the shimmering portal.

Finally, bit by bit, flame by flame, flare by flare, the seam widened and then cracked.

Shards of magic whipped through the air. Case ducked. He knew that was foolish. The magic could hit whether you were physically in its path or not.

He felt the blow of it. Felt the amulet around his neck buzz and bite. Felt his heart boom hard enough to burst.

The gate's magic was still there. Not broken and closed the way Jenny Magic's Bane had done, but pried wide as it could go by drakefire.

Amarpal and Haryath swiftly moved to flank either side of the gate. The Sikhs raised their swords.

Case sent up a prayer to Thor, just in case, and patted the hammer tucked in his belt.

"Steel Clan ready!" Haryath shouted. "We fight for Go No More!"

"We fight for Go No More!" Every voice full-throated bellowed the words back.

And then Tegan gave a long, keening cry and ran, boots churning up earth, straight through the opening.

Case cursed, put on a burst of speed, and followed.

CHAPTER 59
PERIDOT

They were in another, larger space, deep underground. It looked to have been a troll lair at some point in the past, but was now used as a warehouse of sorts, with shelves and racks of weapons, medicaments, and travel-ready foods.

The same torches lit the space, sprinkled here and there with glowing orbs of magic elf-light. It was a utilitarian space, and well suited to purpose, but Peridot was itching to get back up where light shone from the sky instead of from guttering, smoking torches.

The dissidents had agreed to his plan, much to Peridot's surprise. After the Truth Teller's affirmation, it did not take much convincing to get them to trust him. Except for Sapphire, who still seemed to bear a strong grudge against him.

But that was the way of things, was it not? Someone would always be quick to anger at something he had done. Or neglected to do.

Peridot had many things to atone for, and many apologies to make, should he ever get the chance. Should Damson ever again look upon him with kindness, well...there was no time to think on such things now.

Peridot waited as the men and women gathered weapons and water, and the medics packed bandages and other healing supplies. The dissidents had clearly prepared for this day, though Peridot wondered when they thought it would happen. Or what their own plans had been.

He had never been a revolutionary, preferring to play the game as it was written. But he supposed he was a dissident himself now; no longer playing a double game, he was ready to march right off the board and flip the table.

Jacobus approached, cloak over light armor, two wicked-looking troll-forged blades crossed in the dark belt at his waist. None of the people here wore the green leathers of elvish warriors. They were in a hodgepodge of gathered clothing that ranged from rough hemp and wool to supple leathers and well-made boots.

Interesting. Clearly, a few of the nobility had thrown in their lot with this crew.

How much, exactly, had Peridot missed, all the years he worked as spy?

"Ready?" Peridot asked.

"Ready," Jacobus replied, then turned again to the ancient Truth Teller who watched the goings on from a padded stool. "Will you offer us a blessing?"

She snorted. "Do I look like a holy woman? Say your own prayers."

Her grin took the sting from her words, and she raised her right hand all the same.

"Quiet!" Jacobus said. The voices stilled and the clank and clattering subsided.

The Truth Teller's voice was strong. "May the earth guide you. May your hearts beat strong. May magic cradle you. Flow like water. Wind at your backs. Strong arms, stronger legs. Work together. May justice prevail."

She lowered her hand. A hush followed, marred only by the sound of breathing and sputtering torches.

"May justice prevail," Jacobus murmured, and then all was in motion once again.

"Move out!" a voice cried.

One person held the door open as the dissidents filed out into the dimly lit corridor into the warren of pathways that honeycombed beneath Queen's palace.

Peridot wondered where the Queen was now. Still in the Unseelie realms, treating with the Holly King? Back in her own chambers, plotting?

Or with her counselors, preparing for battle?

From up ahead, a glow emerged. A blue light, glowing with magic.

"Halt," hissed Jacobus. Peridot pushed his way forward, having seen a familiar face.

It was Carondel, the alchemist, last seen at the Battle of New Salem. The glow was coming from his hands as he led a straight-backed warrior carrying a body.

Peridot inhaled sharply and Jacobus muttered "Holy Mother."

The body was Princess Elzabetta, whom he could now see was sleeping. And in her arms? She cradled a hunk of wood. A log.

"What happened to her?" Peridot inquired.

Her protector screwed up his mouth as if to answer, but it was the alchemist who replied.

"I believe we have found the princess's missing souls."

"And we are getting her out of here," the elven warrior replied. "Should you wish to stop us, know that you will die."

"No need for that." Jacobus stepped to Peridot's side. "We had plans of our own, but those included helping you with the princess. My name is Jacobus."

"I am Tarioc. Well met. We require help getting back to the gate."

Peridot shook his head. "By my calculations, the Steel Clan will have breached the gate by now. The place will be a battleground. It was one thing when the princess was on her own two feet, but now?"

"Let me through," said a voice down the corridor, followed by the slow *tock tock tock* of a cane on the flag-stone floor.

The Truth Teller emerged from the gloom.

"Well met, Tarioc. My name is Veridite. I knew your mother, several centuries ago. But that is a tale for another time." She gestured down the corridor. "Five turnings down from here is the site of a former gate. The rudiments are there. All we need is the correct combination of magic to open it again. That should buy enough time to get all of us through."

"And we have that combination?" Tarioc frowned, then shifted the princess in his arms.

Veridite jerked her head toward the alchemist. "With this one here, we do."

"And where will this gate take us?" Peridot asked.

Veridite smiled at him as if he were a child. "The gate shall lead us wherever I wish it to. If you can give me coordinates, I will get us there."

This was proving easier than he had feared.

"Lead on, then, Truth Teller."

He just hoped it wasn't too easy. Because too easy always meant subterfuge and betrayal, and a bad ending.

Very bad.

CHAPTER 60

SILVERHAIR

She sat in the throne room, her advisors seated in chairs at the base of the dais, the rest of the room filled with a phalanx of guards in green leather armor. The humans had been seen gathering outside the new gate.

Battle was nigh.

The Holly King had sent in reinforcements but had not come to join the battle himself.

"One of us must stay behind, in order to secure the smooth running of both our realms."

Silverhair saw the truth in his statement, though she did not care for being the one left to lead the charge, so to speak. Nonetheless, he had promised more wyverns, trolls, and the like to help her cause. And, with what was left of Elzabetta's essence to feed her mages, there would be magic enough to defeat the puny humans where they stood.

"Bring my daughter to me," she demanded of her

guards. They shifted uncomfortably, looking to each other instead of to her.

Queen Silverhair snapped her fingers. "Now!"

Finally, the head guard cleared his throat and stepped forward. "My liege, I know not how to say this."

Silverhair straightened her spine and looked down upon the guard, who all but bared his neck for the royal knife.

"Tell. Me." Her voice was a sharp whisper that cut through the room. All rustling stilled and hushed.

"Princess Elzabetta cannot be found."

"What do you mean she cannot be found?" Her fury mounted. She gripped the arms of her chair until the carved wood bit at her skin. "Bring me Tarioc!"

"Forgive me, Majesty, but the guard Tarioc has disappeared as well."

She rushed from her throne, hands outstretched, and with her magic, gripped the guard around the neck until his eyes bulged.

The only sound in the throne room was the mewling from his throat.

She dropped him like a doll upon the gleaming wood floors, where he lay, gasping like a fish pulled from a pond.

"Send for the mages and the necromancers. I want every scrap of magic at our disposal. I want every arrow. Every hammer. Every sword."

The guards near the back of the room rushed toward the doors, eager to leave her presence.

Good. Let them fear her.

Let them fear the days to come.

All that mattered now was shoring up enough power to battle the pitiful creatures standing just outside her gate.

As for her daughter? The girl would be punished once found, and Tarioc, too. She supposed they thought themselves in love and had spirited away to consummate whatever foolish future filled a young princess's dreams.

Well, the girl would find out soon enough that elven royalty did not dream of love and freedom.

They dreamed only of power.

CHAPTER 61
TEGAN

Suddenly they were Underhill. The crackling ozone scent of fire and magic wreathed Tegan's head. Per ran like a demon released, shouting for Go No More. Shouting for per comrades to follow. To fight. To triumph.

"Mboli!"

The power of the river flowed through per. The power of the flame filled per skin. It was more power than Tegan had ever felt. Per only hoped it was enough.

Enough to do what needed to be done. To face phalanx after phalanx of green-garbed elvish knights who stood, fully armored, weapons bristling in the eternal springtime sun.

And there was a tower. And upon the battlements stood the silver-haired Queen. The beautiful. The deadly. But where was the princess, the one they had to save to stop the reaping of human souls?

Tegan only hoped that the traitor elf and the

alchemist would do their jobs. Bring her home to Go No More. Right the balance the drakes and mages said was perilously close to breaking again.

There was no time to think. Tegan had to act.

High on the tower, the silver Queen gestured. Pointed.

"Pull!" One of the elves from the tower cried.

"Shields!" Swan the bowyer shouted.

Tegan had no time for archers or their arrows. No time to duck beneath the shield wall. No time to do anything but listen to the whispers of Mboli in per blood and feel per bond with the lynx at per side.

Tegan knew…per knew which way to go. Feint left, roll, dodge. Right. Spin. Kpinga thrown. A scream. Target hit. Running, wrench per blade from a neck marred with silver blood. Turn. Duck. Dodge. Whirl. Left. Right. Turn. Throw. The arc of another kpinga. Dodge back. Catch a blast of fire from Karaktilla's open maw. Fling it towards a phalanx of elvish warriors who fall. Burning. Screaming.

Scent a stream nearby. Grasp water in the left hand. Fling it towards the grasses where another phalanx stands. Flood the grasses. Marshy ground, sucking boots in place. Yelling. Scrambling to get free.

"Mboli, be with me! Warrior! Mage! Tegan!"

Dodge, run, jump, parry. Screams. The clash of shields and swords and pole arms. The shouts of comrades all around.

Tegan channeled it all. Tegan thrust per machete through it all, wielding magic as per whirled like a dervish from Abyad's realm. Another throw. One of per kpingas hit home, splitting a skull in two. Starlight snarled, hissing and biting and dancing away. Tegan mirrored the lynx's motions.

Run. Leap. Retrieve the blade. Dodge. Parry. Hamstring two warriors with the machete.

The earth. The earth. The earth beneath Tegan's boots. The earth. Filling Tegan. Filling Tegan to bursting. In per mind Tegan saw Bocan, good arm pointing upward, raising up the earth power. The halbtroll chanted. The earth rumbled and began to roll.

"Gods of Earth and Stone, be with me!" Tegan growled.

The marshy earth rolled and bucked. Tegan rode dry land as if per was a child standing on a paddle board on the Willamette. Balanced perfectly, machete in one hand, kpinga in the other. The earth flowing up through per bones. Out through steel.

Shove. Push. Strike this swath of elvish warriors down. Fling magic left. One swath of warriors down. Fling right. Tegan rolled and leapt. Unstoppable. Mboli showing every opening. Every crevice. Every crack.

Tegan slid and dodged between them all, eyes darting to and fro. Looking for the alchemist. Seeking out the traitor elf. Looking for a princess per had never seen....

And all the while, Queen Silverhair stood on her silent tower, flanked by mages. They had singled Tegan out and dropped volley upon volley of magic, guided by the bitch Queen's hand. Magic split the earth around Tegan's boots and caused tree bark and stones to slice at per leathers and the exposed skin on per face.

Tegan bared per teeth and growled up at the Queen.

"You shall not win!" Tegan shouted. "I am Warrior! Mage! Tegan!"

The Queen smiled a wintry smile, unbothered by per taunts.

Then suddenly, there was the bark of a dog, a whirl of wind, and the djinni was there, long staff in hand. Whirling it. Robes swirling as he spun, struck, and whirled again, air pushing outward, flinging bodies away as Abyad's staff cracked against metal and wood.

"Tegan!" he shouted. "Grasp the wind!"

But Tegan had failed at this. Tegan could not. Tegan had only water and fire. A blast of magic from above struck a blow against per solar plexus, driving the air from Tegan's lungs and dazzling per vision until gray spots swum around per sight.

"Tegan!" Abyad shouted once again.

But Tegan could not hear. Just saw his pale lips moving. Saw the battle being waged around per. Saw the Queen, high in her tower. Saw perself, falling in the mud. Slipping. Breathed in. Filled with air. Filled with magic. Per was drowning. Drowning in magic. Drowning in Mboli. Drowning in the way of all things.

Subsumed.

Taken over.

Gone.

CHAPTER 62

CASE

Case saw Tegan fall, and sliced through a warrior's gut with his broadsword, pushed the green-clad elf away. But before he could move, he felt something. Turned to parry.

An Unseelie troll loomed, poised to strike.

"Pig fucker!" Case shouted, and then Jenny was next to him, shoving a buckler up to crack against the troll's nose. The troll roared and lifted his arms. Case thrust his sword into the exposed armpit flesh. A shower of blood drenched him. He gagged with it. Stumbled.

"Go!" Jenny shouted, teeth bared.

Case swiped a hand across his face to clear his eyes, then ran toward Tegan, who was crawling in the mud, Starlight at per side.

It looked as if something was very wrong. More than simply the wind getting knocked from per.

He plowed past an injured elf and leaped over a

downed branch of an apple tree, fruit already rotting, feeding the soil.

His boots slid into the marshy mud, but he caught himself, and bent toward Tegan.

"Tegan. I'm here."

"Case." Tegan reached out, half blind. "You have to help me."

Tegan's hands gripped his arms through his leathers. Per weapons were dropped in the mud at per side. Battle still raged around them, with blasts of magic joining the clamor of metal and scent of scorched earth.

"What do you need? What is wrong?"

"Magic," Tegan croaked out. "Sit me up. The Queen." Tegan's voice cracked. "The tower."

Case looked up and saw the sheen of silver-white hair surrounded by mages.

Fuck. If that was who did this to Tegan? Well, they would pay.

"Tell me," he said. "Tell me what must be done, and I will do it."

Starlight paced back and forth, clearly in distress. No time to deal with the lynx right now.

"Prop me up. Get Abyad and Karaktilla. And Bocan if he's here.

Case saw Jerrod running and shouted to him over the noise of battle.

"Jerrod! We need the djinni and Karaktilla, and Bocan if he made it through the gates."

The halbtroll was supposed to stay back with the

healers, but he was a stubborn fuck, so might have changed his plans when his comrades were otherwise occupied.

Case's thoughts ticked quickly over in his head as Jerrod gave a grim nod and ran off as fast as his long legs would take him.

"Can you feel it?" Tegan whispered. Per back was propped against him as per panted softly.

"Feel what, my love?"

"Love?" Tegan gave a soft laugh. "Am I your love?"

Tegan tilted per head toward Case and gave a half grin, face stained with blood and soot, eyes bright, almost hectic.

"Yes, of course you are, you pig fucker."

And that got a real laugh, that morphed into a cough.

"Water."

Case unstoppered his water skin and squirted some into Tegan's open mouth.

"Feel what?" he repeated.

"The magic," Tegan replied. "It's rising. Can't you feel it?"

Case breathed in and felt the amulet at his breastbone tingling. It was the amulet that every member of the Steel Clan wore, and bound them together. Just like the spoked-wheel-and-wings symbol that was their emblem, the amulet gave them a shared magic. Even Jenny, Magic's Bane.

"Yes," he said, "I feel it."

"Good. You're going to help me use it," Tegan

paused for breath. "As soon as those other pig fuckers get here."

And arrive they did, with a rumble and a clash and much roaring and screaming as they made their way through trolls, a wyvern, and elf upon elf. The mages in the tower lobbed thunderbolt after thunderbolt and spread noxious gas to those closest to them. The Queen turned her silver head, as if wondering whether she should leave.

Or where she should aim her deadly magic next.

"Quickly!" Tegan shouted. "Quickly! Now!"

Case looked up, searching through the tangled melee, and there was Karaktilla's long purple neck and triangle wedge head. Next to the drake was Bocan, damn him, injured arm tied tightly in a sling, flanked by the djinn, who had staff in hand, robes billowing.

Starlight ran to join them, Jenny's faery fox, Flex, racing to meet the lynx. Abyad's dog joined the other animals, and Serena the owl circled overhead.

"More water," Tegan croaked. He squirted more into Tegan's waiting mouth and then, at per gesture, on per face and the coiled knots on per head. Why wasn't Tegan wearing per helmet?

"Stand me up." He got his arms under pers and pulled as gently as possible, but Tegan screamed out in pain.

He stopped.

"Keep going." Tegan was panting hard now, the water running with sweat down per face.

"Fuck!" he cursed, but did his comrade asked. How could he not?

Holding Tegan in his arms on a battlefield like this was much like making love. They were together. They were one in this moment. He was Tegan's spine, and Tegan would be his hands and his sword.

He felt as Tegan inhaled, and braced himself for magic.

CHAPTER 63
TEGAN

Braced against per comrade and lover, Tegan grit per teeth and prepared for the onslaught to come.

Breathing in the smoky, noxious air, per felt the magic kindle in per belly. It was never, or it was now.

Mboli help me. Magic guide me. Ancestors be with me.

"Air! Fire! Water! Earth! Air! Fire! Water! Earth!" Tegan shouted, voice hoarse, over and over, willing the elemental magic to per hands. But nothing happened.

Starlight, Flex, and the black dog worked together, nipping and clawing at any green-clad elf who tried to get close to the trio.

"Case," per said, slumping against him. "They have to help me. The others..."

"You heard Tegan," he shouted. Abyad's head snapped around. The djinni nodded.

Case shouted "Air!"

Abyad raised his staff, and a whirlwind appeared.

Tegan captured the wind in one hand and shoved it towards the tower.

"Fire!" Tegan screamed.

Karaktilla belched out a blast that singed the fine hairs on per face. Tegan caught that too and wove it with the wind.

"Water!" And out of Tegan's skin itself flowed a river, fresh and clean. And Tegan braided that with wind and fire twining above the battlefield in shades of white and yellow, blue and green and red.

"Earth!"

And there was Bocan, shaking the ground, face a rictus of pain, and Tegan grasped that too, though it seemed impossible. Per sent it flying, hands moving, shifting in the air, every part of per souls focused with concentration. Above the battleground, brown and green and blue and yellow and white and orange soared, all the colors, winding, twining, floating, flowing. Magic building upon itself at Tegan's hands. The power built until Tegan heard Case groan, as if he could barely hold on to Tegan anymore.

Serena shrieked, encouraging the magic higher.

But Tegan's body was weak. Per limbs trembled as if per body was about to split into one thousand pieces and fly away. But still, per lover held on tight. Per swayed. The colored braids flying from per hands faltered.

Case spoke urgently in per ear. "Tegan, don't let go! I've got you! I've got you!"

Tegan felt him brace his boots against the rumbling

earth and per caught the magic again. The colored braids grew thick and fat with power.

Tegan raised both arms and shouted, "Now!"

And, with combined roars from the drake, the troll, and the djinn, and per own mouth, the braids shot straight out. The magic hit the tower, split it with a crack so loud it rang Tegan's ears.

Then screaming. Fire. Rumbling. Water. Rain. Mud.

And that silver hair, tumbling, falling, green silk, silver hair, green silk, silver hair...falling to the ground like leaves. Tegan heard a shattering of one thousand crystal cups. The Queen's bones, breaking on hard ground.

Tegan collapsed against Case. He eased them both down to the welcoming earth.

Then, bent over Tegan, per comrade and lover, the one who always had per back, Case wept.

Tegan's eyes filled with tears of per own.

The battle was finally over. Queen Silverhair was dead.

CHAPTER 64
JENNY

Jenny saw the Queen fall. Heard the shattering of her bones. Watched the wyverns and Unseelie trolls shriek and bellow and then run.

Turning, she struck down two warriors in quick succession, but it was clear now that the battle was over. Tegan and the other mages had done their job, and with Queen Silverhair's body lying broken at the base of the tall tower, the elvish phalanx was in disarray.

Soon, the green-armored elves all ran as well.

Jenny turned to help move the Go No More injured and their dead. This was always the hardest part, when exhilaration warred with grief. But this was the part that always must be done.

Tegan looked well cared for by Case and the djinn. Where was Bocan?

Her comrade limped toward her, large blue face wet with sweat and blood.

"The princess?" she asked.

He cracked half a tired grin. "Word came through Aphrodite. Princess Elzabetta is free."

She grinned back and clapped her comrade on his uninjured arm.

"Then let's clean up and get back home."

Tegan had done it. They all had.

Home was a safe haven once more. Plants would grow, children would flourish, and the people could live in peace.

CHAPTER 65
TEGAN

Tegan was propped up on a low couch tucked into an ell in the common room of Case's home, Starlight curled next to per. The lynx was boneless and looked as relaxed and comfortable as if they both had not just barely survived an epic battle.

Oh, to be a cat....

Case's place was larger than per own with one true bedroom, a sleeping loft for his son, Jason, and this little ell for guests. It was also clearly a place that Jason liked to read and play, as there were a few toys and books on the shelves built into the wall, and the cushions looked well worn.

Per had a cup of tea close at hand and enjoyed listening to Case and Jason in the kitchen area, laughing, talking, and playfully giving each other shit.

Father and son. And here was Tegan. Per had never thought such a day would come. Not that Tegan was ready to stop catting around completely, but the conversations per had with Case since coming home assured per that he felt the same.

They would be partners and primary lovers to each other. Tegan would get to know Jason even better. Per had always liked the boy and was grateful to have already earned a modicum of his trust.

But the door was open if, say, a certain djinni wanted to bed Tegan or Case, though hopefully together. Tegan smiled as Case appeared around the corner.

"Would you like to eat back here, or shall I help you to a chair by the wood stove, oh Warrior Mage?"

Tegan pushed perself up, willing down a groan. Everything ached.

"Call me that again, and I'll gut you like a fish."

"You and what squadron of dragoons?"

He leaned forward to help per up. Tegan caught his face in per hands and drew him closer. The kiss was long, slow, and made Tegan ache even more. But in a different way.

"As soon as I'm well enough, that's another thing you have in store."

His ruddy face flushed a deeper red and his lips quirked up at the edges. "Oh, really?"

"Yes."

Starlight grumbled, shifted position, and fell back to sleep.

The sound of boots on the porch was joined by familiar voices.

"You invited people over?"

"Of course. They've been badgering me for two days, Tegan. And you seem well enough."

"No. It's okay. It's...good."

Case helped Tegan to per feet, and stayed with per as Tegan padded toward the main room, which rapidly filled with comrades, smelling fresh and clean from the bathhouse.

"Tegan!" Jenny raced toward per, arms wide, then stopped short. "Guess you're likely not up for a hug."

Tegan smiled. "I'm up for one hug but can't bear the thought of hugging the lot of you pig fuckers."

Jerrod, Case, and Bocan roared with laughter, and Tegan swore per caught a giggle from Jason, who ladled up stew into a raft of mismatched bowls.

Per comrades soon settled Tegan into a chair by the fat iron stove, a bowl of stew in per lap. It smelled like the best thing in the world.

Per looked around, blinking away tears. *This* was the best thing in the world. Battle done. Clean and warm. Food at the ready. Surrounded by comrades and friends, looking at the man Tegan had to admit per fucking loved.

Someone handed per a mug of cider. Tegan raised the heavy cup.

"To Go No More! To the Steel Clan! And to taking down tyrants!"

"To Go No More!" per friends agreed.

No kings. No presidents. No warlords. No rulers.

The Knights of the Steel Clan would bend no knee. They would live free. They would love. They would prosper. They would ride.

Comrades, together.

CHAPTER 66
ELZABETTA

When she finally awakened, Elzabetta was in a strange, dark place. Was she still in the warren of hallways Underhill?

One lantern, wick turned low, sat on a chest of drawers next to the bed. She moved her head, wincing. Her head hurt and her throat was so dry. A pitcher and simple earthenware cup sat on the chest, next to the lantern. She reached, but was too weak, her hands dropping back to some sort of soft quilt.

Sighing, she closed her eyes again and relaxed against the pillow. Whether she was safe or not, she did not know, but was too weary to fight.

The door creaked. Elzabetta's eyes shot open.

In walked a human woman with long, dark hair, wearing rough trousers and a tunic. In her arms she carried the strangest thing. A log, encasing a glowing orb.

"Oh!" Elzabetta said, forgetting to be quiet in this unknown place.

The woman's dark eyes widened, but she recovered quickly, and placed the log on the bed, nestled against Elzabetta's side.

"Thirsty?" the woman asked.

"Yes," Elzabetta rasped. It felt as if she had not tasted water for many days.

The woman propped Elzabetta up on several pillows. The process took quite some time, as Elzabetta felt too weak to offer much assistance, plus, the pounding in her head made her want to faint.

Finally, the woman poured, and held the cup as Elzabetta took three small sips.

"Good," the woman said. "Enough for now."

"Who are you? And where am I?"

"You are in Go No More. Safe. Peridot and Carondel brought you here after you escaped from Underhill. Several more from your realm accompanied them, but that is a story I'll let someone else tell."

Ah. Perhaps that was why there was such darkness. Elzabetta had heard the human realms had shifts of light throughout the day.

"And you?"

"My name is Jimena. I am a mind healer, and with your permission, I think we can free your souls from this orb and mend your mind."

Elzabetta found that she was crying. "No more torture?"

Jimena shook her head. "No more torture. Though I cannot say your healing process will be easy. And Carondel wishes to throw himself at your mercy and has offered to assist you in any way."

Elzabetta frowned.

"But that is up to you, of course. Frankly, I wouldn't give that piece of dung a drink of water. But at any rate, you don't have to decide for quite some time. Just rest now. I have savory broth ready in the kitchen. Would you like some?"

"Yes, please."

The healer nodded and turned to leave.

"Healer."

Jimena turned.

"What of my mother?"

The healer froze like a startled animal. Elzabetta watched as a wash of emotions crossed her light brown skin.

"Silverhair is dead."

Elzabetta blinked. Such a thing did not seem possible. And what could it mean for Underhill and all the Elfland realms?

"And Tarioc?"

"The elf is well. He carried you here and has visited each day, while you were sleeping."

Her breast felt lighter, knowing that.

"Thank you. Thank you for telling me, and for taking care of me."

"Of course."

The healer left the door ajar, and Elzabetta could hear her moving about the kitchen, talking to someone. A low rumbling voice responded. Sounded like a troll.

Elzabetta had never dealt with humans before and had been taught that they were inferior beings. Yet, they had helped to save her. And taken her in.

She supposed she would get used to unlearning the lies she had been fed, just as she would get used to the phases of darkness and light, the strange fabrics, and the way food smelled here.

Her mind skated past the thing she needed to think on but could not bear to.

Her mother. Dead? Was such a thing even possible? Her mother had always seemed eternal. Elzabetta felt a sharp pang of grief, wed with a sense of release.

She wondered what life would bring her way, and who she would share it with. Glancing toward the glowing orb at her side, she wondered what her nursemaid had done to save them—for she was certain now that was what had happened—and what had happened to the hob who had only shown her kindness.

Her mother, it seemed, had much to account for.

But Silverhair was dead now, and Elzabetta was safe. For the first time in her life, she was free.

She would find a life here, in this new place, with these people. She might even make some friends.

She placed one hand upon the glowing orb that held the missing pieces of her soul. It was warm to the touch and felt delicious against her skin, tugging at her, whispering the words *At last.* Elzabetta smiled.

For the first time in her life, her destiny was in her own two hands.

～

IF YOU ENJOYED THIS SERIES, be sure to check out The Witches of Portland!

Danger and corruption stalk the streets of Portland, Oregon. The witches of Arrow and Crescent Coven must face their shadows, harness their magic, and prepare to fight...

Acknowledgments

I give thanks to all readers, everywhere. I'm grateful also for the long line of anarchist and visionary storytellers for being wells of inspiration.

Thanks to Leslie Claire Walker, my intrepid first reader, to Dayle Dermatis, editor extraordinaire, and to expert readers Mala, Sara P., and Mushtaq ali Al Ansari. Any mistakes are my own. Thanks to Shawn and Stefon for further encouragement.

Valerie Herron did the amazing artwork for the series, bringing Jenny, Bocan, Tegan, and their bonded animals, to life. Check out her work at valerieherron.com.

Big, grateful shout out to my Exclusive Readers Group for spreading the word and to Jack for extra typo catching.

And thanks as always to my chosen family, for consistent encouragement and support.

And last...

Thanks to everyone who believes in magic. This series is for you.

ALSO BY T. THORN COYLE

FICTION

The Bookshop Witch Paranormal Cozy Mysteries

Bookshop Witch

Haunted Witch

Tarot Witch

Running Witch

Hallows Witch

Solstice Witch

The Pride Street Paranormal Cozy Mysteries

Sushi Scandal

Flower Frenzy

Muffin Murder

Hairspray Horror

Dandy Distress

The Mouse Thief

Mouse's Folly

Mouse's Fight

The Witches of Portland

By Earth

By Flame

By Wind

By Sea

By Moon

By Sun

By Dusk

By Dark

By Witch's Mark

The Panther Chronicles

To Raise a Clenched Fist to the Sky

To Wrest Our Bodies From the Fire

To Drown This Fury in the Sea

To Stand With Power on This Ground

The Steel Clan Saga

We Seek No Kings

We Heed No Laws

We Ride at Night

Short Story Collections

A Hint of Faery

A Touch of Faery

A Spark of Magic

A Flame for Yuletide

A Hope for Winter

A Time for Magic

A Speculation of Stars

A Speculation of Hope

A Speculation of Time

Risk It All: Queer Stories of Love, Suspense, And Daring

Thresholds: Queer Stories of Love, Suspense, And Daring

Ghost Talker

Cats and Other Creatures

NON-FICTION

You are the Spell

Sigil Magic for Writers, Artists, & Other Creatives

Crafting a Daily Practice

Resistance Matters

Evolutionary Witchcraft

Kissing the Limitless

Make Magic of Your Life

ABOUT THE AUTHOR

T. Thorn Coyle worked in many strange and diverse occupations before settling in to write books full time.

Author of the *Bookshop Witch Paranormal Cozy Mystery* series, the *Pride Street Paranormal Cozy Mysteries*, *The Steel Clan Saga*, *The Witches of Portland*, and *The Panther Chronicles*, Thorn's multiple non-fiction books include *Sigil Magic for Writers, Artists & Other Creatives*, *Kissing the Limitless*, *Make Magic of Your Life*, and *Evolutionary Witchcraft*. Thorn's work also appears in many anthologies, magazines, and collections.

An interloper to the Pacific Northwest U.S., Thorn drinks a lot of tea, pays proper tribute to the neighborhood cats, and talks to crows, squirrels, and trees.

Connect with Thorn:
www.thorncoyle.com

www.ingramcontent.com/pod-product-compliance
Lightning Source LLC
Chambersburg PA
CBHW071353200726
48293CB00008B/2626